"Watch us, kids. Carrie and I'll show you how it's done..."

"I bet you'd like a turn with someone who won't step on your toes." Bryce laughed, drawing Carrie into a dance.

"Cam only stepped on my feet once, and he's not heavy."

"The kid's learning." Bryce dipped Carrie and she relaxed into the music, the dance and her partner.

"I thought men who could dance were almost an endangered species."

"Not in my family. Mom says date nights are important. Along with mutual respect and shared interests, dates help keep the magic and love alive."

Carrie wanted that kind of relationship, one that was a true partnership, and like her parents had.

Bryce turned Carrie in his arms so they were face-to-face and almost cheek to cheek. A hint of his spicy aftershave mixed with her perfume. Her hand trembled in his and her stomach fluttered.

And when the song ended, they were still caught in the moment...

Dear Reader,

One of the reasons I enjoy writing a series is developing a setting and cast of characters through multiple books. *The Cowgirl Nanny* is the third book in my Montana Carters miniseries for Harlequin Heartwarming, following *Montana Reunion* and *A Family for the Rodeo Cowboy*.

Although each book also stands alone, many characters, human and animal, recur, as does the High Valley, Montana, setting and the Carter family's Tall Grass Ranch. I hope you feel at home among this welcoming community of family and friends.

In *The Cowgirl Nanny*, champion barrel racer Carrie Rizzo is taking a break from rodeo and gets a summer job as a nanny for widowed rancher Bryce Carter's two children. As much as Bryce and Carrie like each other, they can't risk their hearts on anything more. She's returning to rodeo and his late wife was the love of Bryce's life. However, friendship can turn to love and an unexpected new beginning might be just around the corner.

I enjoy hearing from readers, so please visit my website, jengilroy.com, and contact me there, where you'll also find my social media links and newsletter and blog sign-ups.

Happy reading!

Jen Gilroy

HEARTWARMING
The Cowgirl Nanny

Jen Gilroy

ISBN-13: 978-1-335-47575-6

Recycling programs
for this product may
not exist in your area.

The Cowgirl Nanny

Copyright © 2024 by Jen Gilroy

For questions and comments about the quality of this book, please contact us at CustomerService@Harlequin.com.

TM and ® are trademarks of Harlequin Enterprises ULC.

Harlequin Enterprises ULC
22 Adelaide St. West, 41st Floor
Toronto, Ontario M5H 4E3, Canada
www.Harlequin.com

Printed in U.S.A.

Jen Gilroy writes sweet romance and uplifting women's fiction—warm feel-good stories to bring readers' hearts home. A Romance Writers of America Golden Heart® Award finalist and short-listed for the Romantic Novelists' Association Joan Hessayon Award, she lives in small-town Ontario, Canada, with her husband, teenage daughter and floppy-eared rescue hound. She loves reading, ice cream, ballet and paddling her purple kayak. Visit her at jengilroy.com.

Books by Jen Gilroy

Harlequin Heartwarming

Montana Reunion
A Family for the Rodeo Cowboy

Visit the Author Profile page
at Harlequin.com.

For Joan, with love from "Jen up the hill."

Thank you for your friendship, wise counsel and staunch support.

CHAPTER ONE

"WHOA THERE, BUDDY." Bryce Carter grabbed the black-and-white goat by its collar. "Where do you think you're going?"

The goat stared at him with a yellow petunia plant half out of its mouth. It bleated and looked back over its shoulder at a miniature red barn by the entrance to Squirrel Tail Ranch's activity center.

"There's always something more interesting on the other side of the fence, isn't there?" Bryce scratched the goat's neck as children's laughter echoed from behind the barn. He shook his head at the trampled flower bed and picked up the rope trailing from the goat's purple collar. "Folks will be looking for both of us." In Bryce's case, those "folks" were his two children—the most important people in his world—and he'd promised them he'd be here half an hour ago.

Leading the goat, Bryce stopped by the red barn and scanned the busy scene. A young woman, likely a college student, drove a tractor pulling a wagon piled with hay and excited children. The principal, who'd been Bryce's fifth-grade teacher at the same school his kids now attended, waved.

"Daddy." Eight-year-old Paisley ran toward him, two blond pigtails bobbing. "When you weren't here when you said you'd be, Cam was scared something bad happened. I said I bet you were rounding up that mean old bull." She wrapped her arms around his waist while her six-year-old brother, Cam, who'd trailed behind, hung on to Bryce's arm.

"It wasn't the bull, and Big Red's not so bad." Not since Bryce's brother, Cole, had taken the animal in hand. "I was checking crops in the far fields, and the truck had a flat tire. I had to stop and change it." He gestured to his mud-spattered jeans. "Sorry I'm late. I couldn't call because I didn't have cell service. I hope I didn't miss too much." He'd wanted to get here early so he could share the last part of this field trip with the kids, but, once again, life had conspired against him.

"It's okay. Everyone's still here," Paisley said. "Where'd you get that goat?"

"He was in the flower bed near the guest welcome area. He must have gotten out of the petting zoo."

Except for the surrounding fields, rented out to grow grain and other cereal crops, Squirrel Tail was more a resort and tourist attraction than a working ranch. Owned by Shane Gallagher, a friend of Bryce's mom who'd moved to Montana from Wyoming a few years ago, Squirrel Tail now hosted events. Besides school field trips like this one, they also held birthday parties and company team building events and offered luxury bed-and-breakfast accommodations and meditation and wellness retreats.

"We went on a nature walk and learned how to build a rabbit hutch. Wanna come see?" Paisley asked.

"Sure." His daughter still hugged him, and Bryce inhaled her sweet little-girl scent. With her blonde hair and pale blue eyes, she didn't look like her mom, but with her outgoing personality, kindness and love of animals, Paisley was like Alison, Bryce's late wife, in other ways. Cam, though, had inherited Ally's bright blue eyes and chocolate-brown hair. He looked so much like the girl Bryce had fallen in love with when her family had moved to town because of her dad's job, and she'd joined his sixth-grade class.

Bryce grabbed his cowboy hat as it caught in a gust of wind and bent to his son's level. "You okay?"

"Yeah." Cam stared at the ground and dug his sneakers into the dirt. "Mr. Gallagher said I'm good with horses."

"You're a natural like your uncle Cole." Bryce ruffled Cam's hair. His son needed a haircut. Something else for Bryce to add to this weekend's to-do list.

As a group of boys around Cam's age raced past, Cam moved nearer to him.

"Has anyone seen a…?" A thirtysomething woman with light brown hair in a high ponytail stopped by Bryce and the kids. "Here you are, Sammy. You're an escape artist, aren't you?" She grinned and glanced at them.

Paisley giggled again. "My daddy caught the goat."

"Thanks." The woman brushed her hands against her faded blue jeans. "It wouldn't be good to lose one of the owner's animals my first time here. You must be Paisley and Cam's dad."

"Yeah, I'm Bryce Carter." He took off his hat and held out his hand. She wasn't one of the regular teachers or classroom assistants. He knew all of them well because he'd either gone to school with them, or they'd been working here when he was a student. He hadn't seen her around Squirrel Tail Ranch before either.

"Carrie Rizzo." When she shook Bryce's hand, his palm tingled as it met the warmth of her strong grip. "Shane Gallagher needed extra help with today's school visit. My aunt and her friend volunteered and brought me along. I've only been in High Valley a few days. I'm here on vacation."

"Welcome." Bryce stuck out his hand to Carrie again before realizing they'd already exchanged handshakes. He was flustered because of the flat tire and being late. It had nothing to do with that unexpected spark of awareness when he'd held her hand in his.

"Can we help you put Sammy back in the pen?" Paisley hopped between Bryce and Carrie. "The rabbit hutch is near there."

"If it's okay with your dad, sure." Carrie glanced at Bryce.

"Please, Daddy?" Cam still clutched Bryce's arm, but there was more enthusiasm in his voice than Bryce had heard for weeks. "I can show you my favorite bunny. He's called Buster. Mr. Gallagher let me feed him."

"That'd be great." Bryce swallowed the lump in his throat. Between work and trying to keep day-to-day life on track, he didn't have much time for fun with the kids. He fell into step with Carrie as Paisley and Cam went ahead. "Who's your aunt?"

"Angela Moretti. She's my mom's oldest sister." As Carrie took Sammy's rope from Bryce, her fingers brushed his, and there was that tingle again.

"Mrs. Moretti's a family friend, but I don't remember you ever visiting High Valley."

"I didn't. Mom and Aunt Angela had a big argument when they were younger and didn't speak for years. They finally reconciled last Christmas." Carrie shook her head. "I'm sorry I didn't get to know Angela sooner. I'm also sorry I won't be here longer. High Valley's a great town and everyone's so kind and welcoming."

Bryce nodded. He'd had a lot of kindness from folks in High Valley since Ally died, but he needed to get better organized instead of depending on everyone's good nature.

"Paisley and Cam are wonderful kids. They were both in my small group today. Paisley's really caring toward her brother. You must be proud." Carrie's smile blossomed.

She had a great smile, like Ally, but it was different than his wife's. And while Ally had been tall and slender, with eyes as blue as the mountain cornflowers that grew wild here from late spring through early summer, Carrie was shorter with a more athletic build. She also had green eyes that sparkled and a dusting of freckles across the bridge of her nose.

Bryce stopped himself. He couldn't keep comparing every woman he met to Alison. Ally was gone, and she wasn't coming back, no matter how much he wished she could. "I sure am proud of Paisley and Cam. They're friends as well as brother and sister and look out for each other. I also try to do my best for them."

"It shows," Carrie said. "In our art session, they used poster paint to make handprints. Paisley said they do them around this time every year and stick them in an album. That's a fantastic idea. A special memory too."

"My wife started that album when the kids were babies." In the past few years, Bryce's mom had added items, but whenever she'd ask him to take a look, he'd find something else to do. The album, along with everything else Ally had made for him and the kids, hurt too much, so he'd packed those reminders away. Now they lurked in boxes stacked in a closet, like ghosts of the life he'd lost. And the album was on a shelf in the guest bedroom where he wasn't likely to see it.

"Look, Daddy." Paisley called. "Sammy must have gotten out here." She pointed to part of the fence where wire had come loose. One of Shane's ranch hands was fixing it, with help from a girl who handed him tools from a red metal box.

A small group of parents and kids patted the other goats, and Angela Moretti and several members of the Sunflower Sisterhood, a local women's group Bryce's mom belonged to, chatted nearby. The penned goats bleated at Sammy, who bleated back, and two horses in a nearby pasture joined the animal chorus.

"The bunny hutch is over here." Cam tugged on Bryce's arm as Paisley held a paper cone with special animal food pellets in front of Sammy to help lure him into the pen.

"Ms. Rizzo has to go home next week, but I want her to stay here longer." Paisley's expression was hopeful. "I also know a way she could. She could look after Cam and me for the summer. Since Grandma can only babysit us on Saturdays, you still hafta find someone else, don't you? I heard you tell Uncle Cole when he came over last night."

"Yes, but…" Bryce hesitated.

"Please?" Cam joined in with unexpected enthusiasm. "Ms. Rizzo said she'd love to see me play soccer."

"I'm sure your dad already has someone in mind." As she closed the pen's gate behind Sammy, Carrie's cheeks pinkened.

"Ms. Rizzo's on vacation. She wouldn't want a job as a summer nanny." Bryce spoke at the same time as Carrie.

"Why not?" Paisley tugged Bryce's right hand while Cam did the same on his left. "Ms. Rizzo said she's looking for a summer job to keep her horse in feed. You don't want Teddy to starve, do you?" Paisley and Cam gave Bryce matching disapproving expressions.

"Job or no job, Teddy will be fine," Carrie reassured the children.

"Paisley's right," Bryce said. "I *am* looking for a summer nanny, but so far, I haven't had any luck. I'd prefer an adult rather than a high-school student."

"Carrie's wonderful with children," Angela said as she and her friend, Nina Shevchenko, joined them near the fence.

Nina nodded. "She's a natural, all right. Kind but firm."

"Your mom says you need help." Angela chimed in again, and everyone nearby murmured agreement.

"If I can find a stable to board my horse, I'd be interested in the job, sure. Teddy's here at Squirrel Tail, now but that's temporary." Carrie knelt to tighten the fastening on one of Cam's sneakers.

"She could board Teddy at our ranch, couldn't she?" Paisley continued tugging Bryce's hand. "Ms. Rizzo's a professional barrel racer. If she looks after me and Cam, she could give me barrel racing lessons too. What do you say?"

"Hang on." Bryce took a deep breath. He'd come to pick up his kids, not look for summer childcare, but as his mom often said, "The Lord moves in mysterious ways." With only a few days of school left, hiring Carrie might be the perfect solution to one of the problems keeping him awake at night.

"Between kids, women and goats, you're outnumbered." Shane Gallagher came out of a shed behind the petting zoo. "Oh no you don't." He grabbed Sammy's collar as the goat tried to escape again.

"If you're free tomorrow, why don't you come out to our ranch?" In the midst of the chaos, Bryce spoke to Carrie in an undertone. "I can tell you more about what the kids and I need. Although Paisley got ahead of herself, we've had a cancellation, and there's a horse boarding space free in our barn. I can hold it if you want."

"That'd be great. Anytime tomorrow would work for me." Carrie's face was still flushed.

"How about eight thirty in the morning? Cam has soccer practice later, and Paisley has gymnastics."

"That's fine." Carrie's green gaze met his. "You've got a lot on your plate."

Somebody told her about Alison. Bryce's breath stuttered. He wouldn't have to explain what was still inexplicable. And when Carrie smiled again—a smile filled with understanding and compassion—it was like the sun slipping out from behind dark clouds.

"See you tomorrow. I'll get directions to your place from Aunt Angela." Carrie gestured to Cam, who, the rabbit hutch and Buster forgotten, leaned against her with his eyes half-closed. "Cam's almost asleep on his feet. You probably want to head home."

"Yeah." Bryce took a step back. For a few seconds, it was like he'd had a connection with Carrie that went beyond the kids. A connection like he'd only ever experienced with one other woman, his wife.

Except, he'd loved once and well. His focus was on his children and the family ranch. The romantic part of his life was over.

THE NEXT MORNING, Carrie took in the view through one of the floor-to-ceiling windows in Bryce's house. Set back from the main road via a tree-lined driveway, the one-story ranch style had an open-concept floor plan with the eating area and kitchen connected to this spacious family room. The window overlooked a pasture, encircled by a split-rail fence, where several horses grazed. Near a water trough, a cute foal nuzzled its mother.

"Take a seat." Bryce came through from the kitchen holding a tray with two mugs and a plate of cookies. He nodded toward a duck-egg blue L-shaped sectional sofa along one wall. "I tidied up last night after the kids went to bed. The place isn't usually this neat." He set the tray on the table facing the sofa and offered Carrie a mug of coffee.

"You didn't have to clean up for me. Homes are meant to be lived in." Apart from a basket of children's books and Paisley's and Cam's backpacks beside a big fireplace, the room was almost too tidy, with none of the scattered toys and games she'd expected. From what she'd seen of Bryce's house so far, from porch planters empty of flowers to this room with the furniture at precise angles, it had an air of sadness as if part of its soul was missing.

"There's lived-in, and there's chaos. We're more the latter." Bryce gave her a wry smile and sat on the other end of the sofa beneath a big TV. In jeans and a white T-shirt, he looked younger than his midthirties. Although Carrie hadn't fished for information, Aunt Angela had told her about Bryce as well as the rest of the Carter family.

Carrie tried to look more confident than she felt. "Where are Paisley and Cam?" The house was silent, and country sounds—cattle lowing, a whir of insects and birdsong—filtered through the half-open windows.

"At my mom's. We've got a big spread here at the Tall Grass. Mom lives at the main ranch house farther along the driveway. She's on her own there except when my sister, Molly, visits from Atlanta. My oldest brother, Zach, and his family live a few miles away in a house our great-grandparents had before they built the main place. Mom needed the kids to come by for a fitting of the outfits she's making them for my brother Cole's wedding."

"Paisley's excited about being a flower girl. She told me about it yesterday." Carrie sipped her coffee. Aunt Angela had mentioned Cole Carter's wedding. Between contributing food, organizing flowers and making decorations for the church and reception hall, the women of the Sunflower Sisterhood were all involved in wedding preparations.

"That wedding is Paisley's favorite topic of conversation. Cole's fiancée and her daughter live in town. With wedding planning in full swing, their house is Paisley's favorite place to be. Cole's moving there after the wedding, but for now he's bunking in one of the ranch's outlying cabins. I joke there are days I'm tempted to join him for some peace." Bryce laughed and set his mug back on the table. "So, about the nannying job." His manner became all business. "I should tell you—"

"It's fine." Carrie set her coffee aside too. "Paisley put you on the spot. I have a lead on a summer job at the Bluebunch Café, and there's bound to be casual work in haying season. I left my contact details at the Squirrel Tail Ranch too. They hire extra staff for special events. I also have a freelance web design and marketing business."

As she moved to stand, Bryce shook his head. "Wait. If you want the nanny job, it's yours. My kids like you, and from what I saw yesterday, you're great with them, but Cam especially..." He rested his beard-stubbled chin in his hands. His short brown hair was damp, as if he'd just had a shower, and an errant curly lock flopped over one of his eyes making him look both rakish and vulnerable.

"What about Cam?" Carrie settled on the sofa again and made herself focus on the children instead of her urge to brush that piece of hair away from Bryce's forehead.

"He's always been a quiet kid, but he used to be a happy one too. The past few months, he hasn't been himself. He's either lashing out in anger or withdrawn. He hardly plays with his favorite toys, and apart from soccer, he isn't interested in the sports or activities he once enjoyed. I talked to the pediatrician and took Cam to see a few counsellors, but none of them have been able to reach him. I don't know what else to do." Bryce looked at his bare feet. "Cam's having trouble at school as well."

"When Cam was assigned to my group yesterday, his teacher asked me to keep an extra close eye on him." Between school staff and a parent volunteer, Carrie had heard lots about Cameron Carter. While he'd been fine with her for the field-trip activities, the word was he spent more time in the principal's office than with his class.

Bryce rubbed one hand across his eyes then looked up at her again. "Yesterday, when Cam was with you, I saw the boy he used to be." He drew in a breath. "My son needs help, and maybe you can help him."

"I'll try." Carrie was one of life's helpers and a giver too, but there was a fine line between giving and people pleasing. Often, she tried to make others happy at the expense of herself. "I heard about your wife. I'm sorry."

"Ally passed three years ago. She had cancer. It should get easier but…" His shoulders slumped. "Cam hardly remembers his mom, and even Paisley has forgotten a lot about her."

"Do you talk about Ally with them?" Having been close to her grandmother who'd died ten years before, when Carrie was in her early twenties, she knew how important it was to keep a loved one's memory alive.

"Not really. It's hard for me too." He shoved that lock of hair away as if daring it to fall forward again. Bryce had a square, serious face with deep-set blue-gray eyes, and Carrie got the impression he didn't smile or laugh often.

She took another mouthful of rich, full-bodied coffee and let it linger on her tongue. She'd half accepted the job without knowing anything about it. That was unlike her, but she was desperate and didn't want to have to dip into her savings. She didn't have new freelance projects lined up, and casual part-time jobs wouldn't pay enough for her to board Teddy. She also didn't want to return to Kalispell and rely on her parents or cross paths with the ex who'd dumped her for a woman she'd thought was a friend.

Although hurt pinched her heart, she straightened, determined to leave the past where it belonged. "What kind of nanny are you looking for? Live-in or daily?"

"Daily to start, but live-in if needed. Monday to Friday mostly but likely some weekends too. Meal preparation, grocery shopping and laundry if you have time."

"That sounds fine." The pressure in Carrie's chest eased. "I'm flexible. Aunt Angela's happy for me to stay with her, or I can live here when you need me to."

Bryce exhaled as if in relief. "Ranching isn't a nine-to-five or Monday-to-Friday job, and things come up unexpectedly. I'm also a volunteer firefighter and do agricultural consultancy. I might need you to work extra hours at short notice." His expression was almost pleading.

"I understand. Although I grew up in Kalispell, my mom's parents had a ranch, where I spent vacations. I can work whatever hours you need. Except for training with my horse, I don't have anything else planned this summer."

And she'd love to stay in High Valley. It would be a chance to prove to herself and everyone else, her parents especially, that her barrel racing career was only on pause. She needed to stop trying to please her folks and follow her own path instead of the one they wanted for her. For far too long, she'd let her parents assume barrel racing and freelance work were temporary. Unless she stood up to them, she'd be in that office in the family construction company before she knew it, wearing a suit and working a desk job. She suppressed a shudder.

"Paisley said you're a professional barrel racer." Bryce's voice broke into Carrie's thoughts.

"Yes." Her stomach quivered at the warmth and interest in his expression. "I had a few minor injuries and need to take time out, but I'm returning to the circuit this fall." Everybody had setbacks. How you handled them was what mattered. This summer was her time to reset, regain her mojo and come back even stronger. "I also went to college and studied business and marketing. That's where my freelance web design and marketing work comes in." It gave her another source of income and added to the money she was saving to buy a small farm or ranch of her own. Once she had it, she wanted to practice sustainable agriculture like she'd learned from her grandparents.

"Paisley's only eight, but she's already set on pro-level barrel racing." Bryce shrugged. "Before he retired with an injury, Cole was a professional rodeo cowboy. My dad rode on the circuit too, so rodeo's in Paisley's blood. I don't want to discourage her from setting a goal and going after it, but I want her to be realistic too. Cole had to sacrifice a lot to make that life work."

"It's tricky, and you have to want it, but I love it. Paisley might change her mind, though."

"Perhaps, but she's a determined girl." Bryce's expression was tight. "Having you around for the next few months will be great for her as well as Cam."

"I'm happy to help all of you." This job would help Carrie too.

"I forgot to mention we have two dogs, and there's always barn cats running around. Are you okay with pets?"

"Love them." Her ex didn't like cats or dogs. In retrospect, it was one of many signs they weren't right for each other.

"Great. Have a cookie?" He passed her the

plate. "They're chocolate chip. My mom made them. Some say she's the best baker in High Valley."

As Carrie took the plate, Bryce's hand brushed against hers, and she drew in a sharp breath. There it was, that same spark of attraction she'd felt yesterday. "I'll have a cookie to go." A door slammed, a dog barked and Paisley's voice echoed from the rear of the house. "With soccer and gymnastics, you have a busy day."

"I do, but..." Bryce hesitated as the kids raced into the family room with their arms open for hugs. "We haven't talked about a start date, but is there any way it could be today? We haven't talked about money either, but I'll pay you more than the going rate. As I mentioned, I'll include horse boarding too. For free, if I didn't make that clear."

"Please say yes, Ms. Rizzo." After hugging his dad, Cam moved to sit beside Carrie.

"Today's fine. I'll let Aunt Angela know." Joy mixed with excitement shot through Carrie at the thought of the money she'd be able to save this summer, but she didn't want to take advantage of Bryce's generosity either. "I appreciate the horse boarding, but you should charge me. Giving it to me for free is too much."

"No, it's not. You're a lifesaver. Horse boarding's the least I can do."

As Bryce's gentle smile wrapped around Carrie like a warm hug, it also reminded her of what she couldn't let herself forget.

Despite that spark of attraction to Bryce, as his kids' nanny, he was her boss. He was also a grieving widower devoted to his late wife. Even if Carrie were ready to date again—which she wasn't—he was off-limits.

The setbacks that had knocked her life off course had made her think about what she truly wanted. From now on, she wouldn't let anything or anyone—especially a man—distract her from her goals. She'd learned that lesson well, and the betrayal still stung.

CHAPTER TWO

"GOOD JOB." In the fenced pasture behind his house, Bryce balanced the bucket as Cam tipped the last bit of water into a horse trough. He raised his hand for a high five, and his son's small palm connected with his. "Get your backpack, and I'll walk you to the end of the lane. You don't want to miss the bus on your last day of school."

"Why can't I stay home with you and Carrie? It's not like we'll do anything important today anyway." Cam's smile disappeared as he took his backpack from where he'd left it outside the fence.

Bryce patted Cam's hunched shoulders. "School's like a job. You have to show up even if you don't feel like it. Besides, you get off early today, and Carrie's picking you and Paisley up to go swimming. Aren't you excited about that?"

"Nope. I don't wanna go to school *or* swimming." Cam dragged his feet in the gravel driveway as Carrie and Paisley came out the front door with Penny and Otis, their beagle-mix dogs.

"I feel sick." He sniffed and gave a hollow cough. "I guess I hafta stay home."

"Oh no, you don't." Bryce ruffled Cam's thick hair. He'd forgotten about that haircut. He'd have to ask Carrie if she could take Cam later this week. After only a few days, Carrie had made a big and positive difference in all their lives. Bryce didn't feel like he was always rushing, and today he'd even eaten breakfast at the table with the kids instead of grabbing something to take to the fields.

"What's with the sad face, kiddo?" Carrie joined Bryce and Cam, and the boy wrapped an arm around her waist. "Don't you like school?"

Cam shook his head.

"You only have one more bus ride and a half day." Carrie's voice was encouraging. "I've got a surprise for you and Paisley this afternoon too."

"What?" Cam finally raised his head.

"It wouldn't be a surprise if I told you, would it?" Carrie laughed and tugged Paisley's ponytail. "Race you to the end of the lane? First one to touch the mailbox wins. Ready, set, go!" She took off, and the kids and dogs followed. "You too, Bryce." She gestured over her shoulder. In the morning sun, Carrie's hair gleamed with golden tints, and her ponytail had a pink ribbon like Paisley's.

Bryce froze and then broke into a jog. Although Paisley and Cam might not remember, he and Ally used to run to the end of the lane with them when Paisley caught the school bus too.

"Go, Cam. We can't keep up with you." Carrie bent and said something to Paisley, and his daughter nodded and slowed her pace.

"I won." Cam touched the mailbox and squealed with excitement.

"You sure did." Carrie hugged him and then Paisley. "And here's your dad bringing up the rear. Early chores tire you out?" She gave Bryce a teasing grin.

"No, it's…" Bryce blinked away the sudden moisture behind his eyes. He had to focus on the present and not mar this moment with sadness or regrets. "Your mom was a fast runner too. Way faster than me."

"I never knew that." Paisley looked him up and down. "What else was Mommy better at than you?"

"Lots of things." An engine rumbled, and the yellow school bus appeared in the distance as Carrie corralled the dogs.

"What things?" Paisley still studied him. "You never talk about Mommy, and I want to know."

"Maybe your dad doesn't—" Carrie glanced at him over the kids' heads.

"It's okay." Bryce forced a smile. "If you want, we could make a list of things your mom was great at after supper tonight."

"Really?" Paisley's expression said she expected Bryce to forget or change his mind.

"I promise. See?" He held up his phone. "I'll make myself a note."

As the bus stopped with a hiss of brakes, Paisley's mouth trembled, and then she flung her arms around him in a tight hug.

Most of all, Ally had been great at loving the kids they'd made together. Bryce's chest compressed. "Off you go. Have a good day. Love you." Paisley let go of him and boarded the bus to join her friends.

"You too, Cam." Carrie gave him a gentle push toward the bus steps. "It's only a few hours until I pick you up. You can manage that."

"I guess I have to." Cam hunched over as if to make himself smaller, trudged up the steps and took the seat closest to the driver.

The driver waved before closing the door, and the bus started up again.

As they turned to walk back along the lane to the house, Carrie broke the silence. "Do you know what that's about?"

"Cam not wanting to go to school, you mean?" Bryce called Otis and Penny back from sniffing a field of new baby bean plants.

Carrie nodded. "He didn't want to get on the bus either."

"He's been that way for a few months now.

I've tried and so have his teachers and the bus driver, but he won't talk about it."

"I'll try too." Carrie patted Bryce's arm and gave him an encouraging smile. "I have the whole summer with him and Paisley."

Bryce's arm tingled like his hand had the day they met, and his gaze caught Carrie's and held. Her green eyes, filled with concern for Cam, were the same color as the bean plants. The color of life, rebirth and hope.

"It's—"

"You—"

Bryce gestured to Carrie to go first.

"That surprise I mentioned to the kids?" Carrie patted the dogs. "I'm taking them for ice cream at the Bluebunch Café after we swim. My mom always did that with me on the last day of school. It was a special treat I looked forward to. If you have time, you're welcome to join us. I'm sure the kids would love it."

Bryce would love it too, and although he didn't have time, Paisley and Cam were more important than ranch work. "That sounds good. Text me before you leave the pool. I'll meet you at the café."

"Will do." As Carrie smiled at him, there was that connection again, even stronger this time.

Although Bryce had never thought about dating or remarrying, he didn't have to shut himself off from fun and happiness—or family and friends either.

Going for ice cream wasn't a big deal. It was the kind of thing Ally would have planned too. Besides, it was for the kids. As long as he focused on the kids and ignored whatever that tingle was with Carrie, he'd be fine.

"I HAVE TO go in here and get something for my aunt Angela before I go home, but I'll be back to make breakfast for you tomorrow morning." Outside the Medicine Wheel Craft Center on High Valley's main street, Carrie knelt beside Cam and used a paper napkin to wipe chocolate ice cream from around his mouth. "I hope you like the lasagna I made. All you and your dad have to do is cover it with foil and heat it in the oven. Easy." She grinned at Bryce. "I used stuff in your cupboards and freezer. The kids and I will pick up groceries tomorrow. Make a list of what meals you'd like, and Paisley and Cam can help me make them."

"That would be great." Bryce straightened his cowboy hat. "Come on, kids. I parked the truck around the corner."

"I don't wanna go home without Carrie." Cam's voice rose in a whine. "Why can't she have supper with us? It's not fair." He stamped one foot in his small cowboy boot.

"Maybe someday soon I can have supper with you. Like if your dad has to work late." Carrie cupped Cam's chin in her hands. "Remember what I said?"

"We don't whine, and when we want something, we ask nicely." Paisley's voice was smug.

"Okay." Cam's grin was sheepish. "Would you read to me tomorrow please? I can pick out books tonight."

"I'd love to read to you tomorrow, and I can't wait to see what stories you choose." Carrie hugged the little boy, and he wrapped his arms around her neck. "Now go with your dad like he asked." She got to her feet. "You're going to make that list about your mom tonight too. It'll be tomorrow morning before you know it."

As the kids put their used napkins in a nearby trash can, Bryce spoke in an undertone to Carrie. "How did you do that?"

"Do what?" She moved toward the craft center's door, which was propped open to let in the balmy June air.

"I thought Cam was going to have a meltdown, but instead he…" Bryce gestured to where Cam and Paisley patted a golden retriever stopped with its owner on the sidewalk.

"I talked to the kids about what they can expect from me, and what I expect from them. I want us to have fun together this summer and for the kids to trust me, but…" Carrie stopped at the expression on Bryce's face. Had she overstepped? She'd never worked as a nanny, but she'd done lots of babysitting and taught pony club. She also remembered what it was like to be a kid.

"It's fine, and you're right. I guess I can learn from you." Bryce's half smile was as sheepish as his son's had been.

"We can learn from each other." Carrie's heartbeat sped up as Bryce rubbed a muscular hand over one of his beard-stubbled cheeks. If she'd met him under any other circumstances, she'd have thought he was gorgeous, but she couldn't let herself think such things about her boss. "You know Paisley and Cam best, but for me kids are a lot like horses. You adapt your training to what the animal, or child, needs but they both need rules. It helps them feel safe and secure."

"You're a wise woman." Bryce's voice had a husky note that was almost intimate. "See you tomorrow?"

"You bet." Carrie put a hand to her throat as her eyes caught his. Her ex, Jimmy, had blue eyes, but not like Bryce's. She'd never met anyone with eyes like his—so soft and gentle but with a teasing glint too.

Her mouth went dry, and warmth suffused her chest as she turned and went into the craft center, brushing a set of wind chimes that tinkled.

"Welcome." A woman's voice came from behind a weaving loom set up by the front window.

"Hi." Carrie swallowed. Despite those beguiling eyes, Bryce was off-limits. "I'm Carrie Rizzo. I'm here to pick up the tapestry wool my aunt, Angela Moretti, ordered. She texted me it was in and asked me to drop by."

"Here you go." The woman stepped away from the loom and blanket she was working on and handed Carrie a paper shopping bag. "I'm Rosa Cardinal. Well done out there with young Cam." A broad smile creased her face as she smoothed her thick shoulder-length gray hair.

"You saw?" Carrie took the bag and slipped the straw handles over her wrist.

"Heard too with the door and windows open. I'm part of the Sunflower Sisterhood and a good friend of Bryce's mom, Joy. You're exactly who Paisley and Cam need. Bryce loves his kids, but he lets them get away with too much." Rosa shook her head. "It's understandable since they lost their mom, but Cam especially needs consistency and routine."

"I hope I can offer him something positive." Carrie glanced around the spacious store filled with beaded dream catchers, framed abstract paintings in bold colors, glass display cases of colorful pottery and silver jewelry, as well as tapestries, rugs and other woven items.

"You already have, and you'll keep on the way you're going. I have three grown children of my own and fostered countless more. I know someone who's good with kids when I see them." Rosa took Carrie's hand and shook it, her grip firm. "I'm glad to meet you. Angela's so happy you're staying for the summer. She hasn't been the same since her husband passed, and it's good for her to have family close."

"I'm glad to be with her." Carrie looked around the craft center again. "You have a beautiful space."

"It is, isn't it? I moved in a few years ago. It used to be the old train station. My business outgrew my kitchen table. Now it's outgrowing this place too." She laughed. "It's a good problem to have. I've hired three women to work with me this summer in the store, and I'll need some high-school kids part-time when it gets really busy in July and August." She stopped and studied Carrie. "Ordinarily, I'd want to interview you, but Angela's opinion and what I heard and saw out there tell me that won't be necessary."

"Interview me for what? I already have a job with Bryce." Although Carrie enjoyed craftwork, it was a hobby, and she wasn't as skilled as Aunt Angela, let alone a professional like Rosa.

"Angela said you do web design and marketing."

"Yes, freelance. Is there something I can do for you?"

"A new website for a start and likely more. Consider yourself hired." Rosa stuck out her hand again. "Flexible hours. Whenever you can fit the work in around those precious children."

"I'd be happy to help you, but you haven't seen my work or asked for a project proposal or quote."

"Oh, I've seen your work. Angela showed me the website you created for that jewelry designer in Idaho and other projects too. She might not show it, but she's proud of you."

"I don't know what to say."

"*Yes* would be a good start." Rosa's warm laugh made Carrie laugh too.

"Then yes, of course." Carrie took Rosa's hand in hers as they shook on the deal. What was that expression about good things coming in threes? The nanny job, free boarding for Teddy at the Tall Grass Ranch and now a freelance job. It was almost too good to be true.

"We'll work out the details later. You'd better get home. Angela will have supper waiting." With a squeeze, Rosa dropped Carrie's hand. "Better days ahead, that's what my mom said." Rosa's dark eyes were as warm as her laugh. "Angela says you've had some bumps in your life, but you've got gumption. I like gumption."

Carrie straightened her shoulders and returned

Rosa's smile. In only a few days, her life had changed for the better, and that was because of High Valley and its people.

But maybe it was also because she'd let herself be open to opportunities. And for the first time in what felt like forever, she was excited about what might happen next.

CHAPTER THREE

JOY CARTER OPENED the barn door and waved at Carrie, who unlatched the back of the horse trailer hitched to a red pickup truck. "Hi. I'm Bryce's mom, Joy." She joined Carrie by the trailer as a rich, red chestnut with a crooked white star between its eyes stuck its head out. "I'm here to lend a hand to get you two settled."

"Thanks. Meet Teddy." Carrie rubbed the horse's neck. "He's my best friend, aren't you, boy?"

Teddy bobbed his head and nickered at Joy in welcome.

"He's gorgeous." Joy studied the quarter horse with an experienced eye. "Looks like just over fifteen hands in height. Good weight too."

"He's also fast and strong. We've won a lot of races together." Carrie's head was close to Teddy's, and he nuzzled her, the affectionate gesture showing Joy their close bond.

"I expect you'll win lots more." Joy took Teddy's lead rope so Carrie could shut the horse trailer.

"Hi, Teddy. Welcome to the Tall Grass Ranch." Standing at a slight angle, she approached him from the left, made eye contact and gave him her hand to sniff. "We've given Teddy a stall on the end near the barn door so he can be part of what's going on." Joy glanced at Carrie. "Bryce cleaned it out last night. He said Teddy's a sociable guy. One of my other sons, Cole, manages the horse barn, but Bryce wanted to take care of Teddy's stall personally."

Bryce rarely had anything to do with the horse barn, so his insistence on getting this stall ready told Joy there was something going on. Offering to be here to help Carrie get Teddy settled was a way for Joy to find out what that "something" might be.

"That's really nice of Bryce." In jeans, cowboy boots and a white T-shirt under a checked flannel shirt, Carrie looked like she belonged on a ranch. Her brown hair was pulled back in a thick ponytail, and her battered brown cowboy hat was working headgear, not a fashion accessory. She smiled as she retrieved the lead rope from Joy and led Teddy toward the open barn door. "I've only worked for him a few days, but Bryce and the kids have been great at making me comfortable."

"You'll be a big help to all of them this summer. You too, Teddy. The kids are excited to meet you." The sweetness of Carrie's smile and the kindness in her expression made Joy warm to her. "Paisley and Cam need the one-on-one attention they can't get at a day camp."

"In you go, boy." Carrie soothed Teddy as he stopped by the stall door. "They're fun kids. Bryce took them to the fields with him this morning so I could move Teddy from Squirrel Tail to here."

"They're lively kids too." Joy hesitated. Carrie seemed sensible and practical. Joy owed it to her, as well as her son and grandchildren, to speak her mind, and if she didn't do it now, when would she? "But the whole family's struggling, and I don't know how to fix it." She leaned on the half door of the neighboring stall and patted Daisy-May, an Appaloosa and the gentlest horse on the ranch.

"Maybe you can't fix it or them." Carrie filled a feed bucket from the container Joy indicated. "You can help, sure, but people have to fix themselves."

"That sounds like the voice of experience." All Joy knew of Carrie was the little Angela had said about her niece at the last Sunflower Sisterhood meeting, supplemented by Paisley and Cam's excited chatter about their new nanny. Bryce hadn't said anything at all and, even though her youngest son was quiet, that told Joy something too.

"I guess so." As Teddy stuck his nose into the feed bucket, Carrie checked the automatic waterer and closed the stall door. "I shouldn't talk. This summer is about fixing myself." She turned to face Joy. "Aunt Angela respects my privacy, but it's not a secret. I had a few injuries, minor ones, but enough to keep me off the rodeo circuit. And then, somehow, I lost my mojo. Along with stuff in my personal life, everything added up. I need time to rest and reset before I return to competitive barrel racing."

"You're smart to recognize what you need." In her early sixties, Joy was only now figuring out what she needed in life—but maybe, and even if she'd started earlier, it would always be a work in progress. "I'm guessing there was a man somewhere in there too?" She wasn't prying; she was only interested because Carrie was looking after her grandbabies.

"You guessed right." Carrie greeted Daisy-May and introduced her to Teddy. "I'm over that relationship, but from now on, I won't let myself think about settling down."

Where had Joy heard that one before? She suppressed a smile. Carrie sounded like Cole, but in a few weeks her restless middle child would marry sweet Melissa and be a stepdad to Mel's daughter, Skylar. He'd only needed to meet the right person. Maybe Carrie did too.

Joy considered the younger woman as she spoke to Teddy and Daisy-May, her voice reassuring and calm. Horses and children both tested boundaries and acted out when they were bored or tired, but they also loved to play. Most importantly, horses and kids lived in the moment. Somebody needed to drag Bryce out of the past and help him live the life he still had. Could Carrie be that person?

"Hey, is that Teddy?" Paisley skidded to a stop by Joy and pointed to the horse.

"It sure is." Carrie overturned two empty buckets so Paisley and Cam, who followed his sister, could stand on them to greet the horse at eye level.

"Can I let him sniff my hand?" Cam asked.

"After you say hello and if your dad says it's okay." Carrie glanced at Bryce, who'd joined them. "Outside the competition arena, Teddy's pretty easygoing." She rubbed the horse's ears. "He's kind too. See the kindness in his eyes?"

The same kindness as in his owner's eyes. As Joy looked between Carrie and Bryce, something flashed between them. Awareness…maybe even a brief soul-to-soul bond. Joy had had that bond with her late husband. From the moment she'd met Dennis as a young girl, she'd known he was the one for her, and that hadn't changed over all their years together.

"Go ahead." Bryce spoke to Cam, who held out his hand to Teddy, and then Paisley did the same. "Whatever you or Teddy need, ask one of the ranch hands or Cole." Bryce waved Cole over to be introduced. "Or me, of course." His cheeks reddened, and he pulled his hat farther down over his face.

"It's all great." As Carrie greeted Cole, her cheeks were pink too.

"You'll see my oldest son around as well, but not until next week," Joy added. "Zach, his wife, Beth, and their daughter, Ellie, are visiting friends in Chicago. That's where Beth and Ellie are from. We all run the ranch together. It's been a family operation for several generations."

"It always will be." Cole grinned at Carrie. "I hear you're a barrel racer. I'm retired now, but I rode rodeo for a lot of years. We might have crossed paths."

"We probably did. I certainly recognize your name. Everybody's heard of Cole Carter."

"Hopefully for the right reasons," Cole joked.

As Carrie and Cole talked about rodeo acquaintances, and Paisley and Cam played with the barn cats, Joy moved closer to Bryce. He stood apart from the group, and his blue-gray eyes were somber.

"Are you okay?" She touched his arm.

"Why wouldn't I be?" His laugh and smile

were too bright. "The crops are doing well, so if we get rain at the right time we'll be set."

"I'm talking about *you*, not the crops." Mr. Wiggins, Joy's favorite barn cat, nudged Joy's ankles, and she picked him up for a cuddle, scratching the black patch on top of his head.

"I'm fine, Mom. You worry too much." Bryce avoided Joy's gaze. "The kids are doing great. Carrie's fantastic for them."

"I'm glad." She gave him a one-armed hug. If Bryce didn't want to talk about his feelings, Joy couldn't make him. "Life goes on, and I want you to be happy."

"I'm happy with my kids and work. That's enough." Bryce shrugged.

"After your dad passed, I thought the same, but life can give you an unexpected second chance. You don't want to miss out."

"I'm happy you and Shane are dating. I like him. We all do. Dad would have too." Bryce kept his eyes fixed on his kids.

"Shane's a good man, but we're taking things slowly." Joy still couldn't believe the kind and handsome owner of the Squirrel Tail Ranch had come into her life and seemed to have every intention of staying there. "I'll grieve your dad for the rest of my life, but that doesn't mean I can't let myself be open to happiness again. It's a different kind of happiness, that's all."

Bryce shook his head. "Zach and Cole are settled, and I am too. If you have to worry about someone, worry about Molly."

"I *do* worry about your sister." As much, if not more, than Joy worried about her sons. Despite having the big-city life and nursing career she'd always wanted, Molly didn't seem happy in Atlanta. "I worry about all of you and always will. It comes with being a parent." And after losing her oldest son, Paul, who'd died from complications of cystic fibrosis in his early twenties, she worried about her other children even more.

Bryce nodded and then stared at the barn floor. "Leave it, okay? I'm not Cole or Zach. I already met the love of my life and married her. I'm not looking for anyone else, so you don't need to interfere."

"I didn't exactly interfere with your brothers. I only—"

"Grandma." Cam tugged Joy's arm. "Teddy likes me. Come see."

"He likes me too, even more 'cause I'm older and know more about horses." Paisley joined in.

"But I'm a better rider than you were at my age and—"

"Teddy likes both of you," Carrie interjected. "Remember what I said about bragging and competing with each other?" She crouched to their level to speak to both kids.

Over the kids' and Carrie's heads, Cole gave Joy a meaningful look and then, as he gestured to his brother, a teasing grin.

Joy shook her head. Carrie *was* fantastic for Paisley and Cam, but she could be fantastic for Bryce too. She wanted all her kids to be happy, and there was nothing wrong in wanting to look out for them, no matter how old they were.

She glanced at Bryce, who stared at Carrie with a new softness and yearning in his expression.

Or in giving people a gentle push when they needed it.

"Don't forget to wash your hands, Daddy. You should change your shirt too. There's yucky stuff all over it." Paisley screwed up her face in distaste as she greeted Bryce at the back door of their house.

"That 'yucky stuff' is good, clean Montana dirt." He pulled off his boots and grinned at his daughter, who wore a pink ruffled bib apron his mom had made for her. "But yeah, I should change." He ducked into the mudroom, closed the door and took a clean shirt and pair of jeans from a hook. They hadn't been there this morning, so Carrie must have left them for him when she'd done laundry. It was the little things she did without him asking her to that made his life easier.

"Where's your brother?" Bryce slid out of his

dirty garments and washed up in the utility sink before getting dressed in the fresh clothing.

"Reading with Carrie." Paisley talked to him from the other side of the door. "We baked chocolate brownies. I helped Carrie cook dinner too, and Cam set the table."

"Something sure smells good." In the six days Carrie had worked for him, Bryce's life hadn't only gotten easier, but his house now felt like a home. A jug of wildflowers sat in the middle of the kitchen table. Delicious meals were ready for him after a long day of ranch work. There was clean laundry when he and the kids needed it. And most of all, he had happy children and more time to spend with them.

"It's spaghetti and meatballs." As Bryce opened the mudroom door, Paisley took his hand, and Penny and Otis tumbled around his feet. "Carrie used her family's recipe from Italy."

"Sounds fancy." Bryce followed his daughter to the kitchen, where the scent of rich spices and meat was stronger.

"No, it's not." Paisley shook her head. "Carrie said it's good, plain Italian home cooking. I wish we were Italian."

"No such luck, kiddo. The Carter family's English, Scottish and Irish. On your mom's side, you're Ukrainian and German with a bit of Dutch thrown in."

"You're a wonderful mix of countries and cultures like lots of Americans," Carrie said as she and Cam came into the kitchen. Cam carried a stack of books and put them on the shelf between the kitchen and the family room. Then he fed the dogs without being asked. "Dinner's ready, and there's a salad in the fridge. I should get going and—"

"Can't Carrie stay? Please?" Cam's expression was hopeful, but his voice didn't have even a hint of what used to be a too familiar whine.

"If you're free, it would be great if you could stay later tonight." Bryce turned to Carrie. "One of my crop-consulting clients called when I was on the way back to the house. I have to work tonight. The guy needs a report by tomorrow morning." After he got the kids to bed, Bryce might have to pull an all-nighter. "I'd pay you extra, of course."

"I don't have any plans, so I can stick around until the kids' bedtime." Like Paisley, Carrie also wore an apron—a green gingham one that had belonged to Ally.

"Yay!" Paisley and Cam shouted.

Bryce opened the fridge to get the salad. There was no reason Carrie shouldn't wear Ally's apron. Bryce had told her to make herself at home, and the apron, like Paisley's, had been in one of the kitchen drawers. It unsettled him, that was all, seeing another woman in Ally's place.

"Wash your hands, kids, and then we can eat," he said, putting the salad bowl and servers one of Ally's cousins had given them for a wedding present on the table.

"Tough day at work?" Carrie untied the apron and hung it from a hook near the kitchen bulletin board. The same hook Ally had once hung it from and the board where he and the kids had pinned the list they'd made of things that Ally was good at. Whenever Bryce looked at that list, his chest tightened and his vision blurred. But having it there made it seem like his wife was still part of the heart of their home.

"It was okay." Bryce rubbed the back of his neck. "I spent most of it on horseback. Since I don't spend as much time in the saddle as Zach and Cole, I'll sure feel it tomorrow." He winced as he pulled out his chair at the head of the table.

Carrie sat in the chair next to Cam's, leaving the seat at the other end of the table empty. "It must be weird for you having me, still almost a stranger, here in your house with your kids. If there's anything I can do to make it easier, tell me, please." Her hair curled in tendrils around her face, and her expression showed concern.

"It's fine, it's…" He hesitated but the kids were still in the bathroom with the faucet running. "I miss my wife, and you cooking dinner and all the rest reminds me of how things used to be. I should be okay with it by now but—"

"There's no timeline for grief." Carrie took paper napkins out of the holder and set them at each place. "The kids showed me the list you made with them where they wrote that their mom was a great cook. Did that apron I was wearing belong to your wife?"

Bryce nodded, suddenly too choked up to speak.

"After I wash it, I'll give it to you to put away. If there are other things you'd rather not see around or have me use, let me know." Carrie got up to drain the pasta.

"It's not that." Bryce stared at his empty plate. "The memories hit me when I least expect."

"I understand." Carrie ladled pasta into a serving bowl.

"Ally was my whole life. I'll never stop missing her."

"The kids showed me pictures of their mom. She was beautiful."

"Beautiful inside and out." Bryce took the bowl of spaghetti, now topped with fragrant meatballs in a tomato sauce, from Carrie as Paisley and Cam sat in their usual places at the table.

"Are you talking about Carrie?" Paisley glanced between them as Carrie poured milk into the kids' glasses. "When we were at the feedstore, Mrs. Taylor said Carrie was beautiful."

"Mrs. Taylor was talking about my barrel racing because she's a fan of the sport." Carrie's face went red. "You shouldn't repeat things you overhear."

"But you *are* beautiful. Almost as beautiful as Mommy." Cam looked between Bryce and Carrie too.

"Let's eat. I'll serve. This salad looks great. Is it another Italian recipe?" Carrie was attractive, and although Bryce was a widower, he was also a man. The sooner he diverted this conversation, the better.

"Yes, it's one of Aunt Angela's favorites. She gave me her recipe." Carrie tucked Cam's napkin into the top of his shirt.

"Wait, Daddy." Paisley bumped his arm as Bryce picked up a serving spoon. "We hafta say thanks for the food first."

"Of course." Bryce bowed his head and said grace, the familiar words comforting and soothing him. Paisley and Cam needed this kind of life and routine.

He did too. As he opened his eyes and looked around the table, he realized how much he'd missed times like this. It was only an ordinary family dinner, but it was the most special meal he'd had since before Ally had gotten sick.

"Promise me?" Ally had looked at him with those blue eyes that had always seen what he was thinking and feeling. "I know you'll miss me, but I want you to find happiness without me."

"I promise." Bryce had clasped her thin hand and lied to her for the first and last time. He'd have said and done anything to ease her passing, but how could he be happy without the other half of himself?

"Daddy?" Paisley nudged his arm again. "I'm hungry."

"Sure. Right." He served salad and then the pasta, busying himself with passing plates and asking Paisley and Cam about their day.

"Please sit up straight and don't gobble your food, Cam. Remember?" Carrie softened the gentle admonishment with a smile.

"'Cause it's good manners and means my tummy won't hurt after eating." Cam's face was smeared with tomato sauce.

"That's right." Bryce straightened too. He'd eaten too many meals on the run or in front of the TV, but a family mealtime, like his mom and then Ally had insisted on, was important.

He glanced at Carrie, who now helped Cam twirl spaghetti around his fork, while the two of them laughed at a joke Paisley had told.

Bryce had never imagined thinking about another woman, let alone being drawn to one like he was to Carrie. However, she was his employee. He had no business looking at her in any way apart from as the kids' nanny.

Carrie laughed again, Otis barked and Penny lay beneath the table at Bryce's feet.

His heart squeezed. Home, family and love were all right here. Not as they'd once been. He'd never get back what he'd had with Ally, but maybe he could find something new.

His gaze drifted to Carrie once more. Something that would be good for all of them.

CHAPTER FOUR

"IS THAT WHEELBARROW too heavy for you?" Carrie called to Cam as she spread clean bedding in Teddy's stall.

From behind the tack room door, with the wheelbarrow still in the middle of the barn's main aisle, the boy shook his head and put a finger to his lips.

"Eli Minden's here for a riding lesson." Paisley grabbed more straw from a bale. "He's mean."

"Mean how?" Carrie used a pitchfork to fluff the straw.

The tack room door slammed shut as Cam disappeared.

"He takes kids' lunches and stuff." Paisley found a broom and swept up straw and shavings into a pile.

"What kind of stuff?" Carrie kept her tone neutral. Cam had seemed happier since school ended, but it was still a struggle to get him to go to his swimming lesson or do other things away from the ranch.

"I don't know." Paisley shrugged. "I've only heard other kids talking."

Carrie put the pitchfork away and went to the open barn door. The Carter family offered riding lessons to locals as well as children and teenagers staying at Crocus Hill, a summer camp for young people with disabilities. One of the camp's riding instructors sat astride a gray horse with a group of children on ponies clustered around her.

None of the kids looked threatening, but appearances could be deceiving. Besides, Carrie was an adult, not six. She turned back into the barn as Cam came out of the tack room carrying several broken halters.

"Uncle Cole asked me to get these out for him. I forgot before," Cam said as he put them on a shelf. "I can move the wheelbarrow now." He stood behind the big barn door, out of sight of the group in the corral.

"It's okay. I can handle it." Carrie poked her head around the door. "After we finish here, want to take a walk to the creek? We could look for dinosaur fossils." Cam loved dinosaurs, and the flat path to the creek was his favorite spot to hunt for traces of the great creatures that had once roamed the Montana plains.

"Fossils are boring. I'd rather have a barrel racing lesson." Paisley looked behind the door too. "What are you doing?"

"Nothing." Cam stepped farther into the shadows, and his lower lip wobbled.

"No barrel racing lesson until I talk to your dad," Carrie said, stopping whatever objections Paisley looked set to raise. "Besides, you have your swimming lesson."

"I don't want to look for fossils or go swimming," Cam said. "Can't we go back to the house and watch a movie?" He poked his head around the door as the riding instructor and students left the corral to ride toward the creek path.

"Swimming first and a movie later. Your dad's already paid for those swimming lessons. You seem to like them once you're in the water. Is it your teacher?" Carrie studied Cam's bent head as they moved the wheelbarrow to the back of the barn.

"Forget it." Cam darted back into the tack room before Carrie could question him further.

After they'd washed up in the tack room sink, Carrie linked hands with both kids. "There's not enough time to go fossil hunting anyway." Cam's tense stance relaxed as they came out into the empty corral. "Why don't we visit Teddy instead?" Each day, Cam and Paisley opened up to her more, but it took time to grow trust.

And only an instant to break it. Carrie's stomach clenched at the memory of what her ex had done. Cheating was bad enough, but doing so with a friend was worse. It doubled the hurt and betrayal. Although she'd convinced herself she was over it, Carrie was warier now and less open with her feelings. She wouldn't risk her heart again anytime soon, if ever.

"Hey, boy." Carrie called to her horse and opened the pasture gate to let Paisley and Cam go through it ahead of her.

Teddy trotted across the field and nickered in welcome.

"How are you doing, Teddy Bear?" He nudged her face with his head, and she rubbed his favorite place behind his ears. Unlike people, horses didn't let you down. And when horses gave you their trust, as long as you continued to respect and treat them well, that relationship was for life. She dug in the pocket of her jeans for treats and let the kids take turns feeding Teddy.

"You're tickling me, Teddy." Cam giggled as the horse nuzzled his flat palm. "He's got a bigger mouth than Paisley's pony."

"A bigger everything." Paisley stood on tiptoe to pat Teddy's neck. "He's a giant compared to Luna." She giggled too.

"Uncle Cole's horse is the real giant." Cam pointed to where Cole led a gorgeous blood bay gelding around a corner of the barn. "We're not allowed near Bandit unless Uncle Cole's there."

"That's a good rule for any horse except your

own." As Carrie ran her hand along Teddy's back, he whinnied and tossed his head in Bandit's direction.

Bandit responded with a whinny of his own, and Cole waved. At his side, his fiancée, Melissa, an animal physical therapist who worked at a clinic in town, checked something on the big horse's right front leg.

"Daddy." Paisley ran to the pasture fence as Bryce's truck pulled up, and he parked and got out of it.

Carrie's heartbeat sped up as Bryce came toward them carrying a paper bag. He was bareheaded and without his usual cowboy hat; the sun made his light brown hair look almost blond. Beneath his checked, snap Western shirt, his shoulders were broad, and he walked with confidence in a pair of worn jeans and boots, his head up and shoulders back.

As she and Cam followed Paisley to the fence, Carrie mentally shook herself. There was no reason for her to act like a high-school girl checking out a cute guy. Bryce worked on this ranch, and she was looking after his kids. They were both doing their jobs. Except, she was more pleased to see him than she should be.

"Hey." Bryce helped Paisley and Cam sit atop the white-painted fence. "Carrie?"

"Hi."

"I was… Teddy…the water trough likely needs filling." Her tongue tripped over itself.

"No problem." Bryce waved to a teenage ranch hand and asked him to take care of it.

"When I was in town, I got you a present. It's for all of you, but Carrie gets to look first. Hold on, kids." He passed the bag to Carrie. "I hope you like it."

She fumbled with the pale-green ribbon that tied the bag's handles together. "What's in here?" She grinned, building anticipation for the kids as she pulled out a swathe of green tissue paper. "Something fabric." She fingered it and drew out a multicolored swirl on a cream background.

"It's an apron. With animals on it and your name." Paisley leaned closer to take a look.

"Three aprons." Carrie took two smaller garments from the bag. "With all our names."

"Except for the names, they're the same," said Cam, nodding his approval as Carrie handed him the apron with his name embroidered in blue on the bib.

"How many different animals can you find, kids? Count them." Carrie swallowed a lump in her throat as the colorful pattern blurred.

"There's a horse and cow."

"A fox and squirrel."

Paisley's and Cam's voices rose and fell with the new game.

"Thank you." Carrie turned to Bryce, who stood by the fence with the children.

"With all that cooking and baking you're doing for us, I thought you could use it. Cam said we only had what he called 'girls' aprons,' so Rosa made these. She thought the fabric would be fun for the kids. And I…well… I thought you'd like it too. The red matches your T-shirt."

"It's perfect." Carrie's breath caught. This gift was sweet, thoughtful and, because it was personal, one of the nicest things anybody had ever done for her. If you had the money, it was easy to buy expensive presents but Carrie had simple tastes. This apron meant more to her than the impractical mini designer bag her ex had given her last Christmas. And way more than the headache-inducing perfume he'd handed to her, still in its airport duty free bag, the day after her birthday. "Red's my favorite color."

"Mine too." He cleared his throat. "I should get back to work."

"Likewise. The kids have swimming." They spoke at nearly the same time.

But Bryce lingered as if he wasn't in any hurry to leave. "Paisley said tacos are on the menu for supper tonight. I won't be late." He stuck his hands in the front pockets of his jeans.

"Great. Tacos. The kids are excited about mak-

ing them." *His* children. The children of a grieving widower.

Even if Carrie liked Bryce, she liked him as a
friend and the kids' dad, she told herself. Nothing more.

BRYCE GUIDED HIS HORSE, Maverick, across the
hilly terrain and drew in a lungful of crisp morning air. He stopped Maverick at the top of a small
rise and scanned the landscape spread out in
front of them. The wheat was a rippling field
of green, and in the adjoining pasture, red and
white cattle grazed in the shadow of the distant
Rocky Mountains.

Carrie liked the apron he'd given her yesterday, but what he'd intended as a friendly gift
had suddenly seemed like more. And why had
he mentioned her red T-shirt? He shook his head
as embarrassment rolled over him again. Ordinarily, he had no problem talking to women, but
Carrie was different. Around her, he was either
tongue-tied or said the wrong thing. It wasn't
like he wanted to date her. He didn't want to
date anybody, and he'd crossed paths with plenty
of nice single women since Ally had died. Yet,
he hadn't reacted to any of them like he did to
Carrie.

Maverick's ears twitched, and a long-billed

curlew stuck its head over a tuft of rough grass before popping back down again.

"It's okay, little one. We don't mean you any harm." Bryce chuckled as Maverick turned his head as if to ask who else was around for him to speak to. His dad had taught Bryce about birds, plants and animals and to respect the natural world. He still tried to live and work by those lessons.

Hooves thudded, and then Zach reined in his horse, Scout, while Cole did the same with Bandit. Bryce greeted his brothers, who, like him, were dressed for ranch work in jeans, Western shirts, boots and cowboy hats.

"That new variety of wheat you tried looks good." Zach gestured to the green field.

"I just checked the moisture, and if Mother Nature cooperates, we should have a bumper crop. The barley's thriving too." Bryce settled his hat more firmly on his head. He and his brothers trusted each other to do their own jobs. While they sometimes worked together, like today when Zach had asked Bryce and Cole for help herding cattle, they never competed with each other.

"Does a good crop mean we can invest more in my rodeo stock contracting venture?" Cole asked. "I've got a lead on a prize bull in Colorado."

"As the saying goes, don't count your chickens, or bulls, before they hatch." Bryce turned Maverick around to follow his brothers to the cattle pasture. "We need a new baler."

"And the roof on the main barn could do with replacing," Zach added.

Cole and Bandit circled the first cow, their movements slow and calm. "It's lucky we have Beth on our team. She's a magician with money."

"She is, but even if she wasn't, I'm a lucky man," Zach said as he and Scout circled several other cows bunched together.

Bryce's chest constricted. His brothers were happy, and soon Cole, like Zach, would be married. Apart from Molly, who was much younger, he was the only one of the siblings on his own. He stared down one cow who gave him the bovine equivalent of teenage attitude. Paisley and Cam were challenging enough now. How would he cope when they reached adolescence?

"Good girl," he told the cow as she reluctantly joined the others. Without Bryce having to do much, Maverick rounded up the remaining stragglers, and now Zach and Scout led the cattle in a slow line as Cole and Bandit brought another group onto the meandering trail. "That's the way." Bryce guided Maverick in a slow, zigzag pattern behind the herd. His job was to keep the cattle calm, moving forward at their own pace and focused on where they were going rather than where they'd been.

That was good advice for life too. Cole, Zach and Bryce were close in age, but Bryce had always been the little brother. Nevertheless, he'd been the first to marry and start a family. But now, while they'd moved ahead, Bryce was stuck in the past.

"You guys need a hand?"

Bryce turned at Carrie's voice. "If you want to join us, sure. Where did you come from? It's your day off." And the kids were with Bryce's mom.

"I hadn't taken Teddy out for a good ride in a few weeks. We both need the exercise." Carrie sat easily in her saddle, at one with her horse like the experienced rider she was.

As Carrie and Teddy matched Bryce and Maverick's zigzag pattern, Bryce waved at Cole to let him know he didn't need more help and for his brother to join Zach at the front of the herd.

"Not that I came looking for you. I wanted to stay within cell service and close to home since I'm on my own." Carrie was intent on the slow-moving line of cattle.

Bryce held back a smile. On a big ranch like the Tall Grass, you could ride for miles without bumping into anyone. While her explanation made sense, something about it also told him she thought she needed to justify herself.

Home. Although it hadn't been long, Carrie already seemed at home on the ranch and in Bryce's house. It was comfortable having her ride beside him too.

"I'm interested in what you're doing with your grain crops." Carrie and Teddy eased a curious calf back into line with its mom. "How often do you leave fields fallow?"

Bryce stared at her and snapped his mouth shut when he realized he'd opened it in astonishment. "Not as often as I'd like to."

As Bryce talked about soil quality and estimated yields, Carrie asked more questions and even suggested a few things he'd considered but hadn't yet tried.

"I used to go out to the fields with my grandpa at his ranch. I learned from him. I've studied on my own too." When they reached the new pasture, Cole joined them at the rear of the herd, riding on Carrie's other side.

"Thanks. Great job." Cole gave Carrie a high five.

"My pleasure." Carrie returned the gesture with a friendly smile. "I like ranch work. Let me know if there's anything else I can do. When I'm not with Paisley and Cam, of course." She smiled at Bryce too. "They come first."

"I expect Zach could use extra help when Melissa and I are on our honeymoon." Cole's expression softened before becoming businesslike. "I'd also like to get your opinion on a mare. I want to breed barrel-racing horses as part of a stock contracting venture."

"Sure," Carrie said. "Let me know when and where."

As she chatted with his brother, Bryce rode ahead. Carrie had many years of rodeo left. Barrel racing was her life, like Paisley, Cam and this ranch were his. Bryce was fooling himself thinking she belonged here.

And despite a flicker of what might have been regret, Bryce couldn't let himself want anything different.

CHAPTER FIVE

"WHAT DO YOU THINK?" At a table in the craft center's workroom, Carrie showed Rosa mock-ups of new logos and color schemes that could be incorporated into her website design.

After a lot of late nights and early mornings hunched over her computer, Carrie was pitching a proposal to her first client in High Valley. If Rosa liked her work, she might recommend her to other business owners. As a freelancer, Carrie relied on word of mouth to build her business and grow her nest egg.

"I think you're a genius." Rosa's eyes twinkled. "I love all your suggestions. It'll be hard to choose only one."

"That's great." The knot in Carrie's chest loosened. She was good at her job but—just as anticipation and anxiety hit her when she and Teddy thundered along the alley to enter the rodeo ring—she got nervous presenting ideas to a new client. "Why don't you ask your employees, crafters and customers for their input? It's useful to get other perspectives."

Rosa nodded and pointed to an image on Carrie's laptop screen. "With this one, it's like you saw inside my head. It's similar to the original medicine wheel design I came up with when I started my business but a lot better. You're talented."

"Thanks." Carrie's face warmed with pleasure. "At each stage, I try to understand my client and their business. No matter which design you choose for your new website, you can then carry the same look and feel over to your business cards, customer packaging and your storefront and gallery signage, so everything is consistent."

"You've made my gallery and craft center look…" Rosa paused. "It feels like my kitchen-table business has reached the big time."

"From what I've seen, you left your kitchen table behind long ago." Carrie gestured to the workroom where craft supplies and products of every description filled the shelves that lined the walls. "You're a successful entrepreneur, so you need to make sure others see you and your business that way."

"I suppose I do." Rosa laughed. "I still get my best ideas at that old pine kitchen table, though. It's also where I feel closest to my family and roots. That table belonged to my mom and her mother before her. When I work there, it's like they're by my side guiding me."

Carrie had lost those connections and roots when her grandparents died and their ranch was sold. More than the house in Kalispell where she'd grown up and her mom had hired a professional to redecorate every few years, that ranch had truly been home. Working in the fields, milking parlor and horse barn had sparked Carrie's dream of having a ranch or farm of her own.

As Rosa looked through the presentation again, Carrie's thoughts drifted to Bryce and how they'd talked when she'd helped herd cattle four days before. She already knew he was smart. Those framed undergraduate and master's degree certificates in his home office said he was good at academics. But he was a working rancher too, and she'd been impressed by how he applied the latest scientific and agricultural research to real-life issues. He understood the ins and outs of sustainable farming too, and she'd almost told him about her own dream. Instead, she'd stopped herself. That dream was too private and special to share with many people.

Her ex, Jimmy, had dismissed it and her, calling it a foolish idea. Like her parents, he wanted her to quit barrel racing and settle down in Kalispell. *Get a real job*. His words echoed in her head. She had a *real* job. Two, including her freelance work.

With a farm, she'd have a third, and she was determined to succeed at all of them.

"If you email me these slides, I'll get some feedback and let you know any other questions and the design I want to go with," Rosa said.

"Sounds good." Carrie gathered up her notes and laptop. Since Bryce had needed her to stay late a few days last week, she had this afternoon off, even though it was a Wednesday.

"Hello, there." A light tap sounded on the half-open workroom door, and Joy Carter came in. She was followed by Paisley and Cam; Zach's wife, Beth; Cole's fiancée, Melissa; and several teen girls, one of whom must be Ellie, Zach and Beth's adopted daughter.

"Carrie." Paisley gave her an exuberant hug. "Are you helping us make wedding decorations? I'm making paper flowers. Grandma taught me." Paisley sat beside Carrie.

"Grandma taught me too, but she asked me to work with her on candles for the centerpieces." Cam sat on Carrie's other side. "That's a very important job."

"Both jobs are important, but no, I'm just leaving to go back to Aunt Angela's." Carrie wanted to update her business plan and email some past clients to ask if she could provide them with anything new.

"Can't you stay, please?" Paisley's puppy-dog

expression mirrored the one Penny and Otis gave Carrie when they wanted a treat.

"We'd love to have you join us." Joy sat across from Carrie and set boxes holding scissors, glue, pastel-colored tissue paper and other supplies in the middle of the table. "By we, I mean the Sunflower Sisterhood." She gestured to the other women who'd joined them, including Aunt Angela and her friend, Nina Shevchenko.

"Please do." Rosa patted Carrie's shoulder as she and Nina set out more chairs. "Consider it your official welcome to town."

"Okay." Carrie wanted to meet more people here, and it had been ages since she'd done any crafts.

She exchanged greetings with the others, who introduced themselves if they hadn't met her before. Lauren, who was married to a Carter cousin, gave riding lessons at the ranch. Carrie nodded at Diana, a ranch owner whose daughter had been in Carrie's group when the school visited Squirrel Tail.

Kristi from the Bluebunch Café waved at Carrie from the opposite end of the table. "I want to talk to you about designing new signs for the café. Rosa says your work is great."

"I'd love to, thanks."

In the hubbub of ten or more women and girls talking at once, Carrie took a deep breath. She was comfortable in the rodeo world, but she knew people there. She wasn't shy, but she was more at ease one-on-one than in groups.

That was another reason she didn't want the job in the family construction company. While she enjoyed her freelance work, leading a team and having to be what her mom called "the face of the company" mingling at cocktail parties and golf days wasn't for her. Somehow, she had to make her parents understand that.

"How can I help?" As Paisley and Cam went to work with Joy, Carrie turned to Beth, who held a roll of white satin ribbon.

"Want to make bows for the church pews with us?" Beth chuckled. "Ellie's at the age where she'd rather be with her friends." She indicated the group of girls who'd set up a workstation at a smaller table on the far side of the room.

"My Lily's the same." The woman beside Beth, Kate Cheng, sighed. "I miss the days when she didn't want to leave my side, but it's part of growing up and becoming independent. At least I still get to be around little ones at school."

"You're a special-education teacher, right?" Carrie remembered Kate from the field trip too.

"Yes. I also cover shifts at the school library when needed. That's where I got to know Cam." Kate gestured to where he was absorbed in sticking white candles in tall clear glass holders.

"He mentioned he spent time in the library at lunch and recess." Carrie took a length of precut satin ribbon from the pile in front of Beth and watched as Beth demonstrated how to make a bow and affix a loop to the back so it could be hung over a pew.

"He did, and that worried me. For kids who love reading, the library's their happy place, but it seemed more like Cam was hiding out." Kate started making another bow. "He sat in a reading nook, but he never had a book. Instead, he stared out the window into the playground. Both the librarian and I tried to talk to him, but he shut us out. After that, he'd take a book off the shelf and pretend to read."

Beth's expression was troubled. "We've all tried to help Cam at home. Even Ellie." She nodded to her daughter. "Ellie's biological mom died, so Ellie went through a rough time too, but Cam wouldn't talk to her either." Beth held one end of the slippery satin ribbon as Carrie tweaked her first, lopsided bow. "We're stuck as to what to do next so we're glad Cam has you in his life. Out of all of us, since you don't know him as well, you might just be the one who can help him."

"WATCH ME GO, DADDY." In the fenced pasture nearest to Bryce's house, Paisley trotted around a barrel pattern with Luna. As girl and horse approached each barrel, Paisley sat deeper into her saddle and pushed her weight into her stirrups.

"Looking good, kiddo." For a girl who loved speed, his daughter rode slowly and carefully, and she talked to Luna as they made the circuit around the small course.

"Carrie says it's better to go slow and steady first." Paisley drew the pony to a halt beside Bryce. "Mr. Gallagher loaned us those boots to protect Luna's legs and this special saddle. He has lots of barrel racing tack, and he said Luna and me could use it as long as we want."

Since Squirrel Tail Ranch was set up for visitors, Shane's stable was fully equipped. He was generous too, but extra generous when anyone in Joy's family needed something. While at first it had been strange for Bryce to see his mom with a man who wasn't his dad, he liked Shane. The older man made his mom happy, and in the past year, Bryce had gotten accustomed to her spending time with him. "That's great. I hope you thanked Shane."

"She did." Carrie joined him by the fence. She wore the apron he'd given her, and it fluttered in the light breeze. "She made him a special card."

"We also made him his favorite peanut butter cookies." Cam held Carrie's hand and wore his matching apron.

"Supper will be ready in twenty minutes. Untack Luna and wash up, please, Paisley."

"We have a yummy surprise for you." Cam grinned as Carrie untied his apron so he could follow his sister.

"I can't wait." Bryce leaned against the fence. "You need help, honey?" he called to his daughter, who led Luna toward the barn.

"Nope," she said over her shoulder. "Carrie says if you're old enough to ride a horse, you're old enough to take care of it. It's about responsibility." She stumbled over the word and then said it again correctly.

"That's right." Bryce tilted his face skyward. The sun hung above the western horizon, and white clouds topped the distant mountains like fluffy meringue on a pie. He loved this place and everything about it, and like his dad had taught him, he taught his children, carrying on a legacy from one generation to another.

At his side, Carrie studied the vista too. "I never wanted to live anywhere but Montana. Although Kalispell has its charms, ranch country feels like home for me."

"Me too." He noted the awe on her face. The same awe that must be on his. "It makes me feel small but big at the same time." He gestured to the vast landscape.

She nodded. "That's why how we take care of

this land matters so much. I'm only one person, but I still have a duty to do my part."

"We're all part of a larger system. Animals too." Bryce didn't often speak about what was in his heart, but something about Carrie made it easy for him to open up to her. "We have to take care of them as well."

"And each other." Carrie paused. "Before the kids come back, I need to talk to you about something."

"Sure." Bryce stopped considering cloud patterns. "What's up?"

"It's Cam."

Bryce's good mood evaporated. "What's wrong now?" He'd thought his son was doing better.

"It's the same as whatever was going on at school. I keep trying to talk to him, but just when I think he's going to be honest with me, someone interrupts us." Carrie rubbed a hand across her face. "I need one-on-one time with him. Yesterday, when I made decorations with the Sunflower Sisterhood for Cole and Melissa's wedding, I talked to Kate Cheng. You know the special-education teacher at the school?"

Bryce nodded. "Kate's great. Even though it isn't her job, she's always been there whenever Paisley needs someone to talk to."

"Although Kate hasn't worked with Cam, she

got to know him because he spent a lot of time in the library this spring."

As Carrie told him what Kate had said, a familiar knot formed in the pit of Bryce's stomach. "That's when I noticed things were off with Cam. I feel so guilty. What kind of dad can't help his child?"

"You're a good dad, the best, so there's no need for guilt."

At Carrie's words, a weight he hadn't realized he was carrying lifted from Bryce's shoulders. He'd felt guilty hiring Carrie to look after the kids, but she made all their lives better. Maybe he was too hard on himself. Since Ally passed, he'd tried to do everything for his children, and except for his mom, he'd never wanted to ask anyone for support. But maybe he needed to admit he was struggling and let himself depend on others.

"Kate thinks Cam has buried whatever the trouble is so deep, he can't talk to anyone about it. She also wonders if someone's threatened Cam so maybe he's afraid to talk."

Anger spurted inside Bryce. "Cam's six. Who'd threaten a little kid?"

"Another child most likely. Remember when you were Cam's age?" Carrie touched Bryce's arm before yanking her hand away and putting both hands in her apron pockets. "Children bully each other, and unless an adult spots what's going on and can intervene, the child being bullied might be so scared they can't see a way out."

Bryce's skin tingled where Carrie had touched him, and awareness of her surged through his body. Not as his employee but as a woman. "I… it's…what can I do?"

"If you plan a special afternoon away from the ranch with Paisley, I'll spend that time with Cam. We need to work together to make the kids understand it's a reward, not a punishment, so neither of them feels singled out or excluded. How does that sound?" Carrie's cheeks were flushed as if she'd felt that awareness between them too.

"Great. Sure. Of course. Anything for Cam." Bryce cleared his throat. "It'll be good for me to have one-on-one time with Paisley." He wanted a close relationship with his daughter, but the years were going by fast. He needed to nurture that father-daughter bond while she was still little. When she entered the preteen years, it would be too late. And he wanted her to feel comfortable coming to him when dealing with the challenges every teenager faced.

"What about tomorrow?" The sun caught Carrie's hair and highlighted gold tints in the brown. Her eyes had gold in them too, like spring green wheat mixed with rich harvest gold.

"Sure. I..." Bryce drew closer.

"Carrie." Paisley and Cam ran toward them, calling as one.

"Uncle Cole's untacking Luna, so can we work on our puzzle before supper?"

As Paisley looked between them, Bryce reared back, and Carrie stepped away too, bumping into the fence.

Carrie waved away Bryce's concern. "Sure, but let's go inside and wash our hands first."

She shepherded the kids to the house and left him by the fence surrounded by sky and fields.

Except now, he didn't feel big *or* small. He felt alone.

CHAPTER SIX

"YOU'RE GREAT AT ART." Carrie passed Cam a green crayon and chose a yellow one for herself. It was another gorgeous Montana summer afternoon, and they sat at the glass-topped patio table on the deck behind the ranch house, shaded by a turquoise umbrella.

"I like drawing pictures. I do art with Mrs. Rosa sometimes." Cam concentrated on coloring a green field, where he'd already drawn several bay horses. "She's nice. You're nice too." Cam drew another horse. "Not like some people."

"What people?" Carrie made her tone casual as she drew a golden sun.

Cam shrugged, gripped the crayon tight and dug it into the pad of paper.

"If you can't tell me, why don't you talk to Penny and Otis?" She called the two beagles from where they lay in the sunshine near the containers of flowers and herbs Carrie and the kids had planted. "Dogs are good listeners." She scratched Penny behind her ears as Otis leaned against Cam's bare legs.

Cam shook his head. "I'd get in trouble."

"Not with me, your dad or anyone in your family." How could Carrie get Cam to open up to her? He had the weight of the world on his slight shoulders, and although she'd expected him to want to go to town with Bryce and Paisley, he'd seemed relieved to stay at the ranch.

"Eli said I'd be in big trouble if I told." Cam made a chopping motion across his neck.

"That's exactly when you have to tell your dad or another adult you trust." *Eli Minden.* The boy Paisley had mentioned and one of the kids Cam had hidden from behind the barn door the day of that riding lesson. Eli was also in another swimming class at the same time as Cam's.

"But Eli's mean and he's bigger than me." Cam picked up Penny and buried his face in the dog's fur. "And him and his friends they…" His shoulders heaved.

"They what?" Carrie knelt by Cam's chair and stroked his hair. "I won't let anything bad happen to you. Your dad won't either."

"They take my lunch, push me into bushes." Cam's words were punctuated with choked sobs. "They say bad things about me, so none of the other kids want to play with me."

Carrie made herself stay calm. "Did anyone

else see or hear Eli and his friends say and do those things?"

Cam nodded and cried harder. "Lots of kids, but they're scared of Eli."

"None of that's okay. It's also not your fault."

"Eli said it was *all* my fault. And then…" Cam gulped. "The first time it happened, I said I'd tell the teacher, but Eli said if I did, something bad would happen to Daddy and Paisley. Like with Mommy."

"Oh, sweetheart." Carrie hugged Cam tight. "Your mommy got sick. It just happened. It wasn't anything to do with Eli or anyone else. Your dad and sister are fine."

"Really?" Cam raised his tearstained face, and Penny and then Otis whimpered, perhaps sensing his distress.

"Really and truly." Carrie took a deep breath. "Were Eli and his friends mean to you every day?"

"Mostly. On the bus too and now at swimming, and he's joined my soccer team." Cam erupted in more sobs.

"No wonder you're so upset." Carrie was upset too, but she had to keep her emotions in check for Cam's sake. "It's good you told me what's been happening because now I can try to fix it. It sounds like Eli hasn't learned how to be kind to other kids. It doesn't make what he's doing right, but maybe there's bad stuff going on in his life, and he hurts others because he's hurting. As for his friends, some kids are followers."

"My dad says you hafta think for yourself." Cam's blue eyes were solemn.

"He's right, but it's okay to ask others to help when you need it." Something Carrie still hadn't fully learned.

"Eli's mom and dad are selling their ranch and moving to town. They're gonna have to live with Eli's uncle in an apartment. I heard Eli say he has to share a bedroom with his baby sisters." Cam rested his chin on Penny's head. "Maybe that's why he's mean."

"It could be." Carrie hesitated. "But for now, we have to think about how we can make things better for you. Can we tell your dad?"

"Yes, and Uncle Cole." Cam gave her a tentative smile. "He was a famous rodeo rider. I bet Eli would be scared of him."

"Your whole family will want to help, and your teachers too, but scaring Eli isn't the answer."

"You mean two wrongs don't make a right? Grandma learned me that." Cam let out a heavy sigh.

"Your grandma *taught* you that, and she's right." Carrie smoothed Cam's tousled hair. "Why don't we make a plan?" Starting with texting Bryce.

"Can it be going to the museum and having

hot dogs for supper? Paisley and Daddy are doing something special, and you said we'd do something special too." His adorable grin popped out. "I didn't get to go to the museum on my class field trip 'cause I was throwing up, but I heard they have amazing dinosaur bones. Big ones."

"Sure, we can. The best plan is having fun." Carrie stood as Cam tossed a ball across the backyard for the dogs to chase.

"Play with us, Carrie." Cam ran after the barking dogs.

"Okay." She followed them across the lawn and retrieved the ball from Otis. "Now you catch." She sent the ball through the air to Cam.

Life was complicated no matter how old you were, but talking about problems helped.

Cam sent the ball back to her, but Otis caught it, mid-throw.

When Cam rolled on the grass with the dogs and laughed, Carrie joined them.

Maybe she hadn't lost her mojo, only temporarily misplaced it. And helping Cam was good for her too.

"WAY TO GO, CAM." At the edge of one of High Valley's soccer fields, Bryce jumped up and down and cheered as his son kept control of the ball before taking a shot on the net.

Carrie joined in the cheering, as excited as

Bryce and the rest of his family, who'd all turned out to watch Cam's game.

"It's only been a week, but what a change in Cam." Under the noise of the crowd, Bryce spoke into Carrie's ear. "He's a happy kid again, and it's all thanks to you."

"Sometimes kids are able to talk more easily to a new person. I'm glad he finally opened up and I could be there for him." Carrie clapped as one of Cam's teammates made another good play. "And while I figured out what's been going on, you talked to the swimming teachers, soccer coach and school principal. Teamwork." She bumped Bryce's elbow.

"Who then all talked to Eli and his parents." Bryce bumped her elbow back. It was a teasing gesture, but for a second it felt like it could have been more. "That poor kid. Eli's been struggling as much as Cam. None of us knew the family was so close to the edge money-wise. Or that the parents have been going without food themselves to feed Eli and the girls and so Eli could still take part in sports."

"Bullying's never right, but it's not surprising Eli acted out." Carrie's voice was warm with sympathy. "I talked to Kate, and she said with all the stress at home, Eli was likely looking for attention."

"In the wrong way. And Cam was a victim, but

Eli's one too." Bryce caught a whiff of Carrie's floral scent. It was fresh, light and had a crisp note, a combination that was a lot like her.

"Now both boys can get the support they need. That the town's pitching in for the Minden family in ways that won't embarrass them is wonderful." As Carrie grabbed a bottle of water from the cooler, her hand brushed Bryce's bare arm, and his skin prickled.

They were talking about his son. That was where his attention should be, not on how soft Carrie's skin felt against his. "For Cam, I'm sure talking to the counsellor the principal recommended will be good. But being able to be an ordinary kid again is best of all."

"It sure is." Carrie's smile lit up her face. "He already seems more confident, and when he goes back to school in the fall, it'll be a whole new start."

The Carter family cheered again as Cam scored a goal.

"Did you see that?" Carrie jumped up and down and pointed to the field.

"Yeah." Bryce's throat was thick as Cam ran around and exchanged high fives with his teammates. Scoring a goal was great, but Cam had achieved something even more important—he'd conquered some of his self-doubt. All made a little easier with Eli taking a break from soccer and swimming.

"That's my brother!" Paisley shouted, and Bryce lifted her up so she could get a better view, while Carrie moved away to speak to Beth, Zach and Ellie.

Bryce's mom looped an arm through his. "It seems things are working out."

"Yeah, life's more settled, and Carrie's fit right in."

"She's good for you." His mom scanned the field, where the game was wrapping up. "You look happier and less stressed."

"Having support at home is great." Bryce kept his tone neutral. "It sure eases the pressure on me."

"In a lot of ways, I expect." His mom's tone was also neutral. "You must—"

"Beth? What's wrong? Mom? I need you." Zach's panicked voice interrupted them.

As Bryce and his mom rushed to join the rest of the family, Carrie knelt beside Beth who lay on the grass. "Did she hit her head when she fainted?"

"No, I caught her and sort of eased her down." Zach's face was pale, and he grabbed a sweatshirt from Bryce to make a pillow to put under his wife's head.

"It's okay," Bryce's mom reassured Beth as her eyes flickered open.

"I'm fine. I just…" She gave Zach a small smile as he crouched on her other side, now joined by Melissa and Cole.

"Low blood pressure again?" Melissa smiled at Beth too as she took out the first aid kit she'd brought to the game as the unofficial team physical therapist. "Paisley, honey? Can you please run to the cooler for a cookie and juice box for your auntie Beth?"

"Sure." Paisley darted away.

Beth looked at the worried faces that surrounded her and Zach. "Melissa already knows because I fainted a few days ago at her place when we were doing some last-minute wedding preparations. Zach and I had planned to tell the rest of you after Cole and Melissa's wedding, but…go ahead, Ellie." She squeezed Ellie's hand.

"Mama Beth and Dad are having a baby. I'm going to be a big sister."

"It's still early days, but that's why I fainted." Beth put her other hand in Zach's as he helped her sit up.

"Oh, my dears." Bryce's mom hugged Zach and Beth and then Ellie too, as congratulations broke out.

"I'm happy for you, bro." Bryce clapped Zach's shoulder. "When are you guys due?"

"Between Christmas and New Year's." Zach's voice was husky. "We were already a family with Ellie, but this baby is an extra special blessing. We're so lucky." He thanked Paisley for the juice and cookie and stayed close to Beth as she ate and drank.

"That baby's lucky too." Bryce spoke around the lump in his throat. "You and Beth are great parents."

"You'll have to give me baby care tips. When Ellie came into my life, she was half grown. This time around, I'm starting from the beginning." As he looked at his wife and stepdaughter, Zach's face was filled with love and pride.

"You've already got the most important thing covered and that's love. The rest of us will pitch in with practical stuff when you need it." Like Bryce's family had done for him and Ally after Paisley and Cam were born.

His gaze drifted to Carrie, who was in the middle of his family group like she belonged there. Paisley and Cam clung to her as she answered their questions about babies and shared their excitement about having a new cousin.

In identifying the bullying situation, Carrie had given Cam a fresh start. Could Bryce let himself think about a fresh start too? And maybe even being happy like Ally wanted?

CHAPTER SEVEN

"I DIDN'T EXPECT you and Luna to learn that new pattern so fast." Carrie clapped as Paisley stopped her pony at the end of the course.

"We've been practicing between lessons."

"I can tell. Your balance is lots better, and you're remembering to focus on where you're going rather than where you've been." So much in horsemanship was relevant to life, and teaching Paisley the basics of barrel racing was teaching Carrie too. As much as she could, nowadays she focused on her future, not her past.

"Where's Cam?" Paisley glanced around for her brother.

"He's with your dad." She'd given Cam a riding lesson earlier, but he'd gotten bored watching Paisley, so Bryce had offered to keep him busy in the barn. "We'll have another lesson after your uncle Cole's wedding." Carrie held Luna still as Paisley dismounted.

"Why not tomorrow?"

"It's the day before the wedding, remember?

Between decorating the church and reception hall and going to the rehearsal and party afterward, we'll be too busy." Although Carrie was happy for Cole and Melissa, part of her would also be relieved when the wedding excitement was over. The place inside her that had once hurt like a raw wound was less tender now, but she wouldn't be human if seeing another couple's radiant happiness didn't make her remember what might have been.

"Sorry? What did you say?" She turned to Paisley and pushed the hurt—and the memories—back where they belonged.

"I asked if I'll be ready to compete in kids' events at horse shows soon." Paisley's expression held hope and the kind of self-confidence Carrie wanted to rediscover.

"Not barrel racing yet, but if your dad says it's okay, you could start showing Luna this fall." When Carrie would have left the Tall Grass Ranch, High Valley and Paisley behind. "I started competing when I was about your age." This job had always been temporary. She couldn't let herself get too attached to any part of it, including the kids. "Events should be fun, though, and not about a ribbon." Part of Carrie getting her mojo back was remembering why she'd started riding in the first place. Like Paisley, it was for a love of horses and rodeo sports. What happened in the competition arena was secondary.

"Why can't I have fun *and* win ribbons? I want blue ones, and I'm going to hang them from a line on my bedroom wall." Paisley gave her pony water. "I bet Luna wants blue ribbons too."

Carrie wasn't surprised Paisley wanted a first-place ribbon, and you needed a competitive spirit to accomplish many things in life—it was certainly needed to succeed in rodeo. However, maybe Carrie had focused so much on competition she'd lost sight of fun and, apart from her freelance work, almost everything else in her life? "Slow and steady, remember? You have lots of time to win ribbons of all colors."

"It would still be good to start with a blue one and…hey, there's Daddy and Cam." Paisley waved. "You want to go riding with us, Carrie?"

"Don't you want time on your own with your dad?" Like all the Carters, Bryce was a natural on horseback. In jeans, a Western shirt, hat and boots, he resembled any other rancher. Yet, even if he hadn't been astride Maverick, Carrie could still have picked him out of a crowd at a hundred feet.

"You're welcome to join us. I finished work early, and it's a beautiful day." Bryce and Cam drew their horses to a stop by Carrie.

"I should get dinner started and—"

"Can we get pizza, Daddy?" Cam asked. Over the past few weeks, Cam had had a growth spurt, and riding Trixie, one of the summer camp ponies, he looked less like a kindergartener and more like a boy ready to start first grade.

"Good idea. Carrie must need a break from cooking for us." Bryce's slow smile made her heartbeat speed up.

"Making meals is part of my job, but I like cooking." She especially liked cooking for a family. When Bryce had to work late, which now happened several times a week, she stayed at the ranch for dinner. She enjoyed being part of family dinnertime too. "Riding would be fun. It'll only take me a few minutes to get Teddy tacked up."

"Already taken care of." Bryce smiled again, and a flock of butterflies took off in Carrie's stomach. "Cam wanted you to ride with us before Paisley asked. Since he was sure he could convince you to say yes, one of the hands looked after Teddy while I helped Cam with Trixie."

"That's great, thanks." Carrie looked beyond Bryce and Cam to see Heidi, a part-time ranch hand, leading Teddy out of the barn. "On the road, I'm used to doing everything myself."

"If we can do something to make your life easier, why not?" Bryce guided Maverick out of the way as Heidi and Teddy approached. "That's what friends and family do, and you return the favor. Giving Paisley and Cam riding lessons and rounding up cattle aren't in your job description."

"I like making people happy." Carrie greeted Teddy, thanked Heidi and swung into the saddle. "Besides, Paisley's doing really well. Cam too." And sharing her love and knowledge of horses with Bryce's kids fulfilled Carrie in ways she hadn't known she needed. "See how he's sitting?" She gestured to the children as they rode ahead of them along the creek path.

"Toes up and heels down. He's got his shoulders back too." Bryce rode at Carrie's side. "I've been trying to teach him that horseman's stance for weeks. How did you manage it?"

"No expectations maybe?" Carrie studied Cam. He had the makings of a good cowboy, but more importantly, there were lots of signs he'd grow up to be a good man. "Since Cam felt bad about himself because of the bullying, it makes sense he wouldn't sit tall on horseback. Hunching his shoulders might have been an unconscious way of making himself smaller so as not to attract attention. He's standing taller too."

"I hadn't made that connection."

"Why would you?" Carrie glanced at Bryce from under her hat brim. "You can't notice everything about your kids. I'm with Cam all day right now, and I'm still getting to know him. Maybe it's easier for me."

"I guess. It seems like yesterday he and Paisley were babies, and look at them now." Bryce's voice hitched. "Before I know it, they'll be wanting to go to horse shows, learning to drive and going on dates."

"Those last two can wait, but Paisley already asked me about entering kids' events at shows this fall." As they walked their horses along the creek path, white butterflies darted alongside, and a crow eyed them from a low branch of a juniper tree. "She's ready, but I told her it's your call."

"So I'll be the bad guy if I say no?" His expression was quizzical, almost teasing.

"That's being a parent, isn't it?" As the path narrowed, Bryce's denim-clad knee brushed Carrie's leg, the brief contact making her nerve endings hyperaware. "Paisley also wants turquoise cowboy boots with rhinestones. She saw a girl on TV with a pair and fell in love."

"Absolutely not." Bryce shook his head and gave a mock glare. "If I say no to the boots, I could say yes to a horse show. What do you think?"

"I think you've got a winner. Then when Paisley says if she can't have the boots, she wants turquoise eyeshadow, you can be outraged and say she can have the horse show or nothing." As they rounded a curve in the path, Carrie's knee bumped his, but Bryce didn't move away.

"Turquoise eyeshadow? At her age? Is there anything else I should know?" His eyes twinkled, but there was a warmth in them too, and the way he looked at her was less teasing and more admiring.

Carrie's breath sped up, and the hairs on her arms quivered as feelings she'd tried to suppress roared into life. "Paisley's a sensible kid, and lots of girls her age like trying makeup. If she—"

"Did you see me and Trixie trot?" Cam called. As if he'd thrown a bucket of cold water over her, Carrie jerked her attention, and her leg, away from Bryce. "Sorry, honey. I missed you. Why don't you go again? I'm watching now."

"I'm watching too." Bryce avoided Carrie's gaze. And, as if by unspoken agreement, when the path widened again, they were both careful to ride a distance apart.

Cam and the pony trotted to where the path ran alongside the creek, and Carrie and Bryce clapped.

"Great job," Bryce said as they joined the kids. "If you keep going as you are, you'll soon be ready for a pony of your own."

Carrie made herself smile and praise Cam before she rested her cheek on Teddy's thick mane, seeking the comfort only her horse could give.

She liked Bryce. It would be easy to fall for him like she'd fallen for his children. However, attraction was easy and fleeting. A lasting relationship was harder and more complicated. That kind of relationship also required opening her heart and giving it fully to someone else. Something she wasn't sure she could risk again.

"You're my guy, aren't you, Teddy?" she whispered into the horse's ear, then rubbed his neck.

She had to fight that attraction to Bryce. It was the only way to protect herself—and keep her tender heart safe.

"STAND CLOSER TOGETHER and smile." In the church lobby, Bryce snapped a photo of Paisley and Cam in their wedding outfits. "I can't remember the last time you two looked so clean." Or the last time Cam looked so much like Ally. He pushed the emotion away. Today was about celebrating and sharing Cole and Melissa's happiness.

"Now a picture with Carrie." He gestured to her to join the kids.

Carrie wore high-heeled beige sandals and a pale green dress that nipped in at her waist then floated out to skim her knees. Bryce almost hadn't recognized her when she'd arrived at the church with his mom, Beth and the children. Along with the dress, which highlighted curves he shouldn't let himself notice, she'd done something new with her hair. It hung in loose curls around her face and cascaded down her back in a silky brown ripple. On an ordinary day, she was pretty, but today she was downright gorgeous.

"Carrie made me have a bath last night and then a shower this morning." With the impromptu photo session over, Cam made an offended face.

"Only because you, Cameron Carter, got into that mud puddle outside the barn after breakfast." Carrie straightened Cam's purple Western string tie, which was a smaller version of the one Bryce wore. "You have to be spic-and-span for your uncle's wedding, and now you're so clean you squeak."

"Squeak how?" Cam looked at Carrie with a puzzled expression.

"Like this." She tugged his arm, made a squeaking noise and Cam laughed. "At the reception, you can take off your suit jacket and have fun, but for now, you need to look and behave like a cowboy in his Sunday best. Like your dad and Uncle Cole."

"You sure do." Bryce took off his son's small white cowboy hat, while Carrie fixed the bow on Paisley's pale purple flower girl's dress. "Cowboys take off their hats in church, remember? Also, as your grandpa Carter would have said, because there are ladies present."

"Oops." Cam put a hand to his mouth. "But Paisley's not a lady."

"Not yet, but since she's your sister, that's even more of a reason for you to be considerate of her, don't you think?" Carrie asked, giving Cam his white satin ring bearer's pillow.

"To grow up to be a good man, a good cowboy and a good rancher, I hafta start now by being polite, honest and respectful to everyone, even my sister." Cam repeated words Carrie had evidently asked him to remember.

"And I hafta be the same, even to Cam when he bugs me," Paisley agreed. "Except I want to be a good woman, a good cowgirl and a good doctor so I can fix Cam and other cowboys up if they get hurt."

"That sounds like a fine plan, both of you." His kids were growing up, and Carrie was helping them become good citizens like Bryce wanted. She had a gentle way of teaching that made lessons stick. She also led by example, and along with Bryce's mom, Molly, Beth and now Melissa, Paisley and Cam had good female role models.

"The car with your aunt Melissa, her parents and the bridesmaids just pulled up." Carrie retrieved Paisley's basket of pink, white and purple flowers from a table near the door and handed it to her. "It's almost time. You remember from the rehearsal what to do?"

The kids nodded with matching solemn expressions.

Carrie turned to Bryce. "Shouldn't you be at the front of the church with Cole and Zach?"

"Yeah, I better see if Cole needs anything." That was the best man's job, and he and Zach shared that role today. He had come to the lobby to make sure the kids were okay when Carrie texted him they'd arrived. "See you guys soon. Mind your manners, remember?"

"Of course, Daddy." Paisley gave him the kind of eye roll he'd thought was reserved for a teenager who was borrowing the family car and being reminded to drive safe.

Over the kids' heads, he grinned at Carrie, and she grinned back. Then he walked up the center aisle and joined his brothers. "All set?" He focused on Cole. That was who he should be thinking of, not how fantastic Carrie looked and the warmth and connection between them when they'd shared that smile.

"I'm more nervous today than if I was waiting in the chute to ride the meanest bull in Texas." Cole's usually ruddy face was pale, and his brother looked as serious as Bryce had ever seen him. "I want to marry Melissa, but this part with all these people is a lot more stressful than I expected."

On Cole's other side, Zach's voice was reassuring. "It's important to celebrate finding the woman you want to spend the rest of your life with. All of us are here for you and to welcome Melissa into our family."

Then the musical trio—a violinist, a guitarist and a banjo player—began to play, and the soloist sang the first words of "Take My Hand," Emily Hackett's "Wedding Song."

"Here goes." Bryce nudged Cole's ribs, but his brother was oblivious. Instead, his gaze was fixed on the back of the church, waiting for his first glimpse of Melissa. Exactly like Bryce had once waited for Ally.

As the romantic lyrics echoed around the church, Melissa's bridesmaids—her two sisters and Molly—walked down the aisle to join the men. They were followed by Cam and then Paisley with Melissa's daughter, Skylar, in matching dresses and awed expressions.

Bryce gave his kids a discreet thumbs-up as they reached the front and turned to wait for the bride.

Beside him, Cole sucked in a breath and then Melissa appeared, escorted by her mom and stepdad. All brides were beautiful, but the love and trust on Melissa's face as she looked at his brother made Bryce's heart flip. He couldn't avoid thinking of Ally and their own wedding.

He also couldn't not think about the unfairness of their life together being cut so short.

Cole greeted Melissa and took her hand as Reverend Ralph stood in front of them and started the service. He'd been their family's minister when Bryce was a child and had come out of retirement to officiate at this wedding.

As Cole and Melissa exchanged their vows to love, honor and cherish each other, Bryce's thoughts wandered. Several generations of Carters had married in this church on the corner of a quiet street in High Valley's oldest neighborhood. And today, half the town had gathered to see Cole and Melissa happily join their lives together.

In a front pew, Bryce's mom patted her eyes with a tissue. She had her own memories of marrying Bryce's late dad here. Shane Gallagher sat behind her, along with Carter aunts, uncles and cousins. All the members of the Sunflower Sisterhood were here too, with Rosa at the end of a row, ready to give a reading. Ranching families Bryce had grown up with, Melissa's coworkers and members of both the bride's and groom's extended family and friends from Montana, California and Canada filled the pews to the back of the church and up into the loft. Weddings weren't only about the bridal couple. They were also about family, friends and community.

Cam held out his ring bearer's pillow for the exchange of rings and then stepped back to his spot between Paisley and Skylar. He beamed at Bryce, who nodded approval.

Bible readings, several more songs and the homily passed in a blur. Although Bryce avoided looking at Carrie, he was still hyperaware of her seated behind Paisley, Cam and Skylar, there for the kids if they needed her.

"I now pronounce you husband and wife. You may share your first married kiss." Reverend Ralph blessed Cole and Melissa. A smattering of applause broke out, the couple kissed and one of Cole's rodeo friends cheered.

"You did it, bro. Congratulations." Bryce patted Cole's shoulder, and Zach congratulated the newlyweds too. Then Bryce was in a line paired with Melissa's youngest sister as the musicians and the soloist launched into Tim McGraw and Faith Hill's moving duet "The Rest of Our Life."

As he waited to recess out of the church, Bryce's eyes smarted, and he dug in his jacket pocket for a tissue. The burning behind his eyes was for Ally and the past, but for Cole and Melissa too, and all they'd overcome to find *their* happily ever after.

When he passed Carrie, his gaze caught hers and lingered.

And instead of thinking of the past, Bryce

thought about the rest of his own life and what it could be. A life he didn't spend alone, but with another good woman by his side.

Moving on from Ally didn't mean letting go of her because she'd always be in his heart. But maybe there was room for someone else there too.

Someone like Carrie.

CHAPTER EIGHT

AT THE SIDE of the dance floor in High Valley's community center, Carrie tapped one foot to "Cowboy Take Me Away" by The Chicks. Since it was a country wedding and a country crowd, she knew most of the songs on the DJ's playlist, including this one. And now that the wedding and formal part of the reception were over, she'd taken off her heels and replaced them with boots, like most of the female guests.

Cole and Melissa danced past her, Melissa's white cowboy boots peeking out from under the ruffled hem of her dress. The couple looked so happy they glowed.

"Want to dance?" Cam held out his hand like he'd seen Cole and the other men do.

"I'd love to." Carrie clasped his small palm and studied his flushed face and the dark shadows beneath his eyes. "It's been a long day, and it's not over yet. You can sleep in as long as you want tomorrow." She included Paisley and Skylar, who stood behind Cam. Skylar was having a sleepover with Paisley, and Carrie was staying overnight in the guestroom at Bryce's to help with all three kids.

"And then can we make blueberry pancakes?" Paisley asked.

"If you want to, sure." Was her pride in Paisley and Cam today how a mom felt? She was as proud of the kids as she was of Teddy when the two of them completed a clean race in a personal best time. Yet, her pride in these children was different, although she couldn't explain how or why.

As Skylar went to dance with her mom and Cole, Carrie took Paisley's hand too. "Why don't the three of us dance together? We don't want to leave your sister out, do we, Cam?"

"'Course not." Cam bowed and drew them onto a quieter part of the dance floor where they wouldn't collide with Bryce, Zach and a group of Carter cousins doing a "Boot Scootin' Boogie" line dance to the Brooks & Dunn song of the same name.

With Cam and Paisley on either side of her, Carrie counted steps. "On four, put your left heel up—that's the same side as the hand you write with, Cam. Clap your hands and then reverse." Their boots echoed on the floor in time to the music. "Nice. You two look like you've done this dance before."

"We have. Lot of times with Daddy. A bunch of other dances too." The tip of Paisley's tongue stuck out of her mouth as she concentrated on the footwork. "Grandma says he's the best dancer in our whole family."

"I can see why." Carrie's gaze slid to Bryce. While the Carter brothers all stood head and shoulders above most of the other men in terms of height and good looks, when it came to dancing, Bryce was also head and shoulders above Cole and Zach. With good rhythm, neat footwork and a smooth style, he seemed to glide across the floor like Fred Astaire in the old musicals Carrie loved.

Focus on the kids. They are the only reason you're here. "I lost my step count. Let's start over." She turned back to Paisley and Cam, and they tried the routine again, getting into the groove of the song alongside the other dancers.

"It's the cowboy cha-cha," Paisley said as the music changed. "That's for two people." Her smile dimmed.

"We can make it work as a line dance with three." Carrie listened to the beat. "I'll show you." She demonstrated, and the kids copied her.

"It's better in a couple, though." Before she realized what was happening, Bryce took Carrie's hands and led her into the dance. "Watch us, kids. Carrie and I'll show you how it's done.

Can you take a picture of us, Paisley? Here's my phone."

Carrie's face heated. Bryce's hands were warm and callused like hers. "I was okay sticking with the kids." They posed for the photo while Paisley took a picture and then gave the phone back.

"But I bet you'd like a turn with someone who won't step on your toes." Bryce laughed and held Carrie close.

"Cam only stepped on my feet once, and he's not heavy." This closeness with Bryce was only because of the dance. It didn't mean anything important.

"The kid's learning." Bryce dipped Carrie, and she relaxed into the music, the dance and her partner.

"He has a good teacher in you." She was used to being independent, but in a partner dance, one person had to lead, and she was happy for Bryce to do it. He had the same confidence on the dance floor as everywhere else, but now he was attuned to her in a way that was new. "I thought men who could dance were almost an endangered species."

"Not in my family." Bryce drew her even closer. Unlike some men Carrie had danced with, who hauled her around like she was a steer they were trying to wrestle, each of Bryce's movements was smooth, as well as gentle and courteous. "My dad was a good dancer, and he and my mom danced together most Saturday nights at home. They taught all of us kids. When my grandparents could babysit, my folks went dancing at a place in town. Mom says date nights are important. Along with mutual respect and shared interests, dates keep the magic and love alive."

Carrie wanted that kind of relationship, one that was a true partnership, like her parents had. Although her mom had given up ranch life to move to the city, marry Carrie's dad and work with him in the family business, she'd always seemed happy with that choice.

The music changed again, and their steps slowed as Darius Rucker's voice wrapped around them singing "History in the Making."

Bryce turned Carrie in his arms, so they were face-to-face and almost cheek to cheek. A hint of his spicy aftershave mixed with her perfume. Under her hand, the muscles in his arm where he'd rolled up the sleeves of his white dress shirt were taut and lightly covered with short hair. Her hand trembled in his and her stomach fluttered.

When the song ended, they stilled, caught in the moment.

"We should…the kids…" Carrie made herself step away.

"Of course." Bryce dropped Carrie's hand and invited Paisley and Cam into their circle.

"You dance almost as well as Daddy." Paisley studied Carrie through narrowed eyes. "Mommy was an excellent dancer. The best ever."

"I'm sure she was." Paisley couldn't be jealous Carrie had danced with Bryce, could she? "If your mom were here, she'd be really proud of how you both handled yourselves today."

"Grandma says Mommy is always with us. In our hearts and watching over us." Paisley glanced between Carrie and Bryce. Her lower lip stuck out, and if her eyes could talk, they would've said, "Leave my daddy alone."

"What a lovely way of keeping your mom close." Carrie laced her fingers together.

"I talk to Mommy sometimes. Cam and I both do." Paisley spit the words out.

"That's great." Carrie was way out of her depth, and from Bryce's uncertain expression, he was as well. "I talk to my grandparents too. I miss them, and that's how I keep them close."

And her grandparents would have wanted her to be happy. When her grandma had left her some money, Carrie had invested the small inheritance in what she called her "farm fund." Thanks to this nannying job, her dream wasn't as far out of reach as it had been.

"Listen. It's my favorite song." Unaware of any undercurrents, Cam did his version of a disco-style dance, his arms and legs flailing to "Electric Boogie."

"Shall we? I remember this one from when I was a kid." Bryce flung his head back as he slid across the floor with Carrie and the kids following.

"An oldie but a goodie." Carrie moved in time to the music. It had been a long and tiring day. Paisley likely wanted to dance with her dad herself. She shouldn't read anything more into the girl's sullen expression. "The DJ at my eighth-grade graduation dance played this song. Whenever I hear it, I remember my science teacher calling out 'boogie woogie woogie,' and all of us joining in."

Bryce, Paisley and Carrie clapped as Cam showed off more moves, and then they joined a conga line with some of Melissa's Californian and Canadian family members.

"I can't remember the last time I had so much fun." As the dance ended, Carrie fanned her hot face and asked the bartender for a pitcher of water and glasses.

"Me neither." Bryce leaned against the bar as the kids joined Skylar and several other children at a table with crayons and coloring sheets. "I could hardly keep up with you guys."

"It's me who couldn't keep up with you." Carrie made her tone light. "It's been a great party."

"Here's the photo Paisley took of us, along with some I got of you dancing with Paisley and Cam." He tapped his phone. "There, I sent them to you."

"Thanks." She'd look at them later when she was alone. That way, she could linger over them and pretend…no. Carrie mentally shook herself. "Aunt Angela's having fun." Carrie gestured to where her aunt danced with a group of friends. "It's been awful for her since my uncle passed, but she says she's ready to get out and mix with people again."

"A small-town party has a way of bringing folks together." Bryce filled glasses with water for them, and Carrie took a long drink, the refreshing coldness slipping down her throat.

"It's like the rodeo community in some respects." Except, for Carrie, this wedding reception was more fun than any after-rodeo party. While rodeo was often called a family, today Carrie had been drawn into the Carter and High Valley families, and that was different. These people were connected not only by bonds of blood, but a history far beyond a shared sport, and she liked the sense of belonging it gave her.

"Lots of rodeo people are here for Cole. This wedding could be good for ranch business too." Bryce finished his water. "I talked to a stock contractor friend of Cole's from Colorado. Heath told me about a new forage barley they're trying. I'd like to give it a shot here."

"I talked to Heath too. He and his wife are a nice couple." Since they were committed to sustainable ranching, Carrie had enjoyed chatting with them and gotten lots of great tips. "I'll take the kids home soon. It's late, and they're high on chocolate cupcakes, excitement and adrenaline. If they color for a few minutes, they should settle down before getting into the car."

"Let's hope so." Bryce's smile was wry. "If you'd like me to—"

"I wanted to say what a wonderful family you two have." A blond woman in her early sixties stopped beside Carrie. "Paisley and Cam have been as good as gold all day, and the two of you are such loving and caring parents. I'm Melissa's third cousin, Marion Koehler, from Calgary." She stopped to take a breath.

"We're not… I'm not… I'm the nanny." Carrie introduced herself. "Paisley and Cam are Bryce's children. Bryce is Cole's younger brother."

Bryce's laugh sounded forced. "Carrie's great with the kids."

"I'm so sorry." Marion put a hand to her mouth as a gray-haired man joined her. "I'm always putting my foot in it, aren't I, Randall?" She looked at the man before introducing him as her husband. "I saw you dancing, and you looked…

anyway…a nanny is almost part of the family, aren't you?" She patted Carrie's arm.

"No harm done." Bryce assured her.

"Bryce and the kids treat me like family." Hopefully, the muted light of the reception hall would hide Carrie's red face. She supposed it was an honest mistake. Zach and Cole were both married, and Molly, who'd arrived the day before from Atlanta, was with a group of her high-school friends. Only Bryce had attended the wedding on his own.

"It's all good then." Marion turned away to order sodas from the bartender.

"I'll check on Paisley and Cam and let them know we're leaving soon." Carrie avoided Bryce's gaze, but as she skirted the dance floor to reach the coloring table, she felt his eyes follow her.

The one time she'd thought about settling down, it had gone wrong. And now, except when it came to horses and work, she didn't trust herself to make good choices.

"Ten minutes until home time, you two." She knelt beside Cam and admired his field of red cattle.

Rodeo and family life also didn't mix, let alone making a go of her own ranch. No matter how good that sense of family and belonging felt right now, Carrie wouldn't give up her dreams. Even if she couldn't quite convince her heart she meant it.

"I CALL THIS meeting to order." At her seat at a table in the Bluebunch Café, Joy tapped a teaspoon against her water glass and tried to sound firm. Although Sunflower Sisterhood meetings weren't formal, there were a few things she wanted to tell the other women at their last get-together before the fall.

"That expression about herding cats comes to mind," Rosa said as the hubbub of female conversation continued. She chuckled and took out the lap blanket she was knitting. "It's been four days, but have you recovered from the wedding excitement?"

"Hardly." Joy laughed too. "It's wonderful having happy and exciting things going on, and I don't want them to end. Molly being able to stay a few days longer is fantastic. She's also lending a hand with ranch work while Cole and Melissa are on their honeymoon."

She glanced at her daughter, who sat at another table with Beth and several younger women. Molly's eyes were purple-shadowed, and she had a new brittleness about her. Whenever Joy tried to talk to her, Molly brushed off her gentle questions. Tomorrow, she'd fly back to Atlanta and a life Joy wasn't truly part of.

"Having Skylar stay with me is fun too." She couldn't help Molly if her daughter wouldn't talk to her. And even if Molly did open up, except for video calls and sending care packages, Joy couldn't do much from two thousand miles away. "With Paisley and Cam in and out as well, it's like having my own children at home again but without so much responsibility."

"Being a grandma is the best." Rosa nodded. "I hope you don't mind, but I invited Carrie to join us. She'll be along as soon as she finishes a few things for my website."

"That's fine. I intended on inviting Carrie to this meeting myself, but I got caught up in wedding planning and then hosting Melissa's family." Cole and Melissa were perfect for each other, and her once restless son was happy and settled like Joy had always wanted for him. If Bryce and Molly could find that same happiness, she could rest easier.

A buzzer sounded, and Kristi, the café's owner, opened the front door and welcomed Carrie. The Bluebunch closed at six, but Kristi let them use the café for evening meetings.

"Sorry I'm late." Carrie hovered in the entryway before Joy patted the empty chair beside hers.

"We haven't started yet." Joy tapped her glass with the spoon again as Carrie greeted Rosa and the others, and the various conversations ceased. Joy stood and scanned the circle of faces. "Since we don't meet in August, tonight's our last gathering until September." Thanks to her college classes, she'd gotten better at public speaking, and she was among friends, but it still wasn't easy. She was pushing herself out of her comfort zone, though, and that was what mattered. "Before we start tonight's icebreaker activity, I have a few announcements. First of all, thank you for your hard work in making Cole and Melissa's wedding so special."

Joy waited until the clapping died down and then remembered to pitch her voice so everyone could hear. "From our support of the food bank, to volunteer placements for our middle-school students at local businesses and ongoing fundraising for our biggest project—making the arena more accessible—we've had a successful year. Thanks to Angela and Nina for leading the arena fundraising project. We all hope you'll stay on." The two widows were contributing to the community again, and getting involved had helped them as well. Joy was happy to see how, like sunflower plants, they'd blossomed.

"We will," Nina said, and Angela nodded.

More applause.

"I handed out the financial report earlier." She acknowledged Diana, who, along with running a ranch, worked part-time as a bookkeeper and kept the group's books. "You can read it at your leisure. Since we keep these meetings fun and informal, Rosa suggested something to round out the year that will help us get to know each other better, especially our new members. Rosa?"

"Some of you may have played 'what's in your purse' before, and if you have, you know it's a lot of laughs." As if on cue, muffled laughter broke out, and several women clutched their bags. "You earn points for particular items on this list. It doesn't include things like wallets or phones because we all carry those around. We're looking for more interesting stuff that says something about who you are. My daughter in North Dakota put the list together, so like the rest of you, Joy and I are seeing it for the first time tonight, although I've agreed to keep score." There was more laughter as Rosa waved a brown envelope and withdrew several sheets of paper. "If you don't have a purse, a backpack is fine."

"But I…" Carrie looked around with an embarrassed expression.

"In this crowd, you won't be the first to carry horse tack around with you. Or paint brushes and pots." Joy sent Rosa a teasing glance.

"I might need them in an emergency." Rosa opened her bag, a patchwork tote of her own design.

"Like painting an SOS sign if your car breaks down on a back road with no cell service," Angela said above more laughter. "It's always good to be prepared for the unexpected."

"Angela's right," Beth said as she cradled her small pregnancy bump.

"Okay. Let's start, shall we?" Joy waved to get the group's attention. "Diana?"

"Nothing too interesting, although I do have a pair of underwear for my youngest just in case." She held up a pair of cartoon-patterned boys' briefs. "A stain removal pen, an envelope with business receipts, a granola bar and safety pins."

Rosa totted up Diana's points.

"You want to go next, Carrie?" Although they'd spoken to each other almost daily at the ranch, either with Paisley and Cam or when Carrie was seeing to Teddy, Joy couldn't say she'd gotten to know her yet. While Carrie was always friendly, it was as if she held part of herself back.

Carrie unzipped her backpack. "A red hair scrunchie." She pulled it out and stuck it on her wrist. "A broken rein, a pack of gum, a USB stick and a picture Paisley drew for me. It's of us riding together." She held it up to show everyone.

As the others admired the crayon drawing of two horses and riders in an emerald green field, Joy flicked a gaze to Carrie's half-open backpack. She wasn't being nosy. She was interested because the pack had a helmet holder similar to one she'd like. Carrie's pack had space for a water bottle too.

Joy drew in a soft breath. Although she'd suspected there was something more than friendship between Bryce and Carrie, she hadn't had proof. Until now. Under the guise of picking up a paper napkin, Joy leaned closer. A picture stuck out from an envelope with High Valley's photocenter logo. Joy had the same envelope in her own purse because she'd printed out wedding pictures to mail to family members who hadn't been able to attend and also didn't use email.

But while Joy's photos featured the bride and groom, Carrie's was of her and Bryce. She'd known they'd danced together because Paisley had mentioned it, but Joy hadn't thought anything of it. But this picture was important. Joy slid her reading glasses from atop her head to get a better look. The tenderness in Bryce's expression, how he held Carrie so close and how the two of them gazed into each other's eyes…

"Joy? We're going around the table clockwise, so it's your turn." Rosa's voice broke into her thoughts.

"Sure. I dropped this." She waved the napkin, but the others were still talking about Paisley's art and how many points Carrie had earned.

"Cam's also good at art. Here's a picture he drew for me." Joy rummaged in her purse for the drawing of her sunflower field Cam had given her earlier. "I have wedding photos, a mini manicure kit and a grocery-store gift card I won at the last bingo night."

As the game continued, Joy stole a glance at Carrie, who was now talking to Diana about irrigation systems.

Although Bryce might not have let himself admit it, he was well on his way to falling in love with Carrie. And all the signs were that Carrie reciprocated the feeling.

After Zach and Beth had gotten together, she'd promised Zach she wouldn't interfere in his life or anyone else's, and so far she hadn't.

Cole and Melissa had only needed a gentle nudge. Would that work for Bryce and Carrie too? Like Joy, Ally had wanted Bryce to be happy. Anything Joy did would be for her son as well as the woman she'd loved like a daughter.

And her precious grandbabies. Although Bryce likely hadn't admitted it, Paisley and Cam needed a nurturing motherly influence, and Carrie would be perfect.

Now Joy had to help her son see what was right in front of him. But first, she had to bide her time, watch and wait for the right opportunity.

CHAPTER NINE

"IT'S ONLY FOR a few hours. Besides, when did you last take a break?" Carrie spoke to Bryce over one shoulder as she hung a ball in Teddy's stall for him to play with.

"I take time off when I need to. Like for the wedding." Bryce finished putting away extra feed buckets and tried to avoid Carrie's intent green gaze.

"You were there for Cole and Melissa, which is what family does, but when was the last time you had fun with your kids?"

"At the wedding." He'd had fun with Carrie too, maybe too much because the more time he spent with her, the more off-balance he felt.

It was like when he was a kid and had taken swimming lessons at the pool in town. While Zach and Cole had run along the diving board and plunged into the water without thinking twice, Bryce had teetered at the edge of the board. Although he'd been scared to dive in, he hadn't wanted to go back to the pool deck either. Yet, when he finally launched himself off the board and sliced into the water exactly as the teacher had shown him, he'd wondered why he'd been so frightened.

Carrie huffed out a breath. "All I'm asking is that you come to Squirrel Tail with the kids and me this afternoon for the children's event. It's like the school field trip but unstructured family fun instead of learning focused." She glanced at the kids playing with the barn cats in the hayloft and lowered her voice. "Paisley and Cam need time with you. Paisley especially. Since the wedding, she hasn't been herself. Maybe she's still tired. It was a lot of excitement and build up for a girl her age, and she's bound to feel flat now it's over. But whatever's wrong, some special time with you might help."

Guilt churned in Bryce's stomach. In the past six days, Paisley had talked back to him twice and slammed her bedroom door after he'd spoken to her about her rudeness. Although that behavior might well be because she was overtired, Bryce couldn't shake the sense something else was also going on.

"I've wondered about Paisley lately. I appreciate you caring about her. About both kids. I'll come to the event with you." Work could wait. He'd devote this afternoon to the children.

"Great. As for caring about the kids? I do care,

truly." For a second, something flickered in Carrie's eyes, as if maybe she cared about him too. Then her tone turned teasing. "Are you sure the ranch won't fall apart if you leave it for a while?"

"Who knows what might happen?" Bryce teased her back. "But yeah, Zach and the hands can manage." He wasn't irreplaceable, and the work would always be there.

"We're leaving right after lunch, so see you back at the house?" Carrie paused at the bottom of the hayloft ladder. "We can take my truck."

"Sure." He hesitated. "You're good for all of us. Me as well as the kids. Thank you." His voice wobbled, and he made a clatter of grabbing a dustpan and broom to cover it.

"It's my pleasure." Carrie beamed before she clambered up the ladder and joined the kids. The sound of their happy voices made him wish he could take the whole day off, not only the afternoon.

Several hours later, in front of a bunny hutch at Squirrel Tail Ranch, Bryce crouched beside Paisley as she explained how she and Cam had helped build it.

"I hammered in this nail right here." She pointed to one of the sides. "I used a drill too."

"You did great," Carrie said. "Shane and I were with the kids the whole time." She reassured Bryce.

"Michael Kim almost chopped his finger off. There was blood everywhere." Cuddling Buster, his favorite bunny, Cam shook his head. "Even on the grass."

"Don't exaggerate, honey," Carrie said. "Michael's finger bled, sure, but he didn't need stitches, and Mr. Gallagher and I took care of it." She turned back to Bryce. "Don't worry. Shane had child-size tools for them to work with, and they wore goggles. Michael cut his finger on the rough edge of a piece of lumber. He wasn't using a saw."

"I wasn't worried exactly. I trust you, and Shane too." Bryce began to protest.

"You weren't there, so I'd be surprised if you weren't worried. Kids have accidents. You must have when you were a kid." Carrie scratched a gray-and-white bunny between its ears.

Like all children, Bryce had had the usual mishaps, but back then he'd felt invincible. After losing Ally to the cancer that came out of nowhere, and his dad in a farm accident, he'd become more aware that life could be short and more protective of his children too.

"Buster's asleep, so can we go in the bouncy house?" Cam tugged on Bryce's arm.

"Sure." Bryce stood and brushed grass from his faded jeans as the kids and Carrie put the rabbits back in their hutch.

He'd changed out of his work clothes, but maybe he should have worn something fancier than his usual jeans and Western shirt. In crisp denim shorts, white sneakers and a white T-shirt with a barrel-racing pattern in glittery pink, Carrie looked casual but more dressed up than she was around the barn or when looking after the kids. No matter what she wore, though, Bryce could barely keep his eyes off her since the wedding. And he kept sneaking glances at his phone and the photo Paisley had taken of him and Carrie dancing. At town and family parties, he'd danced with other women since Ally had passed. Why did dancing with Carrie feel so different and momentous?

"You hafta bounce too, okay?" Paisley gestured to the red-and-yellow bouncy house on the other side of the grassy area from the rabbit hutch and petting zoo.

"Sure." They sat on a bench and took off their shoes as, opposite them, Carrie and Cam did the same.

"Only you and me, okay?" Paisley lowered her voice.

"But we're here as a…" Bryce stopped. He'd almost said "family," but even though they felt a lot like one, they weren't. "A group," he substituted.

"I want to be with you. Not Carrie and Cam." Paisley stuck out her bottom lip.

"Feeling left out, are you, Ladybug?" He tried to ruffle her hair, but she jerked away.

"Mommy called me Ladybug. I thought you'd forgotten."

"I'd never forget something so important." He jerked his chin to indicate to Carrie she and Cam should go ahead. "I've been really busy lately, but I'm never too busy for you and Cam."

"It's always Cam." Paisley picked at the pink nail polish she'd worn for the wedding. "Or Carrie."

"What do you mean? With Eli being mean to him, I thought you understood why Cam needed extra attention. I also thought you liked Carrie."

"I do like her. And Cam, well, he's Cam. It's…" Paisley let out a long sigh. "Forget it."

"I'm your dad. I can't forget it." Bryce hesitated. "If you're upset about something, I want to make it better."

"It's nothing." She gave him a bright smile. "Eli Minden was really mean to Cam. When school starts again, I'm gonna be mean to Eli too."

"No, you won't." Bryce took Paisley's hand as they walked to the bouncy house. "Eli *was* unkind to Cam, but he said sorry, and everyone deserves a second chance." *Even me*. Bryce caught his breath. Although he'd always believed in second chances, that was for others. Why hadn't he given himself the same grace and compassion?

"I guess, but I can still *imagine* being mean." Paisley watched a boy near her age do a series of somersaults.

"You could, but why waste your imagination on something that isn't nice and kind?" Bryce tugged one of her braids as he followed her onto the bouncing area.

"I'd rather imagine being a world champion barrel racer." Paisley held Bryce's hands as they bounced together.

"There you go."

"Hey, watch me, Paisley." The boy showed more acrobatic moves.

"That's Noah. He goes to my school, but he's going into fourth grade," Paisley said. "He's here with his aunt and older cousins."

Bryce watched the kid too, who he now recognized from a youth hockey team Zach coached. And when Noah returned to his family group, and Paisley started talking about barrel racing, Bryce hoped this meant order had been restored. The daughter he knew seemed to be back.

Carrie and Cam joined them, Cam chattering about how high he could jump and taking Bryce's hand to show him.

"Let's jump in a circle holding hands." Cam's mouth and blue T-shirt were stained pink from the frozen strawberry treat he'd eaten earlier, and his hand was sticky in Bryce's. His eyes shone as he twisted his wiry body into pretzel-like shapes. "You too, Carrie."

"Okay." She grinned, and her mouth had a strawberry-pink tinge too.

When her hand connected with Bryce's, he kept bouncing even though the biggest part of him stilled. Although Cam and Paisley continued to talk, the only person Bryce was truly aware of was Carrie. The warmth of her palm and how right it felt in his. How the sunshine on her pretty hair also illuminated her sweet face. The way she smiled at the kids and him too and gave them her full attention. Those freckles on her nose he'd like to trace with a fingertip before kissing. And how he'd like to hold her close like he had when they'd danced, finding safety and comfort in her embrace.

"Bryce? Are you all right?" Carrie's voice yanked him back to reality.

"Are you gonna throw up, Daddy? You look like Paisley did that time at the fair before she—"

"I'm not going to be sick, Cam. It's fine, Carrie." Bryce bounced to a stop and put a hand to his head. "It's hot out here, that's all. Why don't we get lemonade?"

"Good idea." Carrie still looked at him as if he'd grown another head. "We should find some shade too. The kids want to swim, and the children's pool has an awning."

As Bryce left the bouncy house in a daze, he barely heard Carrie or his children. All that jumping around must have really rattled him. That was the only explanation for why he'd let himself think about Carrie in such an intimate way.

As if she were special to him rather than the kids' nanny. As if he wanted her to be part of all their lives forever.

"HERE YOU GO." An hour later, Carrie wrapped a swim towel around Paisley "Is that better?"

Although she still shivered, Paisley nodded and sat on one of the lounge chairs beside the children's pool.

"You'll soon warm up, but I'm done swimming too. I'll stay here with you while your dad plays with Cam." Carrie gestured to Bryce and Cam, who, still in the pool, tossed a beach ball between them. She pulled up another chair under the shaded awning and wiggled her toes. "Our pedicures lasted well, didn't they?" She nudged Paisley's foot with hers.

"Yeah." Huddled in her pink unicorn-patterned towel and with wet hair plastered to her head, Paisley appeared younger than eight.

"You looked like you had fun this afternoon. Especially with Noah in the bouncy house." Carrie hadn't missed Bryce's classic protective dad expression when the boy had shown off for Paisley's benefit. "Are you and Noah friends?"

"Kind of. He's nice. He goes to after-school club with Cam and me. One time, he stopped a kid from pulling my hair." Paisley studied her pink toenails.

"Is he the kind of boy you might like?" Most kids had crushes. Bryce likely didn't have anything to worry about—the kids were so young—but Carrie owed it to him to make sure.

"Just as a friend." Paisley rolled her eyes. "Noah wants to compete in rodeo too, so that's mostly what we talk about."

"If you want to invite him to the ranch, your dad or I can call his parents and set something up. You can invite your other friends too." Now that Carrie thought of it, Paisley didn't mention any friends apart from Melissa's daughter, Skylar. At her age, Carrie had had playdates with friends all the time.

"It's not important." Paisley squeezed water out of her hair.

"Is something bothering you? If so, I hope you know you can talk to me. I might not be able to fix whatever it is, but I've been told I'm a good listener. I remember being your age, and I know sometimes it's hard." Carrie toweled her own hair.

"How could you know what it's like? You had

your mom when you were my age. You *still* have her. Cam and me are the only kids in the entire school, probably the whole town, who don't have a mom. And then at the wedding, when you and Daddy were dancing, I heard…" Paisley gulped and buried her face in the towel.

"Your dad and I danced together because we're friends. We didn't mean to make you sad or upset." Carrie put a gentle hand on Paisley's heaving shoulders and sent Bryce a look, silently telling him to distract Cam a while longer. "Can you tell me what you heard?"

Paisley shook her head.

Carrie patted Paisley's back. She hadn't missed the covert glances she and Bryce had attracted at Melissa and Cole's wedding, and although people in small towns liked to talk about their neighbors, it usually wasn't hurtful.

But while she'd tried to pretend dancing with Bryce was as innocent as when she'd danced with Cole and Zach, it wasn't. She wouldn't have printed that picture of them together otherwise. A picture now tucked in a plain envelope in her bottom dresser drawer beneath a pile of hoodies, where nobody but her would see it.

"Whatever you heard was likely gossip and didn't mean anything important."

"It meant something *very* important. A lady talking to Mrs. Shevchenko called me a mother-

less child. I'm not motherless. I had Mommy."
Paisley raised her tearstained face.

"You did, and you still have her, sweetheart."
Carrie smoothed wet hair away from Paisley's face. "You're not motherless at all." From
everything Carrie had heard around town, Alison Carter had been a devoted mother and wife
whose husband and children were the center of
her world.

"That's what Mrs. Shevchenko said. I like
her."

Carrie liked her aunt Angela's friend, Nina
Shevchenko, too. She'd give her a call tonight
and ask what had been said. If there was anything else Carrie could do to reassure Paisley,
she needed the whole story. "Did Cam hear what
the lady said?"

"Nope. He was goofing around. But the lady
also said if Daddy got married again, me and
Cam would have the mother we needed. Like we
didn't need Mommy." Carrie opened her arms,
and Paisley flung herself into them as her words
came out between choked sobs.

"You'll always need your mommy." Carrie
hugged Paisley tight. "Even if your dad marries
someone else, she wouldn't replace your mother,
not ever. Your dad would make sure of it. He's
that kind of man." As far as Carrie knew, Bryce
wasn't even dating anyone, so the issue was hy-

pothetical, but it broke her heart to think of how Paisley must have worried.

"Really?" Paisley sniffed and rubbed a hand across her face.

"Really and truly, but you need to talk to your dad." She exhaled as she tried to think of how best to help Paisley understand. "Look at Ellie. Her real mom passed too but she and Beth were best friends, so although Beth became Ellie's guardian, she'd never take Ellie's mom's place. Beth's there for Ellie like a mom, but she also keeps Ellie's real mom's memory alive." Carrie didn't know Beth well, but when they'd chatted at the Sunflower Sisterhood meeting, Beth had mentioned talking with Ellie about her mom and displaying photos.

Paisley gulped. "Ellie says she now has two moms."

"There you go." Maybe Beth and Ellie could talk to Paisley too. Carrie had been so focused on Cam and the bullying she hadn't realized Paisley was struggling. "From now on, when you're worried about something, will you promise to tell me, your dad, your grandma or someone else you trust?"

"I promise." Paisley took a tissue from Carrie and mopped her tears. "It's okay if you dance with Daddy. If he does ever get married again, I wish it would be to someone like you."

"I'm your nanny. I work for your dad." Carrie's stomach lurched. "Besides, I'll only be around this summer, but I know…" She rushed on to forestall more tears from Paisley. "You and Cam are the most important people in your dad's life. He'd never share his life with someone who wasn't right for *all* of you." Someone who'd be around all the time to pick up the kids from school, help with homework and tuck them into bed each night.

Carrie's refusal to leave the rodeo circuit had been a recurring argument between her and Jimmy long before he'd gone off with her friend. Neither of them had been willing to compromise.

"For your art project next week, what do you say about focusing on your mom? You could share your memories of her through stories and drawings. If you did it on poster board, we could get it framed, and you could hang it in your bedroom." With Rosa's guidance, Carrie did an art project or craft with the kids each week, and it was fun for her as well as them.

"I'd like that." Paisley sniffed. "But what about Cam? He doesn't remember anything about Mommy, only stuff other people have told him."

"You can tell him about her, and maybe he could talk to your mom's parents and her sister." After Alison's death, her parents had retired to a town in Idaho to be closer to their other daughter and grandchildren, but they video called Paisley and Cam several times a week. "I'll try to think of something special for Cam's art project."

"What kind of something special?" Cam hugged Carrie from behind, his wet arms encircling her neck.

"We were talking about your mom and our next art project. Here's your towel. Dry off, you're getting me all wet again." Carrie caught Bryce's gaze. "I hope that's okay?" She'd wanted to comfort Paisley, but she hoped she hadn't gone too far by talking about Alison.

"Yeah, I can get the old photo albums out," he said, his voice gruff. Then he grabbed his own towel and rubbed his face and hair.

"Those albums in boxes in the basement?" Paisley asked. "You said we couldn't look at them."

"I guess it's time. For all of us." Bryce draped the towel around his shoulders and gathered up the kids' sunhats and backpacks.

Carrie turned away to make sure the children had their flip-flops, water bottles and Cam's ball.

She shouldn't admire the breadth of Bryce's shoulders, or how good he looked in swim trunks, his body fit from daily hard physical work. She also shouldn't think about how a man who was such a good dad would also be a good husband.

Carrie was with this family for a short time and doing her best for them. That had to be enough. Yet, she couldn't help wanting more.

CHAPTER TEN

THAT EVENING, Bryce shut Paisley's bedroom door and rejoined Carrie in the family room. "I appreciate you staying over tonight on such short notice."

"No problem. You have an early start tomorrow. I understand what working with freelance clients is like. When they need to meet with you, you have to be available." Curled up cross-legged on the sofa, Carrie looked both comfortable and at home.

Thanks to her, Bryce's house continued to look more comfortable and homey too. A cozy, horse-patterned blanket was draped over the back of the sofa. Baby spider plants grew in pots on top of a bookcase, and the fridge was decorated with Paisley and Cam's artwork. Nowadays, Bryce liked coming home after work. He also liked talking to Carrie about his day. She knew more than he'd expected about agriculture, and she listened and asked intelligent questions.

"Paisley and Cam had fun this afternoon. They

were so tired they were asleep almost as soon as they got into bed." He sat beside her on the sofa with Otis and Penny snuggled between them. "I had fun too."

"It was great. I'm on the road so much with rodeo, I'd forgotten what it was like to spend time with a family doing something fun." Her smile was pensive. "I love my folks, but when I was growing up, they were often busy with work. My dad's in construction, and my mom has an office job. I spent vacations with my grandparents, so…" She hesitated. "I had some big trips with my parents, sure. New York City, Florida and even Italy once, but it's the little things, you know? They make the best memories."

Bryce nodded. He'd gotten so caught up in work and trying not to think about what he'd lost he'd forgotten those little things and the importance of cherishing the everyday. "Cam liked the bouncy house so much he wants a trampoline."

"You have enough space, and lots of stores are having summer sales, so you might be able to get a deal." Carrie offered Bryce a snickerdoodle cookie. She'd made a batch for the kids, but he must have eaten half of them. "It would also be nice for Paisley and Cam to invite kids from school over to play on it. It might help them make more friends."

"Yeah." His heart sank at the thought of han-

dling a group of kids on his own. He could ask
Beth or Melissa, but he'd gotten used to Carrie
being here and, like today, the two of them working together as a team.

"Paisley wants to invite Noah to the ranch.
She says he's a friend, nothing more."

"Watching Noah showing off for Paisley, I
guess it brought out my protective dad instincts."
Bryce savored the delicious, soft, cinnamon-
flavored cookie. "Sometimes I can't believe how
fast the kids are growing up. How am I going to
cope when they start dating?"

"Try not to worry about the future. Enjoy the
now." Carrie's laugh was light. "Like I should
talk. I worry about the future too, but Paisley and
Cam are showing me how to live more in the moment."

Bryce exhaled. "You're right." She was right
about a lot of things, not only the kids.

Carrie picked up her mug of cocoa and drank.
"Today, Paisley talked to me about her mom and
how much she misses Ally. I tried to help, but
it was tough. There's nothing I can say to make
that kind of loss better."

"I heard part of what you said, and you did
fine." Bryce's throat clogged. "It's hard for me to
talk about Ally with the kids, but, like when the
three of us made that list of things Ally was good

at, today you reminded me I need to make sure we keep their mom's memory alive."

And as he'd overheard Carrie comforting his daughter, saying and doing what he'd never been able to, he realized the magnitude of his mistake. Not only in not talking about Ally with the kids, but also in being so sure he'd never be able to open his heart and life to anyone else. But, like Carrie had said, she was the kids' nanny, and she'd only be around for the summer. He couldn't let himself think about anything long-term.

"Sorry, what did you say?" he asked.

"The client you're meeting tomorrow, what kind of farm do they have?" Carrie looked interested, her expression bright.

"It's small but growing. Spence started with ten acres five years ago, and now he's up to twenty." And as he talked about his work, and Carrie asked questions, Bryce found himself opening up to her.

"I want to have a farm, a small ranch really, but to start, my main focus would be agricultural crops." Having finished her cocoa, Carrie nibbled a cookie. "My grandparents were big on protecting the environment. I want to practice sustainable farming too." She hesitated. "I don't talk about it much. A lot of people, guys especially, think women having a farm or ranch is foolish.

Some still have a problem with women in agriculture."

"They're the foolish ones." Bryce rubbed Penny's floppy ears. "If a ranch is your dream, you should go for it. Don't let anyone hold you back. Look at Diana. She's a better rancher than many men. Ranching's changing and for the better, I say. If Paisley wants to work here on the Tall Grass, I'd encourage her the same as Cam."

"That means a lot." Carrie's voice was low. "Thank you."

The heat of attraction rushed through Bryce. It hadn't mattered he'd never been able to talk with Ally about his work. Their relationship was built on their long history together, the children, friendship and steadfast love. But talking with Carrie, someone who understood what Bryce was trying to achieve, fulfilled him in a way he hadn't known he'd needed. "My oldest brother, Paul, was big on sustainability. He had a vision for this ranch based on environmental stewardship. He had cystic fibrosis and died when I was in my late teens."

"I'm so sorry." Carrie reached across the sleeping dogs and put her hand on top of his.

"If Paul had lived, we'd have worked together on the agricultural side of the ranch, so now I want to carry on what he believed in. He was an artist too. As long as he was able, he'd go out with his easel or sketchpad and draw the landscape and birds and animals."

"Do you have any of Paul's art? It would be nice for Paisley and Cam to see their uncle's work and hear about him. Cam especially has real artistic talent. I wondered where it came from." Carrie gave him a dimpled grin. "Now I know."

"I've got a framed oil of the creek in winter and some of Paul's watercolors of cattle and horses." They were in a box in Bryce's basement because, as with Ally's things, it hurt Bryce to see them. "I guess I could hang them up. That oil would look nice here in the family room."

"If it would be easier, we could do that together this weekend." Carrie squeezed Bryce's hand before letting go. "Get the kids involved."

"That would be good for all of us." He picked up his now cold cup of cocoa and set it back down again. He enjoyed the feeling of Carrie's hand on his and felt an odd sense of loss when she took it away. "Ally would have liked you."

"I'm sure I'd have liked her as well. Everybody around here speaks highly of her."

There was a question in Carrie's green eyes. One that had been there earlier too when she'd talked about Paisley missing Ally. A question—and an issue—Bryce had avoided for too long.

He took a deep breath. "I'd also like to display some photos of Ally and other things, like ornaments. She collected pig figurines." He smiled at the memory. "She belonged to this online group with other collectors. They raised money to support endangered pig breeds. For her birthday and Christmas each year, I'd give her a pig-themed gift. It was a joke between us. One year, we all, the kids too, had matching pig Christmas sweatshirts." For the first time, that memory brought joy and healing instead of pain.

"Why not raise heritage pigs? In Ally's memory." Carrie's voice was light.

"That's a fantastic idea." One Bryce should have thought of himself. "I could try Herefords. They're a great American breed. Gentle and easy to handle. When the kids are a bit older, they could even show them at their 4-H club."

"There you go." Carrie reached for her phone on the coffee table. "It's late, and you have an early start tomorrow. I should get settled in the guest room." She grabbed the mugs and the empty cookie plate to take them to the kitchen. "Text me when you get to the client's farm. The kids like to know where you are."

"Of course." Bryce woke the dogs and went to let them out the back door as Carrie put the dirty dishes in the dishwasher. "I...thank you."

"For what?" Carrie's back was to him, her voice muffled by the clatter of dishes.

"Tonight. It was good to talk." And with that

talk, something important had changed for him and between he and Carrie. Carrie wasn't Ally, and he didn't want her to be. Apart from reminiscing about his wife and their marriage, he'd been focused on Carrie. Ally would always have a special place in his heart, but now Carrie did too.

As a friend, he reminded himself while he let the dogs back in and headed to his own room at the other end of the house.

He set the alarm on his phone and crawled into his king-size bed, which felt bigger and lonelier than ever. Even though Carrie was fast becoming his favorite person apart from the kids, and even though she understood him better than anyone, he could handle this friendship thing. It would be a mistake to want more.

"It looks great, doesn't it?" Kristi gestured to one of the framed posters Carrie had designed that now hung beside a chalkboard listing the daily specials at the Bluebunch Café.

Carrie loved making clients happy, and the thrill of seeing her work in public never faded. For Kristi's new logo, menu and signage, she'd drawn inspiration from both the local area and the café building's history. The design incorporated the old tin ceiling, reclaimed barn board walls, bluebunch wheatgrass and High Valley's "big sky" vista. The result was timeless but also fresh and modern, and it captured the warmth and the whimsical feel of both the café and its bubbly owner. "I'm glad you like it."

"I don't just like it. I *love* it. I called the printer earlier to order postcards of the posters. Tourists have been asking for them." Kristi handed Carrie a bag with three cornbread muffins, the decorated gingerbread cookies Paisley and Cam had chosen and several bottles of apple juice. "After seeing what you did for Rosa, I'd like to hire you to update the café's website too."

"Sure, I'd be happy to take a look and give you a quote." When Carrie nodded, Kristi gave the kids a new variety of trail mix to try. "How does tomorrow evening around seven work for you?"

"Great, see you then. You caught me at a busy time." Kristi turned to a couple who'd approached the counter and asked for half a dozen morning glory muffins to go.

No matter what time Carrie stopped by, the café was always busy. Waving goodbye to Kristi, she held the takeout bag in one hand and guided the kids to the café door with the other. High Valley's charming main street was thronged with visitors, but even in tourist season, the small town had a laid-back, easygoing vibe Carrie liked. From the sidewalk, she waved at Joy, who'd just gotten out of one of the ranch pickup trucks parked in front of Rosa's craft center.

"Watch for cars, kids." When the traffic stopped, they crossed the wide main street at the temporary summer crosswalk and greeted Joy.

"Grandma." Paisley and Cam hugged her, and then Joy wrapped Carrie in a hug too.

"I'm glad to have three helpers." A smile lit Joy's face as she stepped away to take her grand-children's hands.

"It's no problem." With Joy's friendliness, Carrie's heart felt full. "We're happy to pack orders with you and Rosa." She bent to speak to the children at their level. "It's something fun to do before swimming, isn't it?"

"Everything we do with Carrie is fun." Cam's expression was serious.

"It is." Paisley chimed in. "Daddy and us and Carrie redecorated yesterday."

As they went into the coolness of the craft center, where Rosa and two of her summer staff answered questions from a bus tour group, Joy glanced at Carrie and then back to the children. "Redecorated how?"

"We put up pictures of Mommy, and Uncle Paul's art. Daddy also showed us Mommy's pig collection and let me arrange it in a special cab-inet," Paisley said with a tone of importance.

"I helped too," Cam added. "Me and Paisley also named some of the pigs. One's Carrie. She's pink and white with a curly tail."

"That's sweet." Joy's eyes widened with something that looked like speculation, along with approval and maybe hope.

"You named a pig for your mom too." Awkwardness curled in Carrie's tummy. "And your dad. Don't forget to tell your grandma about raising Hereford piglets." She needed to change the subject before Joy got the wrong idea and imagined Carrie could be part of her son and grandchildren's lives longer-term.

Carrie put the food in the small staff kitchen and then regrouped with Joy and the kids in Rosa's workroom. Craft items, packing boxes, paper, customer orders and other supplies were on a big table in the middle of the room, and boxes almost ready for shipment were stacked by the door.

After giving Paisley and Cam rolls of Medicine Wheel address labels and showing them how to stick them to the packed boxes, Joy joined Carrie at the table. "You did a good thing. Bryce and the kids need to remember Ally and Paul. It's part of healing and going on with life." As she covered two dreamcatchers in bubble wrap, Joy's blue eyes were soft with emotion. "I've tried for more than a year to get Bryce to bring out photos of Ally and things that were important to her. Ally's folks and sister have too, but he wouldn't budge. You managed to get through to him, and I'm grateful."

Carrie tucked white tissue paper between the folds of a crib blanket patterned with bears, deer and buffalo. "Paisley talked to me about missing her mom, so I wanted to help. I don't know what I did, not really."

"Maybe Bryce was finally ready to listen, but whatever or however, it's a blessing." Joy patted Carrie's arm. "Bryce was close to Paul, but, like with Ally, it was as if he had to shut that part of himself away to cope with his grief. Then, he got stuck."

"Paul's paintings are beautiful. Did he ever show them in exhibitions?" Carrie found a box and tucked the baby blanket inside, along with one of the gallery's cards.

"No, he planned to, but then…he passed." Joy's mouth worked. "I try to keep Paul's memory alive in whatever way I can. I want to celebrate his life, not focus on how it was cut so short. I have lots of his pictures displayed at the house and around our summer camp."

Carrie closed and taped the box and found the shipping label, checking off the order against Rosa's list. "What would you think of having a retrospective exhibition? It could be a special event with music and refreshments. Not selling the paintings but raising money for a charity?"

Joy's hands stilled on the dreamcatcher box. "That's a wonderful idea. Maybe it could support a charity for children and teenagers with special needs, similar to Camp Crocus Hill. We set up Crocus Hill in Paul's memory."

"Then what about having the campers make art too?" Carrie had only seen them when they came to ride at the main ranch, but someone had mentioned Crocus Hill had an art studio. "We could make the event a showcase for Paul and the camp, along with other local artists. I saw something about an art club in the weekly newspaper."

"That would be perfect. It's too late to organize anything this summer, but perhaps we could hold an event in the fall or for the holidays." Joy's face was animated, and her eyes sparkled. "Everyone will pitch in. Paul was a member of that art club."

"I could design marketing materials. No charge." Ideas popped in Carrie's mind. Although this wasn't the main reason for her offer, it would be a way of promoting her business, and she might make contacts that would lead to new work. "I'll talk to Cole and some of my rodeo contacts. With a Western focus, we might be able to get corporate sponsors interested."

"That's so kind and generous, but you won't be here in the fall, will you? I'm getting ahead of myself." Joy wrapped another parcel of dream-catchers while Carrie tackled a queen-size circle-of-life blanket. "I suppose you could work remotely and, with enough notice, come back to town for the actual event."

"I guess." Carrie had also gotten ahead of her-self. She focused on the card included with the blanket that explained its design and how the colors symbolized different life stages.

"When are you going back to barrel racing?" Joy fixed a shipping label to the box with the dreamcatchers.

"Apart from a small charity event later this month, my first official competition is in Col-orado after Labor Day. I practice with Teddy most days after work, so we should be ready." Carrie felt better than she had in years. Along with increased mental sharpness, she was get-ting back into peak competitive physical form. But, although she was excited about returning to competition, she'd miss being with the kids. And she'd miss Bryce even more.

"I'd love to come and watch. I grew up in Mis-soula, but I spent summers with family in High Valley. That's how I met my Dennis and learned about horses and ranching. Now I can't imag-ine horseback riding not being part of my life." Joy chuckled. "No more jumping, though, so I'm learning dressage. I never tried barrel racing, but

I have a friend who's still doing it in her late fifties. Linda competes in senior rodeo. She loves it, although she says she doesn't bounce as easily as she used to."

"Good for her. I hope that's me someday." Carrie laughed too. "If you're interested, I can give you and your horse, Cindy, a barrel-racing lesson."

"That would be fun. Not that I'll ever reach the heights Paisley's aiming for, but I'd love to try a new sport." Joy gave her granddaughter a fond smile. "I always say there's a time for everything in life. Because you missed out on something once doesn't mean you can't have another chance at it. While it might not feel or be the same as when you were younger, as long as you're breathing, you can still try."

Except for motherhood. Carrie wanted a family and had expected to have one with Jimmy. But he'd said no man would want to be with someone who was away more than they were home. Even if she found the right person, would he accept her wanting rodeo *and* family life? Or had Jimmy and her parents been right all along that sooner rather than later Carrie would have to settle down?

"This blanket's the last." She folded one of Rosa's prize-winning Cree Star blankets into a tissue-lined box and added the information card.

"Ready for snack time, kids?" she called. The children had finished with the address labels and were working in the activity books Carrie had put in their backpacks. "I also brought snacks for you and Rosa." Carrie turned back to Joy.

"Women like you, Beth and Melissa inspire me," Joy said. "You know what you want in life, and you go for it."

"Hardly." Carrie shook her head. "I'm a work in progress."

"You and me both, honey." Joy linked her arm through Carrie's as they moved to the kitchen.

"And me." Rosa's rich laugh rolled out as she joined them. "I say having it all means having what's right for you. If you aren't happy with *who* you are or *where* you are, change it. That's the beauty of life."

As Carrie helped Paisley and Cam set out the food and drinks on the table in the staff kitchen, she considered what Joy and Rosa had said. Who she'd been—yesterday, last month or last year— wasn't who she had to be forever. She *could* change.

High Valley was currently a small phase in Carrie's life. But what if she looked for a property nearby? If she found one in her budget, she could put down more permanent roots here. For things like an exhibition of Paul's art, she wouldn't be a visitor. She'd have a place to come home to, somewhere she belonged. Her new friends—Joy, Rosa, Kristi, Diana and the Sunflower Sisterhood—as well as High Valley could be part of her life for always.

And Bryce wasn't like Jimmy, so she shouldn't judge him by that standard. If she wasn't working for him, who knew what might happen?

CHAPTER ELEVEN

BRYCE DROVE WHAT had once been his dad's red tractor around the outer edge of the hayfield. With the mower hitched to the back of the tractor and a clear blue sky, everything was perfect for haying. These days, though, and even if the weather was overcast, he went about his work with a new lightness in his heart.

As he rounded a corner, he waved at Cole, who drove a green tractor in the next field over. His brother, still a starry-eyed newlywed, raked the hay Bryce had cut the day before. After Cole pulled the hay into rows, Zach would bale it. Haying season meant the whole family worked even more closely together than usual.

Bryce stopped the tractor near a small stand of trees and wiped his face with a red bandanna.

"Here you go, Daddy." Paisley handed him a bottle of water from a cooler.

"Thanks, Ladybug. You guys started raking here. That's great."

Carrie and the kids were involved in haying

too. Although they each had their own jobs, having Carrie alongside him was comfortable. And whenever he spotted her in the distance or, like now, up close, he got warm inside.

"It's hot work." Carrie leaned on a pitchfork.

Bryce nodded as he drank the cold water. In jeans, a light long-sleeved shirt, work gloves and cowboy hat, Carrie looked like one of the extra hands they'd hired for this second hay cutting of the season. She wasn't, though, and he'd never been more aware of her femininity. Her green eyes, framed in thick dark lashes, shone. Her skin glowed, and those freckles on the bridge of her nose continued to tempt him.

"Carrie told us about mice and birds and how this field is a whole…" Cam screwed up his eyes. "Eco something."

"Ecosystem." Carrie took a tube of sunscreen from a bag and applied a dollop to Cam's face.

"We looked at bugs too. Carrie's gonna show us some pictures on the computer when she comes back from visiting her mom and dad." Paisley wrapped her arms around Carrie's waist. "Three sleeps. You promise?"

"I promise. I'll be back around breakfast time on Monday." Carrie hugged the children and then turned to Bryce. "I've got my stuff in the truck. I'm leaving as soon as your mom comes by with lunch."

"Yeah, of course." When Carrie had asked to take an extended weekend to go to Kalispell for her mom's birthday, it wasn't a problem. Now, though, and despite the never-ending work to keep him busy, the time without her seemed like a bunch of empty hours Bryce would struggle to fill. "Have fun."

"I feel bad leaving you on your own at such a busy time. I've put meals in the fridge and freezer for you to heat up. If you have to work late out here, I've arranged for the kids to have a sleepover at your mom's." Carrie paused. "Don't forget Paisley's going to a birthday party tomorrow. Melissa's picking her up to drive into town with Skylar. I already wrapped the present. It's in the basket in the family room."

"It's a mermaid-themed party. We're gonna swim with a real live mermaid. I already packed my swimsuit. Carrie said I need to help you by remembering stuff. While me and Skylar are at the party, Aunt Melissa's taking Cam to the playground."

"And for ice cream." Cam elbowed his way between Carrie and Paisley.

"We'll be fine." Bryce had managed okay before Carrie came into their lives, and she'd only be gone a few days. Why did he now feel like things might fall apart as soon as she left? Like *he* might fall apart. "Mom's pulling up on the other side of the field now. So...bye."

Paisley and Cam hugged Carrie again.

"I'll be back before you know it. Help your dad and don't forget to brush your teeth after meals. Visit Teddy for me too. He'll love those treats we got him from the feedstore. Bye." She straightened and gave Bryce a jerky wave. "Good luck with the baling and everything. The weather looks like it'll hold."

"Yeah." Bryce shifted from one foot to the other.

"You haven't hugged Carrie, Daddy." Cam looked between them. "Whenever anybody leaves or comes back, we always hug."

"Grandma says you can never have too many hugs," Paisley added.

"Sure... I..." Bryce stepped closer to Carrie. "Safe travels." He put his arms around her shoulders.

"Take care." Her warm breath brushed his cheek as Carrie hugged him back, and her hat brim bumped his.

Bryce relaxed into her embrace and deepened it, drawing Carrie closer. He breathed in a faint lemon scent mixed with the hayfield and sunshine. He drew nearer still, and then his mouth grazed the curve of her cheek in a kiss.

"Oops." Carrie jerked back and grabbed for her hat as it tumbled off.

"Daddy's a good hugger, isn't he?" Cam's voice was innocent.

"Uh, he's great." Carrie wedged her hat back on her head.

Paisley giggled behind her hands.

"I better…" Carrie gestured to where she'd left her truck parked on a dirt road behind the trees. "See you Monday." Her face was as red as Bryce imagined his was and not from the sun.

"Yeah." He fumbled with his own hat, which was crooked from hitting Carrie's. "Come on, kids. Let's see what your grandma brought us for lunch."

"Did you kiss Carrie?" Paisley looked from Bryce to the road, where Carrie had already started up her truck.

"No, of course not." His lips had connected with her cheek by accident. It wasn't a real kiss.

"You were holding her really, really close." Paisley tucked her hand into Bryce's.

"I hugged her, that's all. Like your grandma says, the Carters are huggers." But how he'd hugged Carrie was different from how Bryce hugged his family. If the kids hadn't been there, he might have given her a real kiss too.

While Cam ran ahead to check out the field lunch, Paisley squeezed Bryce's hand. "If you want to go on a date with Carrie, it would be okay with me."

Bryce yanked his hat farther down over his eyebrows. "Carrie's your nanny, and besides…" He stopped.

"Besides what?" Paisley skipped at his side.

Bryce's heart flipped. "It doesn't matter. Do you think Grandma brought us a pizza party? Remember she did that last year?"

Distracted as Bryce had intended, Paisley darted after Cam.

If only Bryce could distract himself as easily. His fingers still tingled where he'd held Carrie's shoulders, and his body hummed with awareness of how good it felt to be close to her.

And although Carrie had only just left, without her nearby there was an emptiness inside Bryce neither pizza nor anything else could fill.

"It's so good to have you home safe and sound." In the spacious vestibule of Carrie's childhood home, her mom greeted her with a loving embrace. As Carrie breathed in her mom's familiar floral fragrance, her heart sank. How could she disappoint her mom and dad? She was their only child, and they depended on her.

"How are you doing, Pumpkin?" Her dad gave her a bear hug. "Let's take a look at you." His callused hands lingered on her bare arms. Despite being the president of the family construction company, Frank Rizzo still pitched in on job sites. It was a source of pride he wasn't afraid to get his hands dirty, and he and her mom had instilled in Carrie the value of hard, honest work.

"I'm good." She touched her cheek, still feeling the imprint of Bryce's lips against her skin. All the way to Kalispell, she'd replayed what had happened in the hayfield in her mind. Bryce had only hugged her because Cam had asked him to. That kiss was an accident. It wasn't even a real kiss, only a peck on the cheek. It had also been more than a little awkward because they were both wearing cowboy hats, and the kids were looking on.

"You'll want to change, of course, but you look wonderful." Carrie's mom's heels clicked on the imported-Italian-marble hall floor as they made their way to the family room at the back of the house, which overlooked the patio and pool area. "Ranch life and all that fresh air must agree with you. Your eyes are brighter, and you're glowing."

After leaving Carrie's overnight bag and backpack at the foot of the sweeping staircase, her dad joined them. "Carolina, you are always beautiful, but now there's something extra special. Maybe someone special?" He quirked an eyebrow.

It felt strange hearing her full name, one she'd

always disliked, for the first time in months. "Nobody special." It wasn't exactly a lie, but she couldn't tell her parents the truth without sounding like a teenage girl with a crush. "I like High Valley, and the family I work for is nice." She sounded like she was reciting a school lesson. "The kids, Paisley and Cam, are a lot of fun."

"And their father? You've never said much about him." Her mom's eyes, the same shade of green as Carrie's, narrowed. Sophia Rizzo was astute, and despite their differences, Carrie and her mom had always been close.

"Bryce is a good dad and a good employer." That wasn't a lie either, but Carrie's stomach still lurched, and the spot on her cheek where Bryce had kissed her burned so hot she was surprised her parents couldn't see it. "He's the youngest son in a big family, and their ranch is a family operation. Everyone's made me feel really welcome." Although Carrie hadn't realized how much until now, Bryce and the kids, the ranch, High Valley and the Carter family were all changing her.

Her mom still studied her. "You'll be back home in September, won't you?"

"I'm not sure yet." Carrie took a glass of soda from her dad, who'd busied himself with the drinks cabinet.

"But why not?" Her mom twisted her hands

together, and her diamond tennis bracelet slid on her slender wrist. "I thought everything had been decided. I'm already—"

"We have plenty of time to talk about Carolina's plans, Sophia." Her dad shot Carrie's mom a warning glance. "Now we have a party to get ready for."

Beyond the floor-to-ceiling windows, staff from the caterer and party planner were hard at work. The backyard was already festooned with pink and white balloons, and a small stage was being set up for dancing near the pool house.

Her mom's demeanor and expression were stiff, and tension radiated from her. "I left several dresses for you to choose from on your bed. I remember small-town life. There's likely no place to shop in High Valley."

Not for couture clothing, but the stores there met Carrie's needs. "I planned to wear the dress I wore for Dad's sixtieth birthday. That was only a year ago." She'd never been a dress person, and even at Paisley's age, she'd been happier in jeans, a T-shirt and her beloved cowboy boots.

"I wanted to treat you." Her mom's smile was anxious. "Besides, most of the people who were at your dad's party will also be at mine. You can't wear the same dress."

Carrie held back a protest. As dresses went, she liked the green one she'd bought for her dad's birthday, and that was why she'd worn it to Cole and Melissa's wedding. And how Bryce had looked at her at the wedding now made the dress special. Part of her wanted to have a memory of him here. "I'm sure whatever you chose for me will be beautiful." Her mom had excellent taste and the money to indulge it. "Where's Aunt Angela and the rest of the family?" The house was quiet, although it was so big there could have been a party in the bedroom wing, and she wouldn't have heard it here.

"Angela's having her hair done, your uncles are golfing and the others haven't arrived yet." Her mom's expression softened. "Although I don't understand why you couldn't have gotten extra time off to travel with Angela two days ago, it's been good for us to have time alone together. I have my sister back, and she…you…" Her mom's mouth trembled. "She loves you."

"I love her too. Why don't you and Dad come visit High Valley later this month?" Carrie hadn't told anyone, not even Bryce, how she'd begun to put her finances in order to see what kind of property she could afford. Or how every night before bed, she checked online to see if any small ranches or farms in a twenty-mile radius of High Valley had come up for sale. She didn't want to divert attention from her mom's birthday weekend, and if her parents came to High

Valley, it would be easier to tell them what she wanted to do with her life then. Maybe in the place she intended to call home, they'd understand and support her choices.

Three hours later, dressed in a pale yellow off-the-shoulder cocktail dress paired with white gladiator sandals, Carrie was having more fun than she'd expected. Every aspect of the birthday party had the casual air of elegance her mom had perfected. It was also good to see aunts, uncles and cousins she rarely spent time with because she was on the road so much.

She murmured her thanks to the server, Rob, an acquaintance from the rodeo circuit, who added her empty wine glass to a full tray. Like Carrie, Rob was one of the many cowboys and cowgirls who worked other jobs to earn extra money in between rodeo events. Despite her parents' wealth, as soon as she'd graduated from college, Carrie had been determined to pay her own way rather than depend on her family.

"Want to dance?" Domenic Pasquale, a man around her age she remembered from company holiday parties, held out a hand. When she took it, he swept her into a waltz.

"What are you up to these days?" She made polite conversation. The kind of conversation she'd have to spend her life making if she took that job her folks wanted her to.

"I'm now head of sales." The dance floor was lit with strings of white lights that shone off Dom's dark hair and gleaming white teeth. He wore an open-necked white shirt, sports jacket and dark dress pants along with polished tasseled loafers. "Your dad promoted me last month."

"Congratulations." Dom was attractive, polite and successful. Yet, compared to the men Carrie knew in High Valley, there was something fundamentally lacking about him. Beneath her hand, his forearm was soft, not well muscled like Bryce's, and as he talked about golf and a wine-tasting tour he'd taken on a recent business trip to California, her mind wandered.

As they passed Angela, in a group of Carrie's parents' friends from their neighborhood, her aunt smiled and raised an eyebrow. Angela wore a pale blue dress that set off her silver hair and dark eyes—Carrie's mom had evidently treated her to a new outfit as well.

"I'm sorry, what did you say?" She turned her attention back to Dom.

"Let me know when you finalize your start date. We could have lunch or meet up for a drink after work your first week."

"I haven't signed the paperwork accepting the job yet." Something her parents kept reminding her about.

"From what I hear, the paperwork's only a formality." At Dom's warm smile, more guilt stabbed Carrie's chest. "There's a work trip to New York in September. What do you say about taking in a Broadway show?" His expression was hopeful.

"I guess, but only as colleagues." Carrie stumbled, and Dom eased her closer. He wasn't as good a dancer as Bryce. "I don't date people I work with." *Or work for.* She worked for Bryce, although not for much longer. But at the end of the summer, she'd be going back to rodeo, so she couldn't date Dom *or* Bryce.

"Of course." Dom's smile slipped. "Have you been to New York before?"

"Once, with my parents. It was fun. Our hotel was near Times Square." Carrie kept her voice light. She liked visiting cities, but she wouldn't want to live in one.

"Your dad says you're going to shake up the marketing department. They're a good, creative team, but they need strong leadership. That's where you come in. Your dad's so proud of you. Your mom is too. Together, they've built a company I'm proud to be part of." As the waltz ended, Dom swung her in a circle like Bryce had done at the wedding. "They'll be glad to have you here at home, where you belong."

Carrie tried to smile as she thanked him for the dance and murmured something about wanting to check in with her folks. "Why don't you dance with my cousin? Sabrina's from Seattle and doesn't know many people here." She gestured to a dark-haired woman who stood alone near the bar, and when Sabrina joined them, Carrie introduced her to Dom.

As Sabrina gave her a grateful smile, Carrie backed away before bending to rub a spot on her heel where the new sandals, which her mom had picked out to go with the dress, had rubbed her skin almost raw. A woman like Sabrina would be perfect for Dom. As well as being smart and attractive, she was an avid golfer, and in the card she'd sent Carrie for her last birthday, she'd mentioned taking a wine-tasting class at night school.

Considering she'd done her good deed for the day, Carrie straightened and glanced around for her parents.

"I almost didn't recognize you without jeans, boots and a hat." Rob appeared with a tray of fancy hors d'oeuvres. "You clean up well."

She laughed at his teasing and took a shrimp appetizer with avocado and cucumber. "So do you." As he asked her about Teddy and their next competition, and they talked about rodeo people they both knew, Carrie felt more at ease than she had the entire evening.

"There she is." Her dad's voice boomed, and her parents came toward her holding hands.

Carrie excused herself from Rob and put on her party face again.

"We're treasuring every moment of having our girl home," her mom added. "We only wish you could stay longer."

"She'll soon be home permanently, won't you, Pumpkin?" Her dad's voice rumbled. "I saw you dancing with Domenic. He looked smitten."

"It was only a dance, Dad." Carrie tried to keep her expression neutral. Her dance with Bryce had changed everything, but one dance with Dom had left her unmoved.

"He's got a good business head on his shoulders, and he's ambitious. Reminds me of myself at that age. The Pasquales are a fine family. Dom's grandfather and yours were friends. You should think about—"

"Now, Frank, leave Carrie to make her own decisions. You want her to come home, don't you?" Her mom shook her head, but her expression as she looked at Carrie's dad was loving. "I've convinced your dad to take time off so we can visit you for a few days later this month. We'll stay with Angela, and the two of you can show us around."

"Great." A weight settled in the pit of Carrie's stomach like the rock on the edge of the hayfield where she'd worked with the kids and Bryce. A rock Bryce said was too big to move, so they went around it instead.

Did her mom truly mean Carrie could make her own decisions, and her parents would accept her choices? She couldn't keep going as she had been, letting them think rodeo and freelance work were temporary, but she didn't want to disappoint them either.

No more avoiding or shirking the truth. This weekend wasn't the right time, but when her folks came to High Valley, she'd tell them what she wanted to do with her life, and they'd either accept it or they wouldn't.

But faced with their loving, proud and expectant expressions, the rock in her stomach got heavier.

Somehow, she knew that when she left Kalispell after this brief visit, it wouldn't feel like she was leaving home. Instead, with each mile that clicked over on her truck's odometer, she'd be going back to her true home. High Valley and the Tall Grass Ranch.

CHAPTER TWELVE

AT THE MONDAY morning breakfast table, Bryce pretended to read the local newspaper, but he was really listening to Carrie and the kids. It had only been a few days, but without Carrie, his house had felt empty. He'd managed fine on his own, but now he didn't want to. Carrie was part of his and the kids' lives, and he didn't know what he'd do when summer ended and she moved on.

"The mermaid had a purple tail. We swam with her, and then we had cake and ice cream and played a game, and I won a prize." Paisley squeezed Carrie's left hand while Cam held her right, and both kids tried to talk over each other, as happy to see her as if she'd been gone a year.

"Slow down, guys, and take turns." Carrie gave them both another hug. "I missed you too."

"Aunt Melissa told Ms. Kristi I could have two scoops of ice cream and three different kinds of sprinkles and strawberries. It was too big for a cone, so I had it in a bowl with chocolate sauce." Cam bounced with excitement. "That was after we went to the playground. I went on the swings and right to the top of the new climbing frame. I was so high I could almost see North Dakota."

"Montana is 'Big Sky Country' all right but not quite that big." Bryce laughed and set the paper aside. Carrie was focused on the kids. That was her job. So why did he feel left out because, apart from a brief greeting, he hadn't had a chance to talk to her. "We missed you. The place isn't the same without you around."

Had he emphasized the "we"? He'd almost said "I missed you" but had caught himself in time. As soon as she'd walked into the house ten minutes earlier, his body had responded to her presence, and, like the kids, he'd wanted to greet her with a hug. More than a hug, to be honest. He'd dreamed of her while she was in Kalispell. They'd been in that hayfield in the moonlight, and he'd held her close and kissed the freckles on her nose.

"My folks say hi. They sent you guys presents." Carrie tickled the kids, and they giggled.

"What kind of presents?" Cam eyed the backpack and small suitcase Carrie had left inside the back door.

"You'll see. After you do your chores." She patted Cam's head. "You must have grown while I was away. I'm sure you're taller." She poured herself a mug of coffee from the pot Bryce had brewed earlier and joined him at the table. "Did everything go okay here?"

"It was fine." He made himself focus on her here in his kitchen, not as she'd been in that unsettling dream. "It was a couple of late nights, but we got the hay in." Dreams aside, he could still get used to sitting with her at the kitchen table while the kids loaded the dishwasher.

"That's great." Carrie leaned back in her chair. "I kept checking the weather and thinking about you. About everyone, I mean." She took a mouthful of coffee and turned to the kitchen window. "The herbs and spider plants look like they've grown. Good job with the watering." The curve of her cheek nearest Bryce had a faint pink tinge.

"We watered exactly like you told us. Cam and I took turns," Paisley said, coming to sit in the chair between Carrie and Bryce.

So much for talking to Carrie on his own. Bryce drained his mug. He was attracted to her in all the ways a man could be attracted to a woman. But it was more than just physical. It was a kind of soul-deep pull that drew him to Carrie whenever she was near and made him think about her when she wasn't.

"You could be on Daddy's team for the competition." Cam joined them at the table too, and the dishwasher now hummed in the background.

"What competition and where?" Carrie glanced between them.

"At the rodeo. See?" Cam pointed to a picture in Bryce's newspaper. "It's coming to town on the weekend. We'll be there."

"Our family's going on Saturday," Bryce said. "That's Carrie's day off. Your grandma babysits you on Saturdays, so—"

"I'm not a baby who needs 'sitting,' and I bet Carrie wants to come with us." Paisley nestled into Carrie's shoulder.

"Sure, but it's your family day out. I don't want to—"

"Carrie's like family, isn't she, Daddy?" Cam's voice was hopeful. "And you said you needed someone for your team roping competition. You also said Carrie did great herding cows."

"Yes, but…" Bryce's heart pounded. "If you don't have anything else planned, you're welcome to join us at the rodeo." It wouldn't be a date. His whole family would be there. "Like Cam said, I'm looking for a partner in the amateur team roping competition. Heidi, our part-time ranch hand, sprained her wrist so she had to drop out. It's for fun, not truly competitive, and there won't be any professionals. We're a group of local ranchers raising money for charity." His tongue tripped over the words. "If you want to team up with me, you'd be welcome."

"Grandma's on Mr. Gallagher's team." Paisley snuggled even closer to Carrie. "Grandma said they're going to give the young ones a run for their money. That means make it hard for them to win."

"I've done team roping for fun with friends. It was great." Carrie's green eyes sparkled. "Count me in, as long as you have a horse I can ride that's used to roping. Teddy isn't. We'd also need to practice. My skills are rusty, and I don't want to let you down."

Bryce's mouth went dry. It was an expression, nothing more, and it was only a small-town rodeo and amateur event. Even if Carrie threw the rope too soon and they were disqualified, it wouldn't matter. Yet, she meant what she said. "I don't want to let you down either." *On horseback or in life*. His stomach flipped.

"You won't." Her green gaze held his, and it was as if time stopped. He cared about her, and maybe she cared about him too.

"As a former pro, Cole's not eligible to compete, but there's nothing in the rules that says he can't give us pointers and choose the right horse for you. What would you think about Daisy-May? She's an old girl, but she's steady on her feet, and in her day she loved being in the roping ring."

Bryce heard his voice from far away as if it

belonged to someone else. As one part of him talked to Carrie about different horses and they made plans to meet in the paddock after lunch, the rest of him was trying to figure out what had just happened between them.

He'd always considered himself to be logical and rational. He made decisions with his head, not his heart. It made sense for Carrie to take Heidi's place. It even made sense for her to go to the rodeo with Bryce and the rest of the Carter family.

What didn't make sense were the feelings churning through him, turning him inside out and upside down to leave his usually ordered world in shambles. Feelings that swept logic and reasoning away.

JOY DREW CINDY to a halt in a shady spot by the slow-moving creek and relaxed her hold on the horse's reins. It was already August, and another summer was slipping by. This summer, though, she'd cut back on her usually busy schedule of family and community activities to focus more on what *she* needed. That was one of the reasons she'd told Bryce she couldn't look after Paisley and Cam all the time, and that choice had also been good for her son and grandchildren. Forced to step up, Bryce had hired Carrie, and both he and the kids were better for it.

"If I haven't already said so, you're looking especially pretty today." Shane stopped his horse, Pinto, a gorgeous American paint, beside her.

Joy turned to him with a smile. "You have, but it's always nice to hear." Joy took his hand as he reached across their saddle horns. "You look very handsome too." With his short, steel gray hair, well-fitting jeans, dark cowboy hat and blue Western shirt, Shane looked as good today as he always did. But it wasn't only that he was handsome; she liked him because he was a good person. Kind, honest and trustworthy like Dennis had been, but Shane was also his own man and had his own place in her heart.

"Thank you, ma'am." Shane's grin was boyish, and he gave her hand a comforting squeeze. "What are you fussing about now?" He considered her with the intent gaze that, at first, had made Joy feel off-balance, but nowadays she knew it meant he understood her, cared and wanted to help.

She could have pretended nothing was bothering her, but Shane knew her too well to be fooled. "As always, I'm worried about Bryce. When Carrie was in Kalispell visiting her folks, he looked lost, like he didn't know what to do with himself. He kept working—he always does—but the light in his eyes was gone. What's he going to do when she leaves for good?"

"That's up to him and maybe her too." With his free hand, Shane rubbed Pinto's ears. "Our kids have to live their own lives."

"I know, but…" Joy studied Pinto's brown-and-white pattern, and the horse turned to look at her with his vibrant blue eyes. "Also, something's not right with Molly. I talked to her on-line last night, and although she says she's happy, she's not. A mother can sense these things."

"Molly will be home for her vacation in a few weeks. You'll be able to talk to her then. The computer's great, but a video call isn't the same as in person." Shane's voice was reassuring.

"You're right." Joy pushed her worries aside. She was in a beautiful place with a wonderful man, and she didn't want to spoil it. *Focus on the moment.* She repeated her current mantra to herself.

"I want to talk about us, not our children." Shane dropped her hand and eased Pinto to a walk, and when Joy did the same with Cindy, the two horses meandered side by side along the willow-shaded creek path.

"Us?" Joy's heartbeat sped up. Of course, they were an "us." They'd been dating, if you could call it that at their age, for over a year now, and Shane had become one of the most important people in her life.

"You and me." His breath caught. "You're a

fine woman, and I have strong feelings for you. After I lost my Bonnie, I never thought I could care for someone again like I care for you."

"Like me with my Dennis." Joy edged Cindy closer to Pinto to avoid a low-hanging tree branch. Shane's wife, Bonnie, had passed after a long illness, so he and their children had had time to say goodbye. But no matter how you lost your spouse, whether in an accident like with Dennis or not, after a long and happy marriage, you didn't stop grieving. Rather, you learned to live with the grief and moved on because you had to. Joy had found solace in her family, but lately she'd wondered if that was enough.

Shane took her hand again as they came out into an area where the creek widened and was spanned by a covered bridge. The first Carter family had built it when they'd moved to this part of Montana from Vermont way back in the nineteenth century. In New England, such bridges were known as "kissing bridges," and the Carters had always called this bridge that too.

"I won't ever forget Bonnie, and you won't forget Dennis either. That's as it should be." Shane cleared his throat and took off his hat. "We both have our children, their children and our own places, but I bought more land."

"You did?" Joy blinked at the sudden change

of subject. For a minute, she'd thought Shane was going to ask her an important question. "Where? In Wyoming?" Her heart sank. Apart from his youngest son, who'd moved to High Valley with him, the rest of Shane's family ranched near Sheridan, Wyoming. It would make sense if he wanted to move back there.

"No." He chuckled, and his eyes held a teasing twinkle. "I bought those acres between Squirrel Tail and the western border of your place."

"That's good grazing pasture. It used to be Carter land, but…" She stopped as emotion threatened.

"But you and Dennis had to sell it to pay some of Paul's medical bills." Shane swung off Pinto and then helped Joy dismount from Cindy before tethering both horses to nearby trees.

"How did you find out?" Joy never rode out that way because having to sell that land had been hard and something she and Dennis had agonized over. But Paul was more important.

"Zach mentioned it one day when I met him out there checking the fence line. He only told me because I said it was an odd place for a boundary. Your boy didn't tell me anything private, but I knew it must have been tough for you all."

"It was." So tough, Joy tried not to think about it. "Are you planning on renting out the land or going into the cattle business yourself?"

"Neither." Shane wrapped an arm around her shoulders. "I bought that land for you, so what happens to it is your call. When those acres came up for sale, you never said anything, but I knew you were worrying about who'd buy them and what they'd do."

"Yes." Something else Joy had tried not to think about, but it had wormed its way in like one of those pesky bugs that ate her tomato plants. "But buying all that land is too much. You shouldn't have."

Shane cupped her chin in one of his tanned hands. He had strong hands, and she'd seen him rope a cow with them, fix a fence and lift hay bales. But when he held her hands in his or comforted her grandchildren, they were gentle. Like now, touching her face as if she were as fragile as a butterfly. And as she stared into his eyes, his steady gaze never wavered.

"I wanted to. By rights, those acres are yours, and I have the money, so why not? But when I signed the sale paperwork, all I could think of was you and me and a dream I've had for a while now. One day, I hope we can share a small piece you don't use for grazing or anything else." His face creased in a brief smile. "If you're willing, we could build a house there, and it'd be a place to bring our families together. I love you, Joy, and when you're ready, if you'll have me, I want to marry you." Lines fanned out around Shane's mouth, and his eyes held both love and experience earned from the life he'd lived.

"I love you too." Several tears rolled down Joy's cheeks. "And yes, I want to marry you. I'm crying because I'm happy." Happier than she could have ever imagined. She buried her face in Shane's shoulder, her tears dampening his crisp cotton shirt. "But I can't..." She raised her head to look into his eyes again.

"You can't what?" Shane's expression was tender.

"I don't want to make anything official or tell our kids for a while. At least until September, when Molly's home and your daughters and their families are here visiting. And even then, I don't want them to think we've forgotten Bonnie and Dennis."

"I doubt they'd think that, but I can wait a few weeks. It'll be our secret." He wrapped his arms around her. "I want to give you a ring, so it'll also allow you time to choose one."

"For *us* to choose it." Joy hugged him back and then tilted her face to his. "Yes, we each have our own lives, but I want us to be a team. With our ranches, our families and everything. Except for my college classes. I have to do those on my own." She paused. "I still want to get my degree. If that's a problem for you—"

"Of course, it isn't." Shane looked at her in astonishment. "I not only want you to get your degree, I'll be the one cheering loudest when you walk across that stage in your cap and gown. You're a smart, independent woman, and I love those things about you. Together, we'll be a strong partnership."

"Together." It wasn't like they were young and just starting out. She and Shane had lots of things to figure out, but they'd take it step by step.

Then he kissed her, and as Joy kissed him back, his strong arms holding her close, she was filled with a sense of both love and rightness.

When she finally opened her eyes and saw the love and loyalty in Shane's gaze, the kissing bridge behind him like a benevolent presence, she also felt blessed.

Life, with all its twists and turns, had brought her here. While Dennis would always be a precious memory, with Shane she had a second chance, and she was excited for what lay ahead.

CHAPTER THIRTEEN

"YOU'VE GOT MUSTARD on your face. Hold still a second." Carrie took a moist towelette from her tote, wiped around Cam's mouth and finished with a gentle boop on his button nose.

The boy giggled and booped her back. "What are we gonna do next?"

Carrie checked the time on her phone. "The team roping event is soon. I need to find your aunt Beth and your sister and then your dad." Beth was looking after all the kids while Carrie and Bryce competed. Since Paisley had wanted to hang out with Ellie and Skylar, and Melissa had a volunteer first aid shift, Beth had kept the girls with her while Carrie had had some one-on-one time with Cam. With Joy and Shane competing too, the whole family would reunite in the stands to support them.

"I want you and Daddy to win." In a small cowboy hat, jeans, plaid shirt and cowboy boots, Cam looked like a miniature version of Bryce.

"But I also want Grandma and Mr. Gallagher to win. Is that bad?"

"Nope. You can cheer for all of us." Keeping one hand in Cam's, Carrie scanned the crowd. The visiting rodeo had set up in an open area behind High Valley's riding arena. Along with fairground rides, booths selling food and offering games of chance occupied nearby Meadow-lark Park.

"There's Paisley." Cam pointed to his sister, almost hidden behind a towering cone of pink cotton candy. "And Aunt Beth, Ellie and Skylar."

Carrie waved as they approached. At the same time, Zach and several ranch hands from the Tall Grass passed her carrying saddles. Small-town rodeos were the best, as much about family as the competitive events.

"Sorry we're late." Beth sounded out of breath. "There was a long line for the restroom. We bumped into Bryce and he said he'd meet you in the arena. He's getting the horses ready." Zach paused to kiss his wife, and as he continued on with the other men, Beth shielded her growing pregnancy bump with a protective hand.

Now beyond the first trimester, Beth had a perpetual glow, and whenever Carrie saw her and Zach together, her heart got tight. The love the couple shared was sweet, tender and heart-warming. It made Carrie hope it wasn't too late for her, that one day she'd find that kind of relationship for herself.

"Good luck," Paisley and Cam said, hugging her before joining Beth and Ellie.

"I'll need it." Despite her past experience and daily practice this week with Bryce, Cole, Maverick and Daisy-May, Carrie was far from a roping expert. She jogged toward the arena, greeting friends and acquaintances on the way.

"I'm glad I caught you." Kristi stopped her near the arena's rear entrance, where she was manning an information booth. "I heard through the grapevine the old Sutton farm's coming up for sale soon. It's near Diana's ranch but a lot smaller. If you're interested, I can put you in touch with the Realtor."

"That would be great, thanks." Carrie smiled at the café owner. Apart from Bryce, Kristi was the only person she'd told about her dream of having a small ranch of her own. When Carrie had worked with Kristi on the café's website, they'd discovered a shared interest in sustainable farming. "I have to get ready for the team roping event, but let's talk on Monday. I've got more ideas for branded merchandise. You could sell various sizes of Bluebunch mugs, and I've found more durable, eco-friendly containers for your coffee, tea and muffin-of-the-day club members."

"You're my very own marketing guru." Kristi tipped her white cowboy hat before turning away to answer a question from a visiting competitor.

As Carrie navigated the labyrinth of stalls at the back of the arena, the buzz of conversation melded with the familiar scent of horses, hay and saddle leather. Those sounds and smells gave her the sense of home she'd missed while she'd been away from the competitive circuit.

At the far end of a walkway, Bryce and Cole readied Maverick and Daisy-May.

"Hi, guys." She patted Daisy-May's warm side, and the Appaloosa welcomed her with a soft nicker.

"Hi, Carrie. You saw Beth?" Bryce brushed Maverick, and Cole checked Daisy-May's hooves.

Carrie nodded and made sure the tack she'd packed earlier was in order. "Paisley and Cam are with her. Cam must be going through another growth spurt. He ate two hot dogs, but he was still hungry. I gave him the vegetable snacks I brought with me, and he ate those too."

"You should hear my mom talk about the amount of food she went through with four of us growing boys back in the day. Cam's just getting started," Cole said. Grinning, he turned to Bryce. "Remember not to leave the chute too soon, bro. You're the header, so you have to give the steer enough of a head start." He patted Bryce's shoulder as he left the stall. "And Carrie?"

She lifted her head from adjusting Daisy-May's saddle pad. "Yeah?" She shouldn't be so nervous. It was a demonstration event, not an official competition, but the top three teams would win a donation to the charity of their choice. Bryce had picked the hospice that had given Ally end-of-life care, and Carrie didn't want to let him—or the charity—down.

"You've been great in practice," Cole assured her. "Just relax, take your time and rope both hind legs. Remember, you won't hurt the steer, so keep your rope nice and tight so his feet don't slip out. Mom says she won't hold it against me that I coached you two. After all, Shane's son helped them, and he still rides on the circuit."

"You're sure it's fair for me to take part? I ride on the rodeo circuit too." Carrie had asked Bryce to double-check with the event officials to be certain. She'd never want to do anything that could damage her own or the Carter family's reputation.

"Double- and triple-checked," Bryce said. "You're a barrel racer, not a roper. They're different sports, so today you're an amateur like the rest of us."

Carrie exhaled. "I sure feel like one. Not even an amateur. A beginner."

"Good luck. May the best Carter team win." Cole laughed as he left to join the rest of the family in the stands, and Bryce and Carrie led their horses toward the warm-up area.

"Are you ready?" Bryce held up one hand.

"You bet." She lifted her hand to meet his in a high five. Even this demonstration event on placid Daisy-May reminded her how much she'd missed competing. With guidance from Bryce and Cole, she'd had fun this week rediscovering roping too. Maybe once she was back on the circuit, she'd ask some of the others to train with her. She stopped near a practice chute and drew in a harsh breath.

"What's up?" Bryce stopped too.

"Nothing." *Everything.*

"Let's go on ahead." Carrie ducked around Daisy-May, but it was too late. Her ex, Jimmy, had already spotted her. Brittany, her one-time friend had too. "What are you guys doing here?" she asked, plastering a smile on her face.

"Britt's cousin's competing in junior bull riding." Jimmy jerked his chin to a boy with a red ribbon being congratulated by a couple who must be his parents. "We're spending the weekend in High Valley."

"I'm sorry," Brittany said. "For everything. What I did. What we… I…we didn't realize you were here." She flicked her long blond hair over her shoulder, and her face flushed as she glanced between Jimmy, Carrie and Bryce.

Carrie shrugged. It was too late for apologies. Since she hadn't talked to either of them after Jimmy admitted he'd cheated on her, there was no reason for them to know where Carrie was or what she was doing. "I'm working on a ranch near High Valley this summer." She introduced Jimmy and Brittany to Bryce.

Carrie patted Daisy-May. "We need to warm up. Enjoy the rest of your weekend. If you haven't already, be sure to stop at the Bluebunch Café for breakfast or lunch. The food's fantastic. Check out Medicine Wheel Craft Center too. They sell gorgeous locally-made souvenirs." She nodded politely and led Daisy-May away to where competitors prepared.

"You said that was 'nothing' before. But it didn't look like nothing just now with those two. To me it looked important and…uncomfortable." Standing beside her, with a patient Maverick, Bryce had an expression of concern.

"It was but it's over." And to her surprise, Carrie wasn't upset. "Jimmy's my ex, and Brittany's a former friend. They got together when I was on the circuit, and he 'forgot' to tell me. I found out when I came home a day early, drove by my favorite Kalispell restaurant and saw Jimmy and Brittany kissing on an outdoor patio.

When I calmed down and confronted Jimmy the next day, at first he tried to tell me it meant nothing, but then he admitted he and Britt had been seeing each other for a few months." Carrie shrugged, and Bryce touched her hand in sympathy.

"It's okay," she said. "I'm not even mad any longer. At least I found out what both of them were really like, Jimmy especially. But that's why honesty and trust are more important to me than ever." While having people she'd trusted lie and betray her was never okay, in a way the two of them had done her a favor. She'd have been truly heartbroken if she and Jimmy were engaged or married, and he'd cheated then.

"Still, ouch." Bryce's face was filled with compassion.

"It hurt a lot at the time, but Jimmy and Brittany are in the past." And that experience had helped Carrie learn to trust her instincts. While she hadn't expected to find Jimmy was cheating on her with a friend, she'd sensed something was off with him for weeks. He'd cancelled dates and hadn't texted as often but she'd pushed her doubts aside. She glanced back, and Jimmy was on his phone like always, not paying any attention to Brittany or her cousin. Had he even congratulated the kid for winning a ribbon?

With his dark hair and eyes, athletic build and

charming smile, Jimmy was handsome, and he had a good job in finance. He also had an expensive car, designer clothes and liked splashing money around. However, now it was as if Carrie saw him through new eyes. If she were honest with herself, she'd dated him to please her mom and dad because Jimmy's parents were business associates. And like her folks, Jimmy had always assumed barrel racing was temporary, and never really listened to what *she* wanted. What had she ever seen in him? He was all surface polish and no substance, more focused on himself than anyone else.

As for Brittany, with time and distance, Carrie could even feel sad for her former friend. If a man cheated once, the likelihood was higher he'd cheat again. Besides, everyone deserved a partner who'd put them first, not a guy who spent all his time on his phone and pouted when he didn't get his own way.

She turned back to Bryce and Daisy-May. "I'm fine, really. I only hope the two of them go to the café and Rosa's gallery and spend lots of money. They both like good food, and Jimmy used to go on about the importance of supporting the arts. He should put his money where his mouth is." She chuckled. "Brittany apologized, but it doesn't bother me whether she means it or not. That part of my life is over."

"Good for you." One of Bryce's special smiles spread across his face and made Carrie weak at the knees. "You ready to show everyone what we're made of?"

"Absolutely." Today was about fun, friends and family, and Jimmy and Brittany weren't included. In this new life Carrie was building, instead of trying to please others, she was following her heart and making friends she could trust. Like the women of the Sunflower Sisterhood, Bryce and the rest of the Carter family. And after talking to Kristi, she'd contact that Realtor and ask to visit the old Sutton farm. It was all part of looking to the future, not the past.

She swung herself into Daisy-May's saddle and gave Bryce a thumb's up. "Let's go, partner."

IN MAVERICK'S SADDLE, Bryce made himself relax and eased the horse into the box beside the chute holding the steer. "Just like in practice, buddy." He fingered the rope looped over his saddle horn as the crowd cheered for his mom and Shane. What were the odds of the Carter teams following each other in the charity team roping event?

His mom tossed her cowboy hat into the air and caught it while she beamed at Shane. They'd had a good run, his mom especially, and set a time to beat. But it was even better for Bryce to see his mom happy and having fun.

"Good luck." His mom rode past him on Cindy as she and Shane made their way out of the arena. "And stay safe. No broken bones or other injuries. I went through enough of that worry with Cole."

"I hear you." Bryce laughed, and the tension in his shoulders lessened. He glanced at Carrie atop Daisy-May in a box on the other side of the chute. He was the header, she was the heeler and they were a team. No matter what happened in the arena, they'd handle it together.

As the announcer, a DJ at the local radio station, called their names, Bryce gripped the rope and leaned forward in his saddle. "Here we go." He nodded to the chute attendant and called for the steer.

The chute door swung open, and the steer took off into the arena at a run. Bryce and Maverick followed. Out the corner of one eye, Bryce spotted Carrie and Daisy-May waiting in position. He lassoed the steer's horns and did a quick dally, wrapping the rope around his saddle horn, and pulled the steer off to the left.

The next part was up to Carrie. Bryce held his breath as his gaze found hers for a split second. "You can do it." She couldn't hear him, but somehow he knew she sensed his encouragement.

Then Carrie let her rope fly too and caught the steer under its hind legs.

"Perfect execution." Bryce let out his breath as Carrie dallied up on Daisy-May's saddle horn. "Now for the finish."

He turned Maverick again so they faced Carrie and Daisy-May, and then both horses moved backward. "Gently, that's it." With the steer roped between them, the flag went up, and an official registered their time before releasing the steer, who trotted off.

"Great job." Carrie rode over to Bryce.

"You too." He hadn't compared their time with those of the other teams, but the result didn't matter. They'd shared something more important than a rodeo event. Bryce loosened his grip on his rope and put a hand to his heaving chest. "That was fantastic."

"The way you and Maverick came out of the box and roped those horns. Wow." Carrie's eyes were wide, and her body seemed to vibrate with excitement. "Maybe you missed your calling. Cole's not the only rodeo cowboy in the family."

"I'm happy being a rancher." But her words filled Bryce with quiet pride. Today, he'd stepped out of his comfort zone, and it felt good.

"I'm sorry about skidding on that turn. It was my fault, not Daisy-May's. I held her wrong."

As Carrie talked about their run, Bryce tried to focus. He hadn't noticed a skid, hadn't noticed anything really, except how the two of them had connected. It wasn't through words or even the event itself, but something had bound them together in a way that was soul deep.

"Way to go, guys." As they reached the exit, Cole greeted them. "You're only a second behind Mom and Shane. Looking at the remaining competitors, I'm guessing you'll get second place."

"If not for me messing up that turn, we might have won." Carrie's shoulders slumped and she frowned as she ducked her head.

"You didn't mess up anything. You were perfect." *And not only on horseback.* The thought hit Bryce and caught him tighter than he'd roped the steer. "It's lucky you'd done some roping before, but we didn't have much time to practice. Don't be so hard on yourself. I wouldn't change anything about you or our run." He stuttered to a stop. Carrie and Cole stared at him, along with Melissa and Skylar, Beth, Paisley, Cam, Ellie and Zach. "I should see to the horses." His face must be tomato red.

"Cole and I'll take care of them." Zach stepped forward. "You watch the final competitors and then the result." A small smile played around his brother's mouth, and he exchanged a look with Cole, who smiled too.

"What?" Bryce dismounted and stood shoulder to shoulder between his older brothers.

"Nothing. We're happy for you." Cole sounded like he was holding back a laugh.

Even though they were adults, there were still times Bryce felt like the "little brother" he'd once been. Too young to join the older boys in their adventures, too old to play with Molly—stuck in the middle of the family. He took a step back and patted Maverick before Cole led the horse away.

"You had a good run," Zach said. "You surprised us, and that's good. If you'd wanted a shot at it when you were younger, you might have made it as a roper on the circuit." After Paul's death, Zach had assumed the role of oldest brother and peacemaker. "It's also great to see you having fun and being part of things again." He turned away to take Daisy-May from Carrie, who was getting excited hugs from Paisley and Cam.

After hugging his kids too, and while Carrie chatted with Beth and Melissa, Bryce leaned against the fence to watch the last few teams compete. He'd surprised himself as well. Unlike Cole, who'd always wanted to be a rodeo star, and Zach, who, because of Paul's illness, had been groomed by their folks to take over the ranch, Bryce's role had never been as well-defined. Molly too had always wanted to be a nurse and work at a city hospital.

Had he fallen into ranch work instead of consciously choosing it? He'd been interested in growing things and science since kindergarten, when they'd done a simple experiment to see how plants breathed. Although he'd considered teaching and, with Ally's encouragement, had earned a teaching qualification, he'd never let himself think seriously about any career except crop science and agriculture. Especially after his dad passed, he'd been needed on the ranch, and along with Ally and their family, work had been his life. He'd never let himself think about anything—or anyone—else.

The others cheered, and Carrie shouted and clapped the loudest.

"We did it." She ran over to him and jumped up and down. "I'd have liked to have placed first, but your mom and Shane did great, and the hospice will still get a nice donation."

Bryce joined in the family celebration, hugging everyone and being hugged in return.

Then he found himself beside Carrie again, and it seemed natural to hug her too—and hold her tighter and longer than necessary as he breathed in her sweet scent and savored her softness in his arms.

It felt right. *She* felt right. And it still would have, even if they hadn't won anything for the hospice. Today, Bryce had made a new memory, a good one, and although he hadn't shared it with Ally, that was okay. Maybe he'd begun to understand what she'd wanted for him. And for the first time, that was okay too.

CHAPTER FOURTEEN

"IN ALL THE EXCITEMENT, I haven't had a chance to say how proud I am of you," Joy told Bryce. She'd finally caught up with him in the family room at the main ranch house during the after-rodeo party she was hosting. "You and Carrie were great competitors." Both in the arena and here, her youngest son looked relaxed, happy and like he was having fun.

"I'm proud of you too, Mom. I hope I'm still going strong like you and Shane when I'm your age." He took a juice box and several pretzels from the tray Joy carried.

"We're not that old, but I'll take it as a compliment." Joy swatted his hand away like she'd done when he was a kid. "If you want more snacks, look in the kitchen. These are for the children."

"Yes, ma'am." His cheeky grin reminded her of that little boy too. Bryce was the most serious and introverted of her children, and she and Dennis had called him their "old soul." Although he usually managed to hide it, Bryce was perhaps the most vulnerable and easily hurt of their family too.

"Stop ma'aming me. That really makes me feel old." She shook her head and handed the tray to Rosa, who was keeping an eye on the kids as they ran through a sprinkler on the lawn. "Shane and I only won by a second, and unlike us, you and Carrie have a lot of years of competition left." Joy winced and rubbed her lower back. "Today was fun, but from now on I think I'll stick to dressage. It's more sedate."

"I always thought Cole's rodeo talent came from Dad, but watching you rope that steer, maybe I was wrong." Bryce's eyes twinkled.

"Maybe your dad and I were wrong about you too." Joy drew him into a quiet corner away from the party. "I was sure wrong about myself. After your dad passed, I never thought I'd smile or have fun again, let alone go on dates. It likely sounds silly, but I thought it would be disloyal." If there was a chance to take away what she suspected might be that same sense of guilt from her son, she wanted to try. "I finally realized your dad would want me to go on with my life as best I could. Not only for you kids but for me too."

Bryce rubbed a hand across his face. "Today was great, but…"

"You feel guilty?"

He gave a quick jerk of his chin.

"There's no need." Joy put a tentative hand on his shoulder. "You'll always love and miss Ally, like I'll always love and miss your dad, but that doesn't mean you can't have fun."

Joy glanced around the room. By the stone fireplace, Carrie chatted with Beth, Melissa, Kate and several other members of the Sun-flower Sisterhood. Carrie fit in here as easily as if she'd always lived in High Valley. She'd fit in the Carter family too if Bryce would let him-self take a chance. Today, more than ever, she'd seen the strength of the connection between her son and Carrie. She'd watched and waited for the right opportunity, and now she'd found it.

"Here." She dug in the back pocket of her jeans. "Shane won a pair of tickets to that out-door country music festival on Friday, but we can't go." Joy suppressed a secret smile. They were going to another, larger town to look at en-gagement rings and planned to make a day of it, ending with dinner and dancing at a place they both liked. "Why don't you go with Carrie?"

"With Carrie?"

"Why not?" Joy willed him to take that next step. "There are some great bands playing, and the Wild Prairie Rodeo Chicks are headlining. I've heard Carrie say she likes their music." Joy did too, but even if she weren't going engagement ring shopping, she'd have given up the tickets to help Bryce.

"That would be great. We'd go as friends, of course."

"Of course, but you won't be going anywhere unless you ask Carrie." Joy put her hands behind her back and crossed her fingers for luck.

"Ask me what?" Carrie appeared at their side. "Paisley and Cam have had a long day. If it's okay with you, I'll take them home and get them settled and ready for bed."

"That's fine. I…" Bryce paused. "I won't be here much longer either, but I want to check on Maverick before I leave. Mom…she offered me… us… Shane won them, free tickets to that country music festival just west of town on Friday. They can't go, so would you…like to go? With me?"

Joy forced herself not to bounce with excitement. Despite sounding like a middle schooler asking a girl he had a crush on to go to the PTA dance, her son had done it. Since he likely hadn't asked anyone out since middle school, and back then it had been Ally, his awkwardness wasn't surprising. Asking someone for a date, and going on one, took practice, no matter how old you were.

"That would be fantastic." Carrie's face lit up with a smile. "I wanted to go, but when I tried to get a ticket the event was sold out. I'm a huge fan of the Wild Prairie Rodeo Chicks."

"It's all set then," Joy said. Was Carrie's excitement only about going to the event or was it also to do with Bryce? If she were a betting woman, Joy would put money on Bryce being a bigger draw than any band.

"Thank you, but…" Carrie's happy expression dimmed. "What about the kids? We can't leave them and—"

"Beth and Zach can look after them on Friday night, can't you?" Joy turned to Beth, who'd joined them.

"Of course. We'd be happy to. Ellie loves Paisley like a little sister, and Zach has fun spending time with Cam." Beth exchanged a sideways glance with Joy as if she sensed something was up and was happy to go along with whatever it might be.

"Excellent." Everything was working out exactly as Joy had hoped. "All you and Carrie need to do is go and have fun." She beamed at her son, who looked bewildered but happy, and then Carrie, who was radiant.

With luck, the weather Friday night would be perfect, and under a big, starlit Montana sky, anything could happen. Bryce, who'd had so much heartache, deserved something good…and someone like Carrie to share that goodness with.

CARRIE SWAYED TO the music, and the warm breeze—seasoned with the scents of barbecue, grassland and evergreens—ruffled her hair. Although she'd been born and raised in a city, those summers at her grandparents' ranch meant she was a country girl at heart.

"Having fun?" Beside her, Bryce moved to the music too, his expression as relaxed as Carrie had ever seen it.

"It's the best. The music and the setting are fantastic." *And the company.* She bit back the words that could have taken the evening in a more intimate direction. Even if Bryce wasn't attracted to her like she was to him, it was getting harder and harder to hide her feelings. Her body tingled whenever his arm brushed against hers, and the musky scent of his aftershave tantalized her senses and made her remember that all-too-brief brush of his lips against her cheek. Something she longed to repeat, without the kids looking on… Would his kiss move to her lips this time?

"Montana's beautiful in all seasons, but summer here is extra special." When the song changed, Bryce took Carrie's hand and led her into a country two-step. "I remember as a kid lying in the field behind the house on nights like this and looking at the stars with my dad. It was magical."

"It sounds like it. You must miss your dad a lot."

Carrie followed the step pattern—quick-quick, slow-slow—of the dance her grandparents had taught her as a child.

"I do. Just as I miss my brother Paul, and Ally. Along with my dad, it's a lot."

"I can only imagine." Was that much loss and grief why Bryce seemed so closed and wary of opening up to others?

"Still, like my mom says, life has to go on." There was a bitter note in his voice, gone almost as soon as Carrie registered it.

"It does. But for me, when I think of my grandparents, I hope they'd be happy with how I'm living my life. In a way, trying to live my best life honors their memory." And thanks to that small inheritance her grandma had left her, if the seller was willing to come down a bit on the price, the old Sutton farm might be in her budget. She'd visit the farm once it was officially on the market, but from what the Realtor said, it sounded like the kind of property she wanted.

"This summer, you've shown me how living your best life is important." Bryce guided her through the steps, and the soft, springy grass brushed their boots almost in time with the music.

"I'm happy to help." As they turned in a circle, Carrie tilted her head back to look at the inky sky spattered with stars. She had a sense of safety and belonging in this rural Montana world—and even more so in Bryce's arms— that she'd never felt anywhere else. "Sorry." Not paying attention to where she was going or the pattern of the dance, she stumbled and caught the toes of his boots with hers.

"Not a problem." His voice was low, and his warm hand settled more firmly on her shoulder and drew her closer. "I'm used to Paisley and Cam stepping on my toes. Your little tap was nothing."

His children. She loved the kids, but they were also why she couldn't let herself get too comfortable with their dad. She was leaving High Valley once school started again. She couldn't risk hurting Paisley and Cam by letting them think she could be a permanent part of their lives. "I bet the kids are having fun tonight." The musicians changed pace again, and Bryce moved them seamlessly into the more difficult cowboy cha-cha. "They love spending time with Zach, Beth and Ellie."

"The kids are lucky to have family who are always there for them. Between my family and your support this summer, I've now got a much better handle on everything."

"That's great." Carrie tried to sound happy and enthusiastic. She should be grateful she'd succeeded in her job instead of wanting more.

"Why am I talking about Paisley and Cam? We have a night off." Bryce guided her through the dance steps, one of his arms around Carrie's shoulders and their hands joined.

"We do." Dancing so close together, the warmth of Bryce's body washed over Carrie. If she turned ever so slightly, she could—

"Thanks for supporting the Wild Prairie Rodeo Chicks." The lead singer, a woman with long dark hair and rhinestone-studded pink cowboy boots, took the microphone. "We'll be back after the break with one last set. Our good buddies, and a new band joining us this season, will be here. The Lonestar Runners are a sister act from Texas, and I hope you'll love their music as much as we do." Bryce's hands dropped away from Carrie's as they both clapped. "Get some more food, enjoy a hayride or treat yourself to a souvenir T-shirt or CD, but most of all, kick back, relax and enjoy the rest of the night." She waved as the crowd cheered and more country music, this time a recording, blasted from the speakers around the stage.

The night air had turned cooler, and Carrie shrugged into the pink-and-white "Long Live Cowgirls" sweatshirt she'd tied around her waist. "Earlier, when you were getting us drinks and burgers, and I went to the restroom, I stopped at a souvenir stand. I bought a signed CD for your mom and a T-shirt for Shane. I wanted to thank them for giving us the tickets." She patted the small backpack she used as a purse where she'd put the presents and then, keen to return to Bryce, had forgotten about until now. "I hope they'll be pleased. Your mom said they like the Wild Prairie Rodeo Chicks too."

"They'll be thrilled. That's so thoughtful of you." After putting on his own hoodie, a blue one that matched his eyes, Bryce tucked his hand into Carrie's.

Except for when they'd danced together, Bryce had never held her hand. And the way he clasped it now was different—more intentional and personal. All her nerve endings stirred.

"But right now, I don't want to talk about my mom or anybody else in my family." He gave her a crooked smile. "What do you say we go on one of those hayrides?"

"That sounds great." As Carrie squeezed Bryce's hand, warmth spreading up her arm from his touch, her breath caught at the tenderness in his face.

"I'm having fun." He boosted her up onto one of the hay wagons waiting at the edge of the field and then joined her.

"Me too." Carrie settled into the sweet-smelling hay. The evening had gone too fast, but she wouldn't let herself think about that now. Instead, she'd savor every last moment of being with Bryce, just the two of them. "My grandparents used to take me and my cousins on hayrides. I loved it. Then we'd go back to the ranch house for homemade ice cream."

The driver spoke to the horses, two beautiful Clydesdales, and the wagon moved away along a track that bordered the field.

"That sounds fun." Bryce's leg brushed against Carrie's, sparking the now familiar tingles. "I have an ice-cream maker. If you want to use it, go ahead. I'll be a happy taste tester."

Carrie held on to the edge of the wagon as the horses pulled them down a gentle slope. On the other side of the wagon, their backs to Carrie and Bryce, a family oohed and ahhed at the starlit sky and tried to spot constellations. "I want to try making huckleberry ice cream. I spotted a patch of huckleberries when I was out riding last week. They should be ripe by the end of this month or early September." Around the time her nannying job ended. Carrie's heart squeezed, already anticipating the loss that would bring. Although she'd regain her barrel racing career, she'd lose the kids, Bryce and times like this one.

"I love huckleberry ice cream." The wagon lurched, and Bryce looped an arm around Carrie's shoulders.

"Me too. I'll ask my mom for my grandma's

recipe." Bryce wasn't exactly hugging her. He was only holding her because the wagon ride was bumpy, and like a gentleman, he wanted to keep her safe. But even when the track smoothed, Bryce didn't move his arm, and it was natural for Carrie to lean into his body. "My folks are visiting Aunt Angela and me the last weekend in August. I'd like them to meet you and the kids and see the ranch. They're not horse people, not even my mom despite growing up on a ranch, but High Valley will still be fun for them."

And Carrie would finally tell her parents what she wanted to do with her life, and that it didn't include Rizzo Construction. Her dad would have to find someone else to take on the head of marketing job—and, a few years down the line, someone to lead the entire company—because it wouldn't be her. What had been an ever-present sense of guilt was now replaced with relief and excitement about making her own future.

"I'd like to meet them too. For themselves but also because they're your folks." Bryce's voice was low, almost husky. "Carrie, I...you're important to me."

"You're important to me too." Her heart hammered. Was it possible Bryce felt the same way about her as she did about him?

Bryce twirled a loose strand of her hair around

his fingers. "Your hair's so pretty. You're so pretty. And I…"

"Yes?" Suddenly it was hard to breathe.

"Aww, Carrie."

She didn't know which of them moved first, but they both wanted the same thing. And as their lips met in a kiss every bit as wonderful as Carrie had imagined, she succumbed to the pleasurable sensations engulfing her. Bryce's lips were warm and seeking, and as she returned the kiss, she touched his jaw and ran her fingers across the roughness of his beard stubble.

It wasn't a quick, accidental kiss like the one in the hayfield with the kids looking on. This kiss was purposeful, real and turned every part of her to mush. Yet, it had a steadiness and sweetness too, along with faithfulness, honesty and care.

As they drew apart and stared into each other's eyes, Carrie tipped over that edge from liking Bryce to loving him with every fiber of her being.

She'd worry about what to do about it later. Right now, what she had here was enough.

CHAPTER FIFTEEN

BRYCE FINISHED MUCKING out Maverick's stall and pulled off his work gloves. Less than twenty-four hours after he'd kissed Carrie, guilt had expanded from his stomach to lodge in his windpipe like something hard and physical. Kissing her had been an impulse. And although he hadn't immediately regretted it, after Bryce had dropped Carrie off at Angela's and gone home, he'd tossed and turned all night, playing what had happened between them over and over in his mind. And when she'd arrived at the ranch house for breakfast with him and the kids this morning, despite it being her day off, he could barely look at her.

Wherever he turned on the ranch and in his house, he was reminded of Ally and now Carrie too. Since a big part of him still felt married to Ally, what was he doing kissing Carrie and enjoying it as much as he had? He also liked Carrie in a way that went far beyond friendship, and without consciously planning to, he'd gotten seriously involved with her. Except, she was leaving at the end of the summer so a future for them was hard to see.

He kicked an empty metal feed bucket aside, and it clattered as it hit the barn wall. Two of the barn cats, Mr. and Mrs. Wiggins, darted out of the way and yowled.

"Sorry." He righted the bucket, hung it in its place from a hook on the barn wall and scratched Mr. Wiggins behind his ears.

"Is everything okay?" Saddle leather creaked as Carrie dismounted. She led Teddy into the barn.

"It's fine." Bryce tossed a ping pong ball for the cats to chase.

"It's such a gorgeous day. Teddy and I rode along the creek and then did some training with barrels I set up in the lesson paddock. I waved at you from the paddock, but I guess you didn't see us."

Bryce muttered something incomprehensible. He'd seen them all right, but if he'd waved back, he'd have also gone over to chat. And before he knew it, he'd have been kissing her again, and who knew where that might lead? Sadness when Carrie left, and he was alone again, for sure.

"Can you grab me a hoof-pick, please?" Her sweet voice caught Bryce's heart and made him ache to hold her. "The one with the purple handle. Teddy picked up lots of dirt and gravel on the trail."

Bryce found the pick and passed it to her, making sure to keep a careful distance between them.

"Thanks." She took the pick and bent toward one of Teddy's front hooves. "It's okay, boy. I'll make you feel better."

Bryce should leave the barn right now. There was nothing to be gained from prolonging the agony of having Carrie so close. And it took a lot of effort to stop himself from wrapping his arms around her and maybe even asking her to spend the rest of her life with him. "If you're all set, I need to get out to the wheat field. Enjoy the rest of your day." That was honest, polite and friendly, so why did he feel like he'd taken a hit to the chest with Cam's soccer ball?

"Hang on a second." Carrie straightened and patted Teddy. "Since your mom's looking after the kids today, I wondered if you'd like to have supper with me and Angela? She's making caprese chicken, and I'm taking care of dessert. It's pizzelles and vanilla ice cream. Aunt Angela has an ice-cream maker too, and I want to practice for huckleberry season." Her warm smile lifted the corners of her mouth and lit up her entire face, including her eyes.

A sharp pain shot through what was left of Bryce's heart. Angela Moretti's caprese chicken was famous in High Valley. And he'd tasted plenty of Carrie's outstanding baking, including the crispy Italian butter cookies she'd brought for the kids. For both the company and food, he'd be a fool to say no, but he had to.

"Sorry, I can't. I'm having dinner with the kids at my mom's." Although he hadn't asked his mom yet, she was always happy for him to join them.

"Oh." Carrie's smile slipped. "Another time then."

"Yeah." Bryce swallowed the taste of regret. It was hard, but it was for the best, not only for him but Paisley and Cam. He couldn't let his kids get hurt, either, when Carrie left. "Since I have an early client call tomorrow morning, I'll be working in my office when you get to the house." Carrie hadn't started out working for him on Sundays, but Bryce had taken on a big freelance project. This weekend, he needed her on what should have been his day off. Who was he kidding? He needed her all the time. Not as the kids' nanny but as a partner, someone special in his life.

"Of course." Carrie returned to picking out Teddy's hooves, and her voice cooled. "I forgot to mention the kids and I are volunteering with your mom at the Sunflower Sisterhood's booth at the town's homecoming event tomorrow afternoon. Is that okay with you?"

"No problem. It'll be fun for them. You as well, I hope. A couple of the hands took vacation time, so I'll be busy here." He turned toward the open door. "Hey, girl." He patted Penny who'd followed a scent into the barn.

"I understand." Carrie hesitated, and although Bryce didn't raise his head from the dog, he sensed her studying him. "I'll leave a packed lunch for you in the fridge. Paisley needs new swim goggles, and some of Cam's T-shirts are getting small. I could—"

"Buy whatever they need. I'll transfer you money to cover it." Bryce brushed his damp palms against his jeans. Pretending to be oblivious to how Carrie made him feel was harder than he'd expected, but it would get easier in time. It had to.

"Fine." Was that hurt in her voice? "Have a good day."

"You too. It's sure a hot one." Now he'd resorted to talking about the weather. As Bryce left the horse barn, he mentally berated himself. If he hadn't hurt Carrie, he'd offended her, but it was for the best, wasn't it?

"Who or what ruffled your feathers?" Outside the red barn that housed the ranch's business office, Cole interrupted Bryce's reverie.

"Nobody and nothing." He manufactured a smile as he greeted his brother. "Is Zach inside?

I want to talk to him about the Herefords. They're arriving at the end of the week." Those pigs would keep him busy too. "I also want to see about getting quotes for a new irrigation system."

Cole let out a low whistle. "Zach's at his desk, but an irrigation system will be expensive. With buying that tractor a year ago, is there enough in the budget? You should get Beth's input too. She's a genius with finding extra cash, but she also runs a tight ship."

"She is, and I already have." Did Cole think Bryce didn't know their sister-in-law oversaw the ranch's finances with the same expertise she'd once wielded as chief financial officer for a major corporation? "Don't you have work to do?"

"Whoa. I haven't seen you so riled since Big Red got into the barley field last harvest. What's up, Little Buckaroo?"

"Don't call me that." Bryce usually took his childhood nickname and his brother's good-natured teasing in the spirit it was intended but not today. "As for that bull, if he ever gets into the barley or any other crop again, he's going straight to auction. I'll drive him there myself." Bryce stepped to one side of the barn doorway, and Cole followed him. "What? You're in my way."

"I'm sorry for winding you up. If something's wrong, I want to help. Melissa will too." Whenever Cole mentioned his new wife, his face got a soft, loving expression Bryce usually considered sweet. Now it only annoyed him more. "I don't need your help. I don't need anyone's help. What I *need* is to talk to Zach and then get back to work." He had to focus on work because... apart from the kids, it was all he had.

"Okay." Cole shrugged, but his expression was still remorseful and concerned. "If you change your mind, I'll be in the yard fixing the tractor belt. As for the Herefords, it'll be fun to try something new. I talked to Carrie, and she's excited about them too. She offered to be there when we unload and—"

"Whatever." Bryce entered the dim coolness of the barn, where Zach's voice echoed from the business office. His other brother must be talking on the phone because the conversation, about a cow, was one-sided and punctuated by intermittent silence.

Carrie. Until he'd met her, Bryce's life had been full, and his kids and work had been enough. Somehow, he had to get back to that place again. It was the only way to keep himself, and his heart, safe.

"HERE YOU GO." Carrie handed a woman wearing a High Valley High School, Class of 1992, T-shirt her change along with a reusable shopping bag that held a jar of local honey, two packages of sunflower seeds and a lemon yellow baby blanket crocheted by Aunt Angela. "Thanks for stopping by. Enjoy the rest of your day, and welcome home."

High Valley's weekend homecoming event had started the day before, and the town was busy with visitors. Over the two days, both locals and tourists flocked to the Sunflower Sisterhood's stall on High Valley Avenue in front of the Bluebunch Café.

"Have a seat." Joy indicated one of the folding lawn chairs behind the booth and then took the other one. "You look like you need it. It should be quieter for the next while with everybody heading to the park for the band concert."

Carrie sat and stretched her sneaker-clad feet in front of her. "Thank goodness Beth offered to look after Paisley and Cam for a few hours after lunch. It's been too busy for them to help here, so they'd have been bored. I also couldn't have kept an eye on them and served customers."

"You've been a lifesaver. It would have been hard for me to handle so many people on my own." Joy patted Carrie's arm. "It's good to catch up too. I've hardly seen you these past few days. You'd have been welcome to join Bryce and the kids for supper with me yesterday, but he said you had plans with Angela. I hope everything's okay."

Carrie forced a smile. "Everything's fine. Since Bryce has had to work so much lately, I've almost been living full-time at the ranch. I wanted to spend time with my aunt on my day off." All of that was true, but she'd been disappointed Bryce hadn't accepted her dinner invitation. In fact, since they'd kissed at the music festival—a kiss Carrie still felt on her lips and in her heart— it seemed Bryce was avoiding her.

She feigned an interest in High Valley Avenue. The council had closed the town's main street to vehicle traffic this weekend, and the wide thoroughfare was lined with stalls run by community groups like theirs raising funds for local causes. "If this afternoon's sales are an indication of the weekend total, the Sunflower Sisterhood should be able to make a sizeable donation to the arena's accessibility committee. At least enough to finish putting in more wheelchair-accessible and low-mobility seats."

"Maybe improving accessible parking too." Joy picked up a stack of paper gift bags and began filling them with packages of sunflower seeds, souvenir magnets, pens, notepads and huckleberry-scented tea lights. "I'm glad you and Bryce had fun at that music festival. I love the signed CD you got me, and Shane's wearing his band T-shirt today."

"You two missed a great show." Carrie tightened

the lace on one of her sneakers. She'd dropped off the gifts as quickly as possible and declined Joy's invitation to come in for a coffee. Bryce's mom was savvy. Carrie didn't want her to guess Carrie's relationship with her son was strained. There was a new distance between them Carrie didn't know how to fix.

"Bryce is…" Joy paused and tied a green ribbon around the handles of a filled goodie bag, one of their most popular items. "He's complex, and although he looks fine on the outside, underneath he's a wounded soul."

"Of course." Bryce had lost his wife, his dad and a brother. Anybody would be wounded after so much loss.

"No, I don't think you understand." Joy rearranged a tea-light display. "Bryce can sometimes be like a wounded animal. Although they're different in almost every other way, Cole's the same. When either one of them is scared, hurting or overwhelmed by what they're feeling, they run off and hide. Maybe not physically—although Bryce has spent so much time in the fields this weekend, I've been tempted to ask if he wanted to pitch a tent out there—but emotionally. The few times he's reappeared, he's been like a grumpy bear woken from hibernating too early. We've all noticed it."

Carrie gave what she hoped was a casual shrug.

"My focus is Paisley and Cam." Letting herself care for their dad, and starting to imagine she might become a real part of Bryce's life and family, was her mistake, not his.

"Cole mentioned Bryce made a fuss about nothing with him outside the barn yesterday, and he also had heated words with Zach about housing those Hereford pigs. I was in the business office at the time, so I heard most of it. I stayed well out of it, but from how Bryce was going on, you'd have thought Zach didn't know anything about livestock." Joy shook her head. "Bryce is usually so easygoing. I don't know what's wrong."

"I expect Bryce will figure it out in his own time." Carrie busied herself filling goodie bags too. What was or wasn't bothering Bryce wasn't any of her business. Although Joy sounded innocent enough, something in her tone put Carrie on alert.

"It's such a pity. Bryce has seemed so much happier and almost like his old self this summer." Was Joy's sigh a bit too dramatic? "With taking part in the team roping competition and going to that family fun day at Squirrel Tail, I really thought he'd turned a corner. I know..." Her blue eyes shone. "Shane had a cancellation this week. There's a family bed-and-breakfast suite free on Wednesday night. You, Bryce and the kids should take it. A little vacation might be what he needs to perk right up. What do you think?"

Carrie swallowed. "Bryce and the kids should go, sure. Paisley and Cam would love that one-on-one time with their dad." If they were away, Carrie would focus on her freelance work. She'd add the last touches to Kristi's website and design an advertising poster for one of her rodeo clients.

"It would be a nice getaway for you too. Besides, you're like part of the family. Leave it with me." Joy waved at a couple who'd come out of the Medicine Wheel Craft Center. "I'll talk to Shane and fix everything. He likely won't charge you for the suite either. The family who'd booked already paid in full but had to cancel because their children have ear infections. Poor things." Joy stood and waved at the couple again. "Luckily, the family had cancellation insurance, so neither they nor Shane will be out of pocket. With the suite empty, it would be fun for you to use it."

"Fun," Carrie echoed. As Joy talked animatedly with the couple, old friends who used to live in High Valley, Carrie made an excuse about getting a drink from the café.

Spending time in such close quarters with Bryce as part of the family wouldn't be fun at all. Not now when she was so hurt and puzzled by his behavior. He'd even brushed away her offer to help with the Herefords, although raising those pigs had been her idea originally.

She opened the café door, asked the teenage girl behind the counter for a soda and dug in the pocket of her denim shorts for money.

Whatever was going on with Bryce was his problem. If she ended up going to Squirrel Tail Ranch for that so-called "vacation," she'd be there for Paisley and Cam but avoid any activities that involved Bryce. Thanks to her nannying job and free boarding for Teddy, she could afford a ranch of her own sooner than she'd expected. That was what mattered. Yet, as she took the cold can of soda from the girl, her whole body, not only her hand, chilled. Now she wanted more than that ranch. She wanted Bryce too.

CHAPTER SIXTEEN

THAT EVENING, after spending most of the day at the homecoming, Joy put the first aid box in a kitchen cupboard and patted the bandage that covered Cam's scraped knee. "You were very brave, and in a week or so, your knee will be as good as new. Not even a scar."

"You always make hurts better, Grandma." He wrapped his arms around her, and Joy's heart swelled. Small physical hurts were easy to fix and soon forgotten. The bigger emotional ones, like Bryce's, were much harder. "Get an ice-cream treat and go play with your cars on the porch. I need to talk to your dad for a minute."

"Is Daddy in trouble?" Cam paused by the freezer drawer and looked at her quizzically.

"Of course not." Joy made herself laugh. Bryce was "in trouble" all right but not the kind Cam meant. "I'll come and play soon. If you need anything, ask your aunt Melissa." After Carrie had dropped the kids off at the ranch house because Bryce was still working, Joy had asked

Melissa and Skylar, who'd popped in while Cole did chores, if they could stay a bit longer. Joy wanted some uninterrupted time with her son.

As the porch door shut behind Cam, Joy glanced around her tidy kitchen. It was the heart of her home—and her family—and many of their most important conversations had taken place around the long harvest table. She'd celebrated at that table, grieved there, and in all seasons of her life, received comfort from loved ones there too. When she and Shane had their own house, that table would come with her.

She fingered the diamond-studded engagement ring she wore on a chain around her neck and pictured Shane's face. In a few weeks, they'd share the news of their engagement with their families, but for now Joy had the time she needed to get used to this lovely but big life change.

"I checked those boards on the back deck," Bryce said, coming into the kitchen. "They need replacing for sure. I'll pick up lumber when I'm next in town. Are the kids ready to head home?"

"In a while. Sit." She gestured to one of the chairs, and her beagle, Gus, and elderly collie, Jess, sat too.

"Okay." Bryce laughed, pulled out the chair and patted the dogs. "What's up?"

"I was about to ask you the same question." Joy grabbed the bowl of peas she'd picked earlier, sat across from him and started shelling the firm green pods. The evening light slanted across the kitchen floor and accented the lines on her son's face. "Has something happened between you and Carrie? When she volunteered with me at the homecoming stall, she was different. Evasive even. I thought you two were friends." More than friends, although it wasn't Joy's place to say so.

"We are, but…" Bryce exhaled and rested his head in his hands. "It's a mess and all my fault."

"If it is, you can fix it." She studied his bent head and the silver strands amongst the brown. Dennis had gone gray early too, but in Joy's eyes, it had only made him more handsome and distinguished.

"I had a great time with Carrie at the concert, and I really care for her. As a lot more than a friend." His voice was almost a whisper.

"Grief and guilt are funny things. They ebb and flow and swirl and slither around until you can feel like you're tied up in knots inside. If you're anything like I was, taking that next step is hard." She set aside the peas and covered Bryce's hands. "The first time Shane kissed me, I felt like I was cheating on your dad. For a few days afterward, the guilt was terrible."

"It was?" Bryce raised his head, and his eyes were troubled.

Joy nodded. "Then I talked to my friends and my grief counsellor, and they made me see guilt is another part of grief. It comes in stages. First there's going out and having fun without your loved one. That's a big hurdle. Then there's letting yourself care for someone else in a special way, and that's even bigger."

"But you did it?" His voice cracked.

"Shane and I both did. He misses his wife like I miss your dad. But although our loved ones were taken too soon, they'd have wanted us to be happy in all ways. I can't live my life as I once did, but that doesn't mean I can't have a new life." The ring tucked beneath Joy's T-shirt testified to that.

"If Carrie makes you and the kids happy, you should see where things go. We both know you can't plan everything in life, so what about instead letting yourself be open to opportunities?" She squeezed Bryce's hands and returned to shelling peas. "Letting yourself care for Carrie doesn't diminish your love for Ally. It doesn't make you a bad person either. Rather, it makes you human and someone who needs comfort and companionship like we all do."

Bryce rubbed a hand across his weary face. "Thanks, Mom. You always know how to make things better. I'll talk to Carrie tomorrow and start by apologizing. I've been weird to her this weekend. To all of you."

Joy chuckled. "We're a family. We can put up with weirdness from time to time. You might want to apologize to your brothers too. Zach and Cole were pretty steamed about what you said to them yesterday."

"It wasn't anything they said or did." Bryce's expression was sheepish. "I took my own stuff out on them."

"They'll understand. I certainly do. It's hard when you're on your own and surrounded by loving couples, but we each have to find our own path."

"I'm happy for Zach and Beth, and Cole and Melissa, but sometimes it hurts, you know?"

"Reminders of any big loss always will, but you learn to live with it. Besides, it's only been a few years, and you've had the kids to worry about. Grief doesn't have a timeline, and you could only grieve in bits and pieces. You couldn't even think about a new relationship because you needed to be strong for your children." Joy came around the table and hugged her son as tight as she'd hugged her grandson. "But you're never too old for a fresh start."

She only hoped her kids would be as happy about her fresh start, and Shane becoming part of their family, as she was.

"YOU TWO ARE doing great with your swimming." Near midday on Monday, behind the wheel of Bryce's pickup truck, Carrie spoke over her shoulder to Paisley and Cam, who were buckled into their booster seats. "Your front crawl is lots better, Cam, and so is your diving, Paisley."

"I'm scared about the test." Cam's voice was small.

"Everybody gets scared before tests. I still get scared each time I go into a rodeo arena to compete," Carrie said. "Take a deep breath and do your best. That's all anyone can ask of you."

That was all Carrie should ask of herself too. She'd hoped to find a quiet moment to talk to Bryce earlier and try to understand what was wrong. But some cattle had gotten loose, so he'd left the house with Cole as soon as she'd arrived.

"Your teacher said you'll pass no problem," Paisley assured her brother. "I'm scared for my test too. Can we go to the pool again tomorrow afternoon to practice? Aunt Melissa's bringing Skylar then, and we could practice together. Skylar's excellent at swimming. She's younger, but she's way better than me."

"Skylar started swimming lessons earlier. Her grandparents in California have a pool too." Carrie slowed the truck and stared at a ranch on the right-hand side of the highway, where black smoke billowed from one of the barns. "Hang on." She pulled onto the gravel shoulder as an emergency siren squealed, and a fire truck raced past.

"It's a fire. Daddy might be there." Cam bounced in his seat and pointed.

"Or on his way," Paisley added. "Some kids who go to the high school live on that ranch. They rode on our bus last year."

Carrie's body chilled as she spotted flames coming from the barn roof. In the distance, someone led a horse to safety in a nearby pasture. "Sit tight, kids. Here comes another emergency vehicle. The fire department will soon have things under control." She tried to make her voice calm. They had to quell the fire fast before it spread to nearby fields, other barns or the ranch house, but she couldn't leave the children to go and help. She fumbled with her cell phone and scrolled to Bryce's number.

She was driving his pickup because hers was in for a service, and Angela's car didn't have enough space for the two booster seats. If Bryce was here, he'd have taken Joy's car or one of the ranch's trucks.

His phone rang and went to voicemail. Without leaving a message, she tried Joy's number and then Melissa and Beth.

"Hello?"

"Thank goodness." When Beth answered, Carrie exhaled. "I've been trying to reach everyone. A barn's on fire a few miles this side of town and—"

"I just heard. Joy called me. I'm at home with Ellie. If you want to come here with the kids, we're staying put. Bryce responded to the first alarm, so he's already there in his gear. Zach and Cole left around the same time."

"I'll stay here for now. Joy's car's pulling up behind me." The phone slipped in Carrie's sweaty palms, and even the kids were quiet. "Here's your grandma." She got out of the driver's seat and met Joy outside the truck.

"Almost as soon as the emergency call came through, the town sent out an email, and there's a lot on social media too. Everyone wants to support the Irving family." Joy spoke in a low voice to Carrie. "I thought if I drove out this way, I'd meet you coming from swimming. I can take the children back to the ranch if you want to lend a hand moving the horses and other stock."

"Thanks, I do." Before Joy had finished speaking, Carrie was pulling her hair up into a ponytail and taking off her sneakers and replacing them with one of the pairs of barn boots Bryce kept in the back of his truck.

"I have a batch of chocolate chip cookies fresh from the oven." Joy helped the kids unbuckle their seat belts. "How does cookies and milk sound?

Your dad will be back before you know it, so we can save some for him."

Paisley, older and more aware than Cam, glanced between Carrie and Joy, and a worried frown creased her face.

"Your dad and the other firefighters will keep everyone safe." Carrie knelt to Paisley's level. "And I'm going to keep the animals safe. I'll be home as soon as I can. Can you save cookies and milk for me?"

"Lots of cookies in Grandma's special tin. The one with the tractor on it." Easily diverted, Cam let Joy lead him to her car.

"You go on," Carrie said to Paisley. "It'll be okay. Your dad needs you to be brave and help Cam and your grandma. Can you do that?"

Paisley nodded and hugged Carrie before she joined Joy and Cam.

Carrie ran down the long driveway toward the barn. Bryce had to be okay. She couldn't lose him. Although she'd tried to fight her feelings, she loved him, and she wanted that love to have a chance to grow. "What can I do?" She met Jon Schuyler, a local veterinarian, by the pasture fence.

"We're loading these guys into a trailer to take to a neighbor's place." He gestured to two beautiful chestnut Morgan horses who stomped and pawed the ground and showed the whites of their eyes. "I could use a hand."

"You've got it." The frightened horses would give Carrie a focus beyond Bryce. Still, her gaze strayed to the barn where firefighters in protective gear trained hoses on the burning structure while several others did the same in the hayloft, where the roof was partly gone. "Easy, boy. You're safe." She soothed the nearest horse and guided it gently toward the waiting trailer.

In a few minutes, Cole appeared with a gray pony, and they worked together to load the precious cargo. "Luckily, most of the cattle are in a far pasture, but Zach and a couple of ranch hands are getting a few calves and some other stock out."

"And Bryce?" Carrie's hands shook, and she fumbled with the first Morgan's trailer tie.

"Last I saw, he was headed into the barn fire." Cole's expression was grim. "He knows what he's doing. He's been trained for it. It's not his first fire either. Try not to worry."

Carrie gulped and went back for the second Morgan, further conversation made impossible by several more emergency vehicles screeching to a stop beside them.

As she focused on horses and then calves, chickens and several pigs, time lost all meaning. Cole made several trips to the neighboring ranch with the loaded horse trailer while Carrie worked on and tried not to look at the inferno that had now spread to the barnyard and an empty chicken coop. *Where are you, Bryce?*

An hour later, Jon, the vet, rubbed a hand across his soot-streaked forehead. "The worst of the fire's out. All the animals have been relocated, and they saved the crops, except an acre or so of the barley field and a vegetable garden. Luckily, the wind didn't change direction, or they might have lost the house too. I was here on a routine visit when the fire broke out. It spread so fast. It's also lucky you turned up when you did. Cole and I couldn't have gotten the horses to safety so quickly without you."

"I was happy to help." Pitching in when neighbors were in need was part of small-town and ranch life. "Did the family have insurance?"

Jon nodded. "If there's anything insurance won't cover, the rest of us will share what we can now, and for animal feed throughout the winter. I heard Joy Carter and Rosa Cardinal are organizing the Sunflower Sisterhood to deliver meals and divide up garden produce."

Carrie would be part of that effort as well, but her priority was to find Bryce. She shaded her eyes with one hand and lifted her damp ponytail from the back of her neck with the other. Most of the firefighters were still clustered by the barn.

But at this distance, and with them wearing all that equipment, she couldn't tell them apart. "If you don't need me for anything else, I'll—"

"Carrie. What are you doing here?"

She swung around at Bryce's voice. "Helping. Your mom's looking after the kids." Apart from a yellow safety helmet, he'd removed his outer gear and wore a blue short-sleeved T-shirt with dark pants and boots. "I was so scared for you." She swayed toward him, and her eyes filled with tears.

"Hey, it's okay. The fire looked bad, but I've been called out to worse." Bryce opened his arms, and she almost fell into them.

"I…you're safe… I thought I'd never see or talk to you again." Her voice cracked, and tears slipped down her cheeks. And as she kissed him, and he kissed her back, she was oblivious to any curious onlookers.

She and Bryce had another chance, and that was all that mattered.

CHAPTER SEVENTEEN

AFTER SAYING GOODNIGHT to Paisley and Cam,
Bryce sat beside Carrie on the front porch swing.
His house faced west, and the sun was a red-gold
ball against the far horizon. "When one of my
crew said you were at the Irvings' farm today,
and then I saw you with Jon and the horses, I was
both proud and terrified. Proud because you'd
pitched in, and without your help the Irvings
might have lost stock, and terrified something
could have happened to you."

While Bryce wanted to keep Carrie safe, having her nearby steadied him. She'd been his calm
and anchor amidst the chaos of the fire. And
now he wanted to tell her at least part of what
he was feeling.

"Anybody would have done the same. If your
mom hadn't come by, I'd never have left Paisley and Cam. But since she did, I couldn't go on
home without doing what I could."

The setting sun picked up matching gold and
red glints in Carrie's pretty hair, and in a red-

and-white polka-dot sundress he hadn't seen her wear before, she looked feminine and almost delicate. She was strong and tough when she needed to be, though, and Bryce liked that and everything else about her. More than liked. Could he love her? The rush of emotion he'd experienced in the aftermath of the fire, when she'd tumbled into his arms, hadn't subsided. If anything, it had grown stronger.

"What did you say?" He stared at Carrie, mesmerized by the soft curve of her cheek and the bow of her kissable mouth.

"I asked if the kids had settled into bed okay. They were both more worried about you than they let on. They love you so much."

Carrie's expression was puzzled, and Bryce tried to rearrange his face into a more neutral countenance. "I love them too. I…" He stopped himself. He'd almost said he loved her as well, but for a cautious and logical guy like him, it was too soon, and the feelings were too new. "Cam was asleep as soon as his head hit the pillow. Paisley took longer, but reading a story calmed her."

The swing creaked as it moved back and forth in a gentle motion. The past few summers, Bryce hadn't spent much time on this porch. However, Carrie and the kids had planted petunias in the previously empty containers and brought out this swing from where he'd stored it in the garage. Along with a cheerful, sunflower-patterned welcome mat, a low table with a candle lantern and strands of white lights twined around the railing, the porch was now as homey as the rest of his house.

"It's a pretty night." Carrie's voice was low. "Peaceful."

No matter what they were doing, or what else was going on, simply being around Carrie gave Bryce a sense of peace. "I meant it when I said I was terrified for you at the fire." As a younger man, he'd never admitted to fear, but life and loss had changed him. "At the music festival, I said you were important to me. What I should have said is I have important feelings for you. When I kissed you on the hayride, it was great, but then I panicked, so I backed away. I'm sorry for being weird."

"It's okay. I think I understand." Her eyes were soft and filled with compassion. "Am I the first woman you've kissed since Ally?"

Bryce nodded. While some women might have been jealous or uncomfortable, Carrie was intuitive enough, and caring enough, to get and accept where he was coming from. Already slow to open his heart and his life to someone else, Bryce also had baggage most other men his age didn't.

"I have important feelings for you too." She

slipped her hand into his, and they rocked quietly together for a few moments. "That's a big part of why I don't want to leave High Valley. I've got an appointment with a real estate agent to see the old Sutton farm tomorrow after work. When I'm not competing, I'd like to make my home in this area."

"I'd like that." He took a deep breath. "Shane had a cancellation, and he offered me a free, two-bedroom family suite at Squirrel Tail on Wednesday night. It would mean a lot if you joined the kids and I there."

"Your mom mentioned that as well, and now... yes. I'd love to come with you." Her words came out in a rush, and her green eyes shone.

"It could be the start of seeing where things might go between us." Instead of panic, Bryce felt calm and a fundamental sense of rightness. "I don't want anything to spoil our friendship or upset the kids, but what do you think?"

The only other time he'd gotten serious about a woman, he'd been a teenager, and he and Ally had grown up together. It was different with Carrie. He was different, and this relationship, as it should be, was also different from the one he'd shared with his late wife.

"I think that sounds good." The honesty and trust in Carrie's face touched a part of his heart he'd thought was gone forever. "I know you need time, so I don't want us to say anything to the kids or anyone else right now. Let's take things slowly. I won't be working for you much longer, and after that…" Her face went pink. "Today, at the fire, I was afraid I'd never have a chance to tell you how I feel about you. I want us to have a chance to explore those feelings, Bryce."

"I want that too." He moved closer and read the invitation in her eyes. And then he kissed her, better than any of the kisses they'd shared before because now they were also sharing what was in their hearts.

IN THE TRANQUIL river behind the main guest house at Squirrel Tail Ranch, Carrie dipped her paddle into the water, and the kayak slid forward.

"Are you guys having fun?" From a three-person kayak moving in tandem with hers, Paisley and Cam, who wore orange life jackets, gave Carrie a thumbs-up. Bryce grinned and raised his own paddle in salute. Beneath a yellow life jacket, he wore a white T-shirt with the Tall Grass Ranch logo and black swim shorts. A ball cap had taken the place of his standard cowboy hat, and aviator sunglasses finished the look.

"It's fantastic, isn't it?" She let her kayak drift to watch a pair of ducks paddle into a clump of reeds.

"You got the hang of kayaking real fast." Bryce

nodded approvingly. He looked as at-home on the water as he did on horseback or working in the fields.

"You're a good teacher." He was kind, patient and had a way of explaining things that made it easy for Carrie to understand.

"I once thought about teaching high-school science. I did a teaching qualification part-time after I finished college. School in the winter and ranching in the summer would have been a good fit but…life happened." A shadow flitted across his face. "I'm teaching several agricultural workshops next winter. One of my consulting clients asked me for them, and I thought why not?"

"You'll be great." Carrie turned her kayak around to follow Bryce and the kids back toward the rental area. Although life didn't always turn out how you expected, there were all kinds of ways to make dreams come true. You had to take a fresh perspective, that was all.

As they neared shallower water, she rested her paddle across her knees. Before today, she'd only ever been on tourist boats, and they were motorized and much bigger. Kayaking was different. It brought her closer to nature, and the slow pace brought her closer to herself too.

"Here you go." Bryce, already out of his kayak, pulled Carrie's onto the sandy shore and helped her out.

"What did you think?" Carrie gave a hand to Paisley as she scrambled out of the bigger kayak while Bryce did the same with Cam.

"It was awesome." Paisley grinned.

"Look, there's a frog." Cam darted toward the grassy area beyond the small beach, and Paisley followed.

"Your life jackets, you need to—" Carrie stopped.

"They'll be back in a minute, and they'll also be extra safe if they get close to the water, even though we can still see them from here." Bryce laughed and pointed.

Since they'd talked on the porch swing about the feelings they had for each other—feelings both of them had been careful not to name—there was a new easiness between them. And on this brief vacation, Bryce seemed happier and more relaxed than Carrie had ever seen him. He was even more attentive to her too, and with each private glance they shared or brief touch of hands behind the kids' backs, she fell a bit more in love with him.

And this feeling *was* love, she was sure of it. With Jimmy, it had been infatuation, intense but fleeting. Although she hadn't realized it at the time, she hadn't been herself with Jimmy, and over time, she'd downplayed her barrel racing success and freelance client portfolio to be the kind of girlfriend he wanted. Now, more confident in herself, she could be the woman she truly was. Bryce liked the real Carrie, and he was interested in her career too, which Jimmy never had been.

"Are your folks still coming here the weekend after this one?" Bryce pulled both kayaks farther up onto the beach, tucked the paddles beside them and took off his life jacket.

"Yes, Mom said they should be here next Friday night around ten. She'll make sure Dad doesn't work late." As Carrie shrugged out of her life jacket, Bryce helped her, and his hands brushed her arms, making her skin quiver. "They'll likely want to go to bed soon after they get to Aunt Angela's. We can give them a tour of the ranch on the Saturday morning. I'll introduce them to you then too." Afterward, she'd find a private moment to tell her folks she didn't plan on coming back to Kalispell to live or taking that marketing job at Rizzo Construction. She grabbed a towel from her bag and rubbed water droplets off her arms and legs. The water was cold, that was why she was shivering. It had nothing to do with that looming conversation. Still, her parents' visit was more than a week away. She didn't have to think about it now.

"It's too bad your mom and dad can't get here earlier. They could cheer you on at your event at the charity fundraiser. The kids and I will cheer extra loud to make up for their absence." Bryce toweled his muscular legs, and Carrie's stomach somersaulted. He looked good in ranch clothes, but he looked even better in casual sportswear. "How are you feeling about returning to competition?"

"I'm excited." Carrie squeezed river water out of the hem of the oversize T-shirt she'd worn over her swimsuit for kayaking. "Teddy's in great shape, and it'll be a fun event." One she hadn't told her parents about. Preferring she give up rodeo altogether, they weren't likely to cheer her on as Bryce suggested. They'd be upset enough once she finally told them the truth about what she wanted in her life as well as in her career.

At least she wouldn't have the added stress of showing them the Sutton farm. A few hours before her scheduled viewing, the family had gotten and accepted a preemptive offer that, according to town gossip, was far higher than what Carrie could afford. "My folks are looking forward to meeting you and the kids." Except, she also hadn't told them Bryce was more than her boss. That one was easier, though, because she hadn't told anybody and neither had he.

"It'll all work out." As if he'd read her thoughts, Bryce gave her a quick hug and kissed her cheek.

"I hope so." Carrie made herself smile as Paisley and Cam rejoined them. She and Bryce helped with their life jackets and then returned the equipment to the rental place as the kids talked about the frog and getting mud between their toes.

If things didn't work out, what was she going to do? She had an open invitation to stay with Angela as long as she liked, but Carrie wanted her own place to come home to between competitions. And although her parents wouldn't disown her, they'd be disappointed, and she never wanted to do anything to hurt them.

"Like my mom says, don't borrow trouble." As they walked to the main part of the resort to get ice cream, Bryce gave her a supportive smile.

"Why would you borrow trouble?" Paisley giggled. "It's not like a library book."

"You don't really borrow it. It means don't worry about something before you need to." It was good advice, and for now, Carrie would set her worries aside. "But we don't need to worry about anything because we're on vacation."

"And we're having ice cream and then doing goat yoga and having a barbecue and roasting marshmallows and lots more." Cam took Carrie's hand to lead her to the ice-cream stand.

"We sure are." Carrie laughed with the others at Cam's "schedule" for their day.

As Paisley and Cam went ahead to choose ice-cream flavors, Bryce drew closer to Carrie.

"After the two of them are in bed, what would you think about stargazing with me? The patio outside the bedroom the kids and I are sharing would be perfect. It's supposed to be a clear night, and we'd still be close enough to hear them."

"I'd love that."

But most of all, Carrie loved spending time with him and Paisley and Cam. This mini vacation felt like being a couple and a family she wanted to be part of for the rest of her life.

CHAPTER EIGHTEEN

BRYCE LAY ON a blue yoga mat while a curious brown-and-white young goat bleated and nudged his shoulder. "You want to join in, buddy?"

"Mine does, Daddy. See?" On a mat to his right, Paisley lay on her back with a small white goat sprawled on her chest.

As the goat continued to study him, Bryce rolled onto his stomach and glanced at Carrie. She sat cross-legged with a tiny black-and-white goat in her arms while Cam used her phone to take a picture.

"I've never had so much fun doing yoga before. Since these guys are rescues, and Shane puts their welfare first and foremost, they'll still have a good life here when they get too big to cuddle. Maybe goat yoga is something I could offer at my ranch someday. For locals, not tourists." As the special family class, a few beginner yoga moves and lots of animal cuteness, ended, Carrie set the goat aside, got to her feet and stretched in a graceful arc.

Bryce's mouth went dry. Right now, what he wanted most was to kiss her breathless, but he couldn't. Keeping their relationship secret was hard, but it was also the right decision. He wasn't one to rush into anything anyway, and he had the kids to think of. What if he got their hopes up that Carrie would be part of their lives longer-term, and then things didn't work out?

"I'm sorry the Sutton place fell through, but don't be discouraged. Another property will come up." It likely wouldn't be as close to High Valley and the Tall Grass Ranch as the Sutton farm, though. Given Carrie would often be away with rodeo, when would they be able to spend time together?

"I'm impatient. The Sutton farm seemed perfect, but there must be something else out there that will be even better." Carrie secured Paisley's flyaway ponytail.

Bryce had abundant patience, but unlike Carrie, he wasn't so certain better things lay ahead. However, what if he let himself think that way? It was early days, and he and Carrie would figure things out as they went along. A positive mindset could make all the difference. "What's next, guys?"

"Swimming, visiting the rabbit hutch and Buster, and going on the trampoline." Cam bounced around him.

"Then an arts-and-crafts session for the kids before the barbecue," Carrie added. "I'd also like to visit the horses. Shane has a new mare he's excited about. He thinks she has the makings of a champion barrel racer."

"Mr. Gallagher said he'd let me ride her when I'm bigger," Paisley said as she took Bryce's hand. "Isn't this the best day ever, Daddy?"

"Yeah, it is." And for the next few hours, Bryce focused on each magical moment, especially ones like now when he and Carrie had a few minutes by themselves.

"You missed a spot. Here, let me." He grabbed the bottle of sunscreen from the patio table in their suite's small garden area. "Got it." He checked, and they were still alone, so he dropped several quick kisses on her nose.

"You're very distracting." Still, Carrie kissed him back until they both reluctantly drew apart. "I'll check on the kids. They should be changed for the barbecue by now, but it's way too quiet in there."

As Carrie moved to the screen door, it slid open, and Paisley and Cam came out.

"Don't you two look clean and tidy. Good job." Bryce clapped. "Are you ready for the barbecue and marshmallow roasting?"

"Almost." Paisley had her hands behind her back, and both kids looked as if they were bursting with suppressed excitement. "While you and Carrie went to see the horses, we made something for you in arts and crafts. We hid it in Cam's backpack so you wouldn't see and it would be a surprise."

"For me?" Bryce glanced between his kids.

"For Carrie too. Really, it's for all of us. See?" Paisley took her hands from behind her back to show them a piece of art paper covered with colorful drawings. "It's to remember our vacation."

"There's the frog I saw after we went kayaking." Cam pointed to a picture near the top. "Didn't I choose a good green color?"

"You sure did." Bryce's throat was tight as he and Carrie admired the children's work. "You've got the goats from yoga and your ice cream." He indicated a chocolate cone held by a boy who looked like Cam.

"There's our kayaks and my pink baseball cap." Carrie put a hand to her head and then the drawing. "And Buster and the other rabbits and you kids on the trampoline."

"We drew all of us too. There's me and Cam between you and Carrie." Paisley showed them four stick figures in the center of the paper. "There's Mommy too. She's the angel in the sky watching over us." She pointed to a brown-haired figure perched on a cloud with purple wings on the back of her purple dress.

"I drew the wings, and Paisley did Mommy's dress." Cam leaned into Bryce's side. "Paisley said angels don't have purple wings, but nobody knows for sure, not even the minister."

"Purple was your mom's favorite color. She'd love those wings to match her dress." Bryce hugged both kids as they told him more about the picture. "You did a great job and made a wonderful memory." He blinked away moisture behind his eyes. If Ally could see the kids now, he hoped she'd be proud of them and him too. "I'll get this artwork framed so we can hang it up at home."

"I smell barbecue grilling. Has everyone worked up an appetite?" Carrie glanced at Bryce like she knew he needed a distraction.

"I'm starving. I could eat three hamburgers." Cam rubbed his stomach.

"Let's start with one, okay?" Carrie laughed as they made their way to the main patio, which housed a fire pit and barbecues.

"Today's been great. Thanks for everything." Bryce greeted Shane, who stood behind a buffet table loaded with salads, while Carrie took care of their hot dog and burger orders at a separate food station.

"My pleasure." Shane handed Bryce a tray. "You're welcome at Squirrel Tail anytime. All of Joy's family are." His expression softened before he turned away to serve another guest.

As Bryce filled bowls with mixed salad greens and toppings, he couldn't shake the sense there was something more going on between his mom and Shane than either of them had let on. It was the way the older man had said Joy's name and how his gaze had lingered on Bryce in an almost fatherly way. Still, it was their business, and given his relationship with Carrie, Bryce wasn't one to talk.

After he added a bowl of grated cheese and a glass of breadsticks to the tray, Bryce returned to the picnic table where the kids waited.

"All set?" Carrie arrived with her tray and began handing out plates of food. "Please don't reach in front of your sister, Cam." She passed Bryce his burger and then set out her own meal.

"But I want cheese, and she's taking it all," Cam said.

"No, he's taking it," Paisley argued.

"Quit it, kids. There's enough cheese for both of you, but if you keep on, neither of you'll have any." Bryce made a mock annoyed face, and Carrie choked like she was trying to hold back a laugh.

As the kids settled and they ate the delicious food and talked about the day, Bryce was at peace in a way he hadn't been in a long time.

And several hours later, as he sat on a patio chair and stared into the glowing coals in the fire pit, that peacefulness, along with comfort and bone-deep contentment, wrapped around him like one of Carrie's hugs. "You're my sleepy boy." Cuddled on Bryce's lap, Cam mumbled something unintelligible.

Without disturbing his son, Bryce gestured to Paisley and Carrie, who'd joined a group to listen to a bedtime story.

"I didn't realize it was so late." Carrie collected their belongings.

"I'm not tired." Paisley's mouth was smeared with chocolate, marshmallow and graham cracker crumbs from the s'mores they'd made earlier.

"You will be when you get to bed." Carrying Cam, Bryce led them back to the suite along a path lit by solar lights.

"Cam left his cow in the truck. Can you find it while I get him into his pajamas and brush his teeth?" Carrie flipped on lights that illuminated the spacious living and dining area as well as the hall leading to the bedrooms.

"Sure." Bryce made sure he had his keys and went back out into the night to the parking lot. Opening a rear door, he found Cam's cow, which his son needed to sleep with, as well as Paisley's bear.

He scooped up the toys, closed the truck door and looked at the starry sky. Maybe Ally was up there watching over him, an angel like in the kids' drawing, but now her memory brought him more solace than pain.

Returning to the suite, voices murmured from the larger bedroom with a queen-size bed and bunk beds he shared with the kids. Carrie was across the hall in her own room.

"Your dad will be back soon with Cow-Cow," Carrie said. "What was your favorite part of today?"

"I had lots of favorites." There was a pause as Cam thought. "But the best part was being with you, Daddy and Paisley."

"That was the best part for me too," Carrie said.

"I love you." Cam's voice was so soft Bryce strained to hear him. "I wish you could be my second mom."

"I love you too." Carrie's voice was muffled. "Right now, I'm your nanny, but even when I don't work for your dad, I hope I'll always be your friend and maybe like an adopted aunt. How does that sound?"

"Daddy?" The bathroom door swung open, and Paisley stepped out ready for bed in horse-patterned pajamas. "Thanks for finding Buttercup. I thought he was in my suitcase."

"What? Oh." Bryce looked at the bear and cow in his arms. "Yeah, here you go." He passed her the teddy.

"Did you get bitten by a mosquito or something? Your face is all red and itchy looking."

"No, it's nothing." *Or maybe everything.*

There was no more uncertainty or doubting his feelings. He loved Carrie too, and like Cam, he wanted her to be a permanent part of their family. Happiness and a sense of rightness surged through him.

As Paisley continued to the bedroom, Bryce glanced at Paisley and Cam's artwork on the coffee table. The pictures they'd drawn were more than a memory. They could also be his future, their future.

A second chance and a new family, together.

A WEEK AFTER her mini vacation with Bryce and the kids, Carrie waited with Teddy in the arena's alleyway and visualized the run one more time. Unlike some of the other horses waiting to race, Teddy stood quietly with no jumping or rearing up.

"You can do it, Teddy Bear. *We* can do it." She rubbed his ears how he liked and shifted in the saddle. Although this rodeo was only a small event—and as a fundraiser for a horse rescue, it wasn't part of the official competition schedule—it still felt good to be back. Having Bryce and the kids here to support her was better still—something she wouldn't have at her first official event since Colorado was too far for them to travel once school started.

The crowd applauded for the previous competitor, and Carrie walked Teddy to the gate, where he again stood quietly. Although Teddy was calm and attentive by nature, a calm rider also made for a calm horse.

"Let's show them what we can do." She spoke softly into Teddy's ear and then straightened in the saddle, focused on the job at hand.

The gate swung open, and they raced into the arena and around the first barrel. "Good job, easy now."

Teddy's hooves thudded in the dirt, and the wind rushed past Carrie's ears as Teddy sailed around the run like he'd gained wings. And Carrie was in what she called "the zone" with him like she used to be before things had gone wrong.

"Go, Carrie. Go, Teddy," Paisley's voice rang out.

"That's it, boy." Teddy finished the cloverleaf pattern, and then they raced to the finish. "Great job." She patted his heaving side. They'd done it. She hadn't hesitated, hadn't doubted herself or Teddy, and they'd had a clean run without touching a barrel. She'd gotten her confidence back, and whether she won a ribbon or not, that combination of mental and physical strength was a personal best in all the ways that counted.

As her name and time were announced over the loudspeaker, she waved to the crowd and three people in particular. Bryce and the kids had come from their seats in the stands to greet her at the gate, all of them talking at once and clapping and cheering.

"Way to go." As soon as Carrie had led Teddy out of the arena and dismounted, Bryce hugged her. "You were fantastic. I don't know much about barrel racing, but even I could see you and Teddy nailed it."

Paisley hugged Carrie too. "I bet you win a blue ribbon for sure."

"There are still some good riders and horses left to compete." Carrie had learned early on to be confident but never overconfident. The latter led to taking unnecessary risks and, possibly, a career-ending accident. "There's Kim Padilla on Mustang Maddie, for instance." She gave a good luck thumbs-up to the two of them. "Besides, the most important thing is how much money we've raised for the horse rescue, right?" And for Carrie, it was proving to herself that she deserved her previous success and was ready to compete professionally again.

From behind the fence, Paisley studied the other waiting riders and horses. "I'm gonna be out there someday. You'll see."

"I don't doubt it." Carrie wrapped an arm

around Paisley's shoulders as Bryce and Cam took Teddy into the barn. "But don't forget what's important in life outside the rodeo arena. That's your family and friends. A place to call home. And following your heart and doing what's right for you."

"Why would I forget those things?" Paisley looked bewildered. "Anyway, Cam's gonna be on the circuit with me. We'll have a truck and trailer together. There'll be space for our horses and to live." She turned away to clap for Kim and Mustang Maddie.

"You never know." Carrie spoke under her breath as she clapped too. What you wanted at one point in your life could change. Or you could lose sight of what you wanted and have to redis-cover it. Maybe other people wanted different things for you, and you tried to please them in-stead of being true to yourself. She exhaled and studied the scoreboard.

Since their stay at Squirrel Tail, she and Bryce had spent all their free time together, and for these last few weeks of her nannying job, Car-rie had moved into Bryce's guest room to have as much time as possible with him and the kids. They watched movies after Paisley and Cam had gone to bed. Bryce had abandoned his home of-fice to work at the kitchen table, where Carrie did her freelance projects. And on Carrie's day off, she'd gone to the fields with Bryce to check the crops, learning from him for her own ranch. They spent time in companionable silence too, either watching the stars from the porch or over cups of coffee the next morning.

Unlike Jimmy, being with Bryce made Carrie's life better. And since he gave her the acceptance and space to be herself, Bryce made *her* better too.

"Teddy's comfortable." Bryce and Cam rejoined them, drawing Carrie out of her thoughts. "We left him with Heidi to get settled. Heidi says congrats. She watched your run with some of the other hands."

The part-time ranch hand at the Tall Grass loved Teddy, and the horse returned her affection. Since Heidi was a barrel racing fan, she'd come today to help.

"You and Teddy are still in first place." Paisley jumped up and down and pointed to the scoreboard.

"Yes, but there's one more competitor to go," Carrie said. "Digby Dare's a great horse, and his rider's no slouch either."

"Even if you don't win, you and Teddy are still best to me." Cam took one of Carrie's hands and squeezed it.

"Me too," Paisley chimed in.

"Aww. Thanks, guys." Carrie glanced at Bryce.

"Me three." His voice was gruff, and if the look in his eyes wasn't love, she didn't know what it could be.

She held his gaze, and the same look of love must have reflected back at him in her eyes.

"Yay, you did it, Carrie. You won!" Paisley yelled. "Did you see? Digby Dare knocked over a barrel and got a penalty. It's you and Teddy, then Kim Padilla and Mustang Maddie."

Carrie glanced at the scoreboard. She'd missed the race because she'd been caught up in Bryce. That look, that feeling between them and having him and the kids at her side. It made a great day even better. And while it was fantastic to win, it was even better to share her victory with people she loved.

"It's good to have you back." Kim congratulated Carrie.

"Thanks, it's good to be back. You had a great run." As Carrie introduced Kim to Bryce and the children, the other woman gave her a sideways glance and smiling nod of approval.

"What's next?" Paisley wondered after asking Kim for her autograph.

"We'll be presented with our ribbons. There'll be photos too. It's fine with me if you want to head home." As competitors, Carrie and Teddy had traveled to the event before Bryce and the kids, who'd arrived later in his truck. Heidi had also traveled separately because she was spending tomorrow in the area visiting friends who lived nearby.

"Why would we go home early? We want to see you get your ribbon and watch the rest of the events together," Bryce said.

"You saw us get our certificates for passing our swimming tests," Paisley added.

"I did." Paisley and Cam were children and needed adult supervision, but even if they didn't, Carrie would still have stuck around so they could celebrate.

"We'll soon be as good at swimming as Mommy was like we put on our list," Cam said.

"You sure will." Paisley and Cam talked about their mother more often now and those casual references warmed Carrie's heart.

"But right now I'm starving. Lunch was hours ago, and Daddy said we could have supper here," Cam added while rubbing his tummy.

"I did." Bryce laughed. "We'll go home in a convoy together. That's the Carter way." His voice was warm. "Besides, there aren't many houses or towns along that stretch of highway. I don't like to think of you driving it alone at night. I'd worry."

Although Carrie was used to driving long distances alone, knew how to change a tire and do basic maintenance and had a roadside rescue plan for anything more serious, it was nice to have someone who cared and wanted to make sure she reached home safely.

Letting Bryce look out for her and accepting his help didn't mean giving up her independence. It was part of being a team and made her feel closer to him.

She held his steady gaze again, and in it she read trust, commitment and love—everything she'd always wanted but never found. And he came with a family too. She looped arms with Paisley and Cam as they walked toward the prizewinner's area. Children she loved like they were her own.

As Kim chatted with Chelsea, the third-place winner, bits of their conversation reached her. She didn't know Kim well, so she hadn't realized Kim had a husband and kids, and Chelsea, who Carrie hadn't met before, did too. If they made barrel racing and family life work, there was no reason Carrie couldn't. And if she asked, they'd likely be generous with advice and support.

Bryce and the kids wouldn't be alone when Carrie was on the road. They had the whole Carter family.

"It's the Carter way." His words echoed in her head. That "way" was about more than making sure people reached a travel destination safely. It was a way of life and about stepping

in when others needed help. If Carrie became part of their family, Joy and the others would do whatever was needed as soon as Carrie asked—maybe even when she didn't. But they'd never be intrusive or take over either.

She joined Kim and Chelsea for the ribbon presentation and smiled for photos.

With some creativity and flexibility, she could have barrel racing *and* Bryce and the children. All she had to do was figure out how.

Starting with talking to her parents.

CHAPTER NINETEEN

BRYCE EXAMINED HIS reflection in the mirror over the utility-room sink at the main ranch house. Should he have gotten his hair cut? Carrie had texted him she and her parents would be here soon, and he wanted to make a good impression.

"You look good." As he came into the kitchen, his mom studied him and then straightened his shirt collar like she'd done when he was a kid.

Wearing the apron Bryce had given her, Paisley stood behind his mom's baking island, stirring a wooden spoon in a big mixing bowl. "After you and Carrie show Mr. and Mrs. Rizzo the ranch, we're having a tea party for them with cookies and lemonade on the porch."

"I'm decorating the cookies and drawing them a special picture." At the kitchen table strewn with colored markers, Cam was intent on a drawing pad.

"That's great." Bryce glanced at the kids.

"Be yourself, and it'll be fine." His mom gave Bryce an encouraging smile.

"It's strange, you know?" The last time Bryce had met a girl's folks, he was twelve. Now he was in his midthirties. Carrie wasn't a girl, and he wasn't an awkward middle-school boy either.

"It was strange for me when you kids met Shane for the first time too." His mom patted his back.

"It's not the same." Who was Bryce kidding? Carrie was important to him like Shane was important to his mom.

Her expression teased him. "If it isn't, you have nothing to be worried about, do you?"

As Bryce went out the back door, a white SUV pulled up and parked in the driveway by the house.

Carrie clambered from the rear seat, and her parents got out the front. Her dad, a barrel-like man with thinning steel gray hair, paused by the driver's door and spoke into his phone. Her mom pointed to the pasture and spoke to Carrie.

Bryce walked toward them with a welcoming smile. Maybe he should have brought the kids with him, but at the time it had seemed easier to meet Carrie's parents on his own. At least Paisley and Cam would've been a distraction and taken attention off him. "Mr. and Mrs. Rizzo. Welcome to the Tall Grass Ranch. I'm Bryce Carter." He extended his hand, and Mr. Rizzo took it in a beefy grip.

"We're so pleased to meet you." Carrie's mom, an older version of her daughter with brown hair threaded with silver, greeted him too. "But please, call us Sophia and Frank." She clasped his hand in turn. "We feel we know you. Carolina's told us so much about you and your sweet children."

Carolina? Bryce glanced at Carrie, who made an embarrassed face.

"We named our Carolina after my mother." Frank grunted and put his phone away. In a white open-necked shirt, dark dress trousers and shiny loafers, he looked like he should be at a wine-tasting evening at Squirrel Tail rather than on a working cattle ranch. "My parents, Carolina and Antonio, came to America with nothing, but with hard work they—"

"Dad." Carrie interjected. "You and Mom are here for a tour, and Bryce is taking time out from a busy day. Would you like to start with the horse barn?"

"I'd love to see the horses," Sophia said. "I had a pony when I was small. She was called Mabel." Her smile had the same warmth and sincerity as Carrie's.

"You never mentioned anything about a pony." Carrie stared at her mom in astonishment.

Sophia's laugh was light. "It was a long time ago. Another life."

Bryce cleared his throat. "Let's head over to the pasture. The horse barn's beyond it."

Despite Sophia's smile, Carrie's mom and dad were a lot different than he expected, and it wasn't because they lived in a city. They had an air of wealth and sophistication that would set them apart anywhere, not only here. Carrie had said her dad worked in construction, but Frank looked like he'd be more at home in a boardroom than on a building site.

As for Sophia, her "office job" must also be pretty high-powered. An expensive-looking watch and several bracelets sparkled on her arms, while diamonds twinkled in her ears, at her throat and on her wedding finger. In crisp jeans, a pale pink T-shirt with a floral-patterned scarf looped around her neck and immaculate white sneakers, she too looked like she'd been headed for Squirrel Tail and ended up at the Tall Grass Ranch by mistake.

"Carrie says you've got a big spread." Frank fell into step beside Bryce. "Ever think of expanding into corporate ranching? I hear there's good money in it."

"The Tall Grass Ranch has always been a family operation. We want to keep it that way." Bryce kept his voice even. "Watch your step." He gestured to a mud puddle. Frank, to his credit, moved around it unfazed.

"Family operations can grow into multinational corporations. I'd be happy to—"

"That's Bryce's horse, Maverick, with Teddy," Carrie broke in. "The other ones are Scout and Bandit. They belong to Bryce's older brothers. Bandit's retired now, but he was a rodeo horse. Bryce's brother, Cole, was a cowboy. He rode professionally on the circuit." Carrie's words came out in a rush, unlike her usual more measured way of speaking.

"Teddy looks wonderful." Sophia stood by the pasture fence and held her hand out, palm up.

"He's a fantastic horse," Bryce said as Teddy came to greet them. "You should have seen Carrie and him competing in a charity event a few days ago. How the two of them raced around those barrels set the standard for sure. My kids and I almost cheered ourselves hoarse when Carrie and Teddy came first. We're so proud of them."

"You raced in a charity event?" As she patted Teddy, Sophia raised a groomed eyebrow, and her expression was puzzled.

"It was only a small thing. To raise money for a local horse rescue." Carrie's cheeks were pink.

"Don't be so modest." Maverick, Bandit and Scout sidled up to the fence to check out the visitors too, and Bryce dug in his pocket for treats. "It was small, but it attracted talent. The kids and

I are excited to see Carrie compete in official events this fall. My daughter's keen on barrel racing. It's wonderful for her to have Carrie as a role model. Carrie gives Paisley lessons too, between pitching in with chores, rounding up cattle and working in the fields. We couldn't have managed without her at haying time."

"I…" Carrie stuttered, and she glanced between Bryce and her parents. Instead of the humble pleasure he'd expected, her expression was more one of horror.

"Haven't you been working as a nanny?" Frank stepped away from Scout's nose while keeping his gaze on his daughter.

"Of course, I have, but the whole Carter family is involved in ranch work. Paisley and Cam have daily chores, so I'm in the barns with them. Besides, I'm boarding Teddy here, and I—"

"There must be staff to look after Teddy." Frank shook his head, and he, like Sophia, looked puzzled. "What about your freelance business? Have you given your clients notice you won't be available after Labor Day?"

"I…not yet." Carrie seemed to shrink into herself.

"Where are your priorities, Carolina?" Frank tutted. "And what's this about rodeo competitions in the fall? You'll be back in Kalispell."

"Which reminds me," Sophia said. "You still

haven't told maintenance the color of paint and carpet you want in your office. And Human Resources is waiting for you to sign the paperwork they emailed. My assistant needs to book your trip to New York City with Dom and arrange theater tickets. The client's a fan of Broadway shows. If you fly out a few days after Labor Day, you can rent a car and check on that hotel project upstate too. It's running behind, and the civil engineer says—"

"Mom. Dad." Carrie sounded anguished. "Let's talk about this later, okay?"

Dom. New York. Office. Human Resources. Theater tickets. Hotel project. Bryce tried to make sense of the words. "What's...you're going to New York and not that rodeo in Colorado after Labor Day? With Teddy? Who's Dom?"

"Not with Teddy. At least, not to New York City. Dom...works for my parents. It's complicated. I need to talk to my folks. I planned to do that later today. Nothing's been decided yet. Not officially." Carrie's lower lip wobbled.

What was going on? Carrie wouldn't have lied to him, not after her ex and former friend had hurt her with their dishonesty. There was a big misunderstanding somewhere.

"It's not complicated at all." Frank's tone was decisive. "You're returning to Kalispell as soon as this nannying job ends to start your role as head of marketing at Rizzo Construction. We've been more than patient with you to get barrel racing and freelancing out of your system, but now your duty is to your family and our business. We'll work together these next few years so you can take over the whole shebang when I retire. That's always been the plan, and as far as I know, nothing's changed."

"Frank, honey, Carrie's right. We should talk later." Sophia looked almost as distressed as her daughter.

"Carrie?" Bryce took her hand and then dropped it. Her folks thought he was their daughter's boss. As long as she looked after Paisley and Cam until the time they'd agreed on, it shouldn't matter to him whether she went to Kalispell, New York City or anywhere else. It did, though, more than anything.

She stared at him, and although her mouth worked, nothing came out.

And as he waited for her to speak, he read the truth in her eyes. If Carrie hadn't outright lied to him, she hadn't told him certain things about herself and her family. Important and life-changing things.

Her dad didn't only work in construction, her family owned a construction company. A successful one that had made them wealthy. Her dad and mom expected her to work for that company and live a life a world away from rural Montana. They likely wanted her to marry a man from that world too, maybe even that Dom guy.

Bryce swallowed and rubbed Maverick's ears. "I should get going. Like Carrie said, I have a busy day. It was good to meet you both." He touched his cowboy hat to Sophia and Frank. "Carrie can finish showing you around. After your tour, Paisley, Cam and my mom, Joy, will have a tea party set up on the porch. The kids are making and decorating cookies for you."

"Bryce, I'm sorry. I can explain. I meant to tell you about my family and their plans for me, but I…it was never the right time." Carrie sounded choked, like she was fighting back tears.

"I don't understand." Her dad looked between them. "Was Bryce expecting you to keep on being a nanny for his kids? Didn't you only take this job for the summer?"

"I did, but… I didn't mean to mislead any of you." Carrie gave Bryce a pleading look.

"It's fine." It wasn't, but Bryce wouldn't get into that now. "Enjoy the rest of the weekend." He made himself look at and speak to Carrie as if she were any other employee. "I'll see you Monday morning. Can you be at the house around seven thirty? I have a meeting in town at eight." It was cold, businesslike and as effective as putting a bandage meant for a minor cut on a mortal wound.

"Of course." Carrie took a step toward him and then stopped.

Bryce turned on his heel. He didn't know where he was headed, only that he had to get as far away from her as possible. And everything that reminded him of what he'd thought they'd shared.

"I WANTED TO talk to you before. I should have, but I thought you wouldn't understand." From her perch on the sofa in her aunt Angela's tidy living room, Carrie reached for another tissue from the box on the coffee table. She rarely cried, but now she couldn't seem to stop.

Her parents sat in matching green-upholstered armchairs on the other side of the table. When they'd returned to Angela's after an awkward tea party with Paisley, Cam and Joy, Carrie's aunt had evidently realized something was wrong and excused herself to work in her garden.

"We still don't understand." Her mom dabbed her eyes with a tissue as well. "From everything you said, we thought competing in barrel racing was temporary. Like your freelance work was temporary."

"I let you think so because…" Carrie couldn't think about Bryce and the betrayal and hurt in his eyes and on his face. She'd meant to tell *him* the truth too, but she hadn't wanted to spoil the magic of their quiet moments together. Because she couldn't face the reality, she usually avoided hard conversations and wanted to please instead. The real reason hit her in the solar plexus. And now, because she hadn't stood up for herself and been honest about who she was and what she wanted, she'd messed everything up. In some ways, she'd been as dishonest as Jimmy and Brittany. "I didn't want to disappoint you." But she'd disappointed herself, Bryce and her folks anyway.

"So instead, you as much as lied to us? I thought we raised you to tell the truth." Her dad's face was red, and her mom put a soothing hand on his forearm.

"You did, but…" Carrie took a deep breath. She was an adult, not a child, and it was more than time she took a stand. "I'm sorry."

Her father harumphed. "Don't fuss, Sophia. Carolina knows where her responsibilities lie."

"I do." But from now on, she wouldn't let herself be pushed around either. "I'll always love, respect, care for and support you as a daughter should. However, I can't work for Rizzo Construction as head of marketing or anywhere else in the company. Not now and not ever. I'd hate working in an office all day, and I wouldn't be good at it either. Being CEO would be even worse. You need someone who can grow the business like both of you have done." As a vice president and head of business development, her mom was as much a part of the company's success as her dad. "That person isn't me." There, she'd said it, and despite everything, it was as if a weight had lifted off her shoulders.

"But, but…what will you do? How will you live?" her dad sputtered.

"I want to compete in barrel racing as long as I can, continue with my freelance work, and with money I've saved and what Nonna left me, I want to buy a small farm or ranch of my own." Now that she'd started, the words weren't as hard to speak as she'd expected, and more weight lifted.

"Your dad and I are worried for your future." Her mom's tone was conciliatory. "A ranch is fun for a summer vacation but not to build a life, at least not for you. It's hard, rough and exhausting work."

"Don't you understand, Mom? I'm not you. You couldn't wait to leave the ranch, and you love the life you and Dad made together." She glanced between them. Her folks were a team, and it was understandable they wanted the best for her. However, it was up to Carrie to decide what that "best" was.

"I know you're not me, and I don't want you to

be. I love you for who you are." Her mom sniffed and patted her eyes again. "Your dad and I both do, but what about a pension plan and benefits? Healthcare and everything else?"

"Your mother's right." Her dad's expression was more sad than angry, and Carrie's heart pinched. "You have to be sensible. The Carter family's ranch is scenic, and from the sounds of it, they're doing okay now, but what happens if there's a drought or something else beyond their control? Like barrel racing and freelance work, agriculture's risky. If you don't want to join us in Rizzo Construction, surely you can see you need a permanent and secure job? When you come back to Kalispell, I'll talk to my friends, and we'll get you fixed up with something else. You can still ride Teddy as a hobby."

"Dad." Carrie exhaled. "I know you care and want to help, but it's my life and I need to live it my own way."

"Looking back, I was the same, Frank." Her mom's voice sounded both resigned and concerned. "My parents wanted me to stay on the ranch, but I wouldn't hear of it. If I'd done what they wanted, I'd never have met and married you. Carrie needs to make the right choices for her."

"But when we're gone, who will look after you, Carolina? You're over thirty and still on your own. Since you didn't hit it off with Dom, I can introduce you to someone I met at the golf club. Gino's a good man from a fine family. He'd love to meet you. He has a secure, well-paying job as an attorney with the county and a pension too. Say the word, and I'll—"

"Pappa." The Italian name from Carrie's childhood came out unprompted as frustration mixed with love. "I don't need a man or you and Mom to look after me. I can look after myself." She didn't want any man but Bryce, not that she could tell her parents. And even then, she'd imagined they'd be equal partners looking out for each other, and she'd still have her own agricultural business.

"You're our only child, our daughter. Part of me will always see you as my little girl, no matter how old you are." Her dad let out a heavy breath. "And your mother and I aren't getting any younger."

"What your dad's trying to say, badly, is we miss you." Her mom's mouth trembled. "If you lived nearby, we'd see more of you."

"And I miss you, but I can't do what you want."

Her dad stood and muttered something about going out to see Angela in the garden.

"Frank…" Her mom raised her hands in a helpless gesture and came to join Carrie on the sofa.

"I'm sorry I've upset you," Carrie said. "But if

I come back to Kalispell, I won't be happy." She rubbed her face as her dad's footsteps echoed on the tiled floor of the hall and then the front door shut with a sharp click. "I don't want to live a life like yours."

Her mom gave Carrie a crooked smile. "Each generation thinks they're different, when, in reality, we're much the same— even your pappa."

"I didn't mean to judge you." A knot hardened in Carrie's stomach. "You're happy with your life, and that's great, but it's not for me." Had her mother ever had regrets? If so, she'd never voiced them in Carrie's hearing.

"Your grandfather Rizzo didn't want me to work in the business. He was very traditional and thought a woman's place was in the home. Your dad overruled him. Just now, you sounded as your father did with his father." Her mom sighed. "We each need to make our own choices, as well as mistakes. I have regrets, yes, but they're likely not the ones you think." As if she'd read Carrie's mind, her mom stared at Angela's collection of angel ornaments displayed in a glass-fronted cabinet. "I love your dad and you, and I love being a wife and mother. I love my job too and how I've worked with your dad to build the business into what it is today."

"But?" Although Carrie and her mom were close, they'd never talked this honestly.

She took Carrie's hand. "Your dad works too hard, and he won't listen when I tell him he needs to slow down and ease into retirement."

"So that's why you've been pushing me to join the company?" Carrie leaned into her mom's shoulder like she'd done as a child.

"In part. There's the family legacy, of course, but I thought if you came on board, your dad would be able to relax. I want us to have a lot more years together and time to have fun and enjoy life. When your dad went with Zach to see the ranch's office setup, and you took Paisley and Cam to wash their hands, I talked to Joy. She and her husband had all sorts of plans for their retirement, but then she lost him. Along with you getting hurt barrel racing or on the road, losing your dad is my biggest fear."

"Oh, Mom." Carrie hugged her. Why hadn't she realized her parents were vulnerable? And why hadn't she also realized how similar she and her dad were, both of them determined to do things themselves and their own way? "I can't imagine Dad not working, but I have an idea. Instead of me, why don't you ask Sabrina to join the business? At your birthday party, she asked lots of questions about the company, and she just finished her MBA."

"Your cousin Sabrina?" Interest and maybe even relief sparked in her mom's eyes. "Your uncle Marco and aunt Lynn never wanted her to have anything to do with Rizzo Construction. Marco has always been set on Sabrina moving to Washington and working in politics. You're too young to remember, but Marco once had political ambitions himself." She stopped and laughed. "You really think Sabrina would be interested? She lives in Seattle."

"I don't think there's much to tie her there." Between the job and how she'd looked at Dom, Sabrina would probably book a moving company before the contract paperwork was even final. "If you ask Sabrina, and she says no, then we'll have to come up with another plan." Carrie grinned. "I doubt it, though. I bet she and Dom would be perfect for each other, or if not, Dad could introduce *her* to that Gino guy."

"Your dad shouldn't have interfered. I told him it was a bad idea to try to set up you and Dom and now Gino. Your dad isn't as traditional as his parents were. Even though I come from an Italian family too, my ancestors are from the north of Italy, whereas the Rizzos are from the south. It sounds silly now, but when we got engaged, there was upset because your dad's parents wanted him to marry the daughter of a friend whose family came from the same village back in Italy."

"Really?" Carrie shook her head. "It sounds

like something that would have happened hundreds of years ago, not in the twentieth century."

"Oh yes." Her mom's smile was bittersweet. "It worked out eventually, but at the time it was hard. Your dad only wants to see you happy and settled, but he's always been a fixer and problem solver. Even though he goes about it the wrong way sometimes and doesn't listen, he has what he thinks are your best interests at heart. Like the company. Like Domenic." Awareness dawned on her mom's face. "It's Bryce Carter, isn't it?"

Carrie nodded. "I love him, Mom. I love Paisley and Cam as well. But I made a big mistake in not telling him the truth about you and the job and everything. And I don't know how to fix it." *If* she could fix it. Some of her dad's problem-solving ability would come in handy right now, but she'd created this mess, so it was up to her to deal with it.

"All you can do is try. Like you did with your dad and me today." Her mom's voice was comforting.

"What if Bryce doesn't forgive me?"

"That's up to him, but if he doesn't, forgive yourself and focus on the future. *Your* future and that ranch you want to have. Life's a journey, remember? There are lots of mistakes along the way, but hopefully we learn from them. I didn't realize it then, but growing up on the ranch was idyllic. As I grow older, I miss it. Not the work, mind you, but if that's your dream, I won't stand in your way."

Carrie hugged her mom tight, too choked up to speak.

"Now, let's go find your dad, and you can tell us about your plans for this ranch." Her mom's voice was thick with tears. "Send me your competition schedule. I'd like to come and see you ride at as many events as I can. I'm planning to go part-time with work in a few months, and when I do, maybe your dad will see sense and join me." She gave Carrie a watery smile. "I'll talk to him about Sabrina and everything else. It'll take time but he'll come around. Despite that nonsense about wanting to look after you, he knows you're a strong and independent woman, and deep down, he wouldn't want you to be any other way. My only true regret is being so busy with work that I missed out on things in your life. If you'd be open to it, I'd like us to spend more time together."

"I'd like that." Enveloped in her mom's embrace, Carrie felt the warmth, security and love she'd always found there. But now, she also found new strength and confidence. As far as work went, she'd gotten the life she wanted.

Now she had to figure out the rest—the love

and family that would make a happy life even better. And as soon as her parents left, she'd do whatever it took to earn back Bryce's trust.

CHAPTER TWENTY

LATE ON SUNDAY AFTERNOON, Bryce spread fresh straw in Maverick's stall and cleaned the automatic waterer. Carrie's parents would be on their way back to Kalispell by now, and since Teddy wasn't in his stall or the pasture, she must be out with him. Bryce had spent most of the weekend working, and in between tasks, he'd stayed home with the kids to be sure he wouldn't bump into Carrie or her folks in town.

So far, he'd avoided her at the ranch, but he still had no idea what he'd say when he saw her. And having left it that she'd turn up as usual for work tomorrow morning, he had to figure out a strategy soon.

How could he have been so wrong about the woman he'd planned to propose marriage to? He'd thought he'd known her, but he hadn't, not at all. He patted Maverick, left his stall and latched the door.

Outside the barn, the air was cool and fresh, and although it was still summer, the seasons had begun to turn. A horse's hooves clattered, voices rang out and Bryce swiveled in the direction of the creek path. One of those voices was Carrie's, and that distinctive whinny belonged to Teddy. Even though she hadn't seen him yet, it was too late to duck back into the barn or continue on to the ranch house to pick up the kids.

"Thanks, but I'm heading in." Carrie waved to Melissa, who rode Daisy-May, and Cole, on Bandit, before saying something else Bryce couldn't catch. Then she turned and spotted him in the barnyard.

He made his expression neutral. He had nothing to be embarrassed or ashamed about. He wasn't the one who'd hidden big parts of who he was.

"Hi." She stopped Teddy beside Bryce and dismounted.

"I'm on my way to the house. If you need anything, Heidi's in the barn." He rubbed Teddy's ears to avoid looking at his owner.

"I do need something. I need to explain." Carrie's face flushed red. "I wanted to come and talk to you as soon as my parents left, but you weren't at your place, and I didn't want to text."

"I've been working today. Harvest's coming." Bryce put his hands in the front pockets of his jeans so she wouldn't see them shake.

"Of course. The wheat's looking great." She

hesitated. "I wanted to apologize and say sorry again." She fiddled with Teddy's saddle. "But I also wanted to say I never meant to lie to you. My parents kept pushing me to join the family construction company, and for this summer, I wanted to avoid thinking about it and what they expected of me."

"Head of marketing's a big leap up from nannying." Bryce swallowed and tasted betrayal.

"Not for me." Carrie moved toward him, and Bryce made himself step back. "I'd hate that job or any other kind of office work. I wouldn't be good at it either, but I was too afraid of disappointing my parents to tell them the truth. That's why I let them think barrel racing and my freelance work were temporary. I'm working on it, but I've always been a people pleaser. My only true act of 'rebellion' was wanting to be a professional barrel racer. I even went to college to please my mom and my dad."

"I get they must worry about you, but…" Bryce stopped. If he kept talking, he'd be drawn to her again. She hadn't been honest with him once, what might she not be honest with him about again? He couldn't take that risk. Not for himself and not for Paisley and Cam either. "Apology accepted so let's consider the matter closed." It sounded formal, cold and unfriendly, but it was what he had to do.

"You don't understand. I'm not going back to Kalispell or taking that job with my folks or any other one. I told them the truth. When I'm not competing in rodeo, I'm staying here in High Valley. At first, I'll live with Aunt Angela, but I'm still looking for a farm of my own nearby."

No matter how much it hurt, Bryce had to tell her what he'd decided. "It was a mistake for us to develop a personal relationship. You're the kids' nanny, and I should have respected that. I put you in an awkward position." Paisley and Cam had gotten way too attached to her, but a clean break would be best for all of them. He tipped his hat. "If you'll excuse me, I'll—"

"You didn't put me in an awkward position. I'm a temporary nanny, and we didn't tell Paisley, Cam or anyone else in your family we were more than friends." Carrie's breath came out in short jerks.

Only Bryce knew he'd been a fool. That should have been comforting, but it wasn't. At least he didn't have to give uncomfortable explanations. Being with Carrie right now was hard enough. Being around her for another week—in his house and at meals—would break his shaky resolve. His mind raced, and he glanced across the barnyard to the ranch house. The T-shirt Cam had gotten ice cream on at lunch flapped on the clothesline. As Bryce watched, his mom came out of the house carrying a laundry basket.

"I'll still see you tomorrow morning, then? Around seven thirty like you asked?" Carrie's voice was hesitant. "I planned to take the kids to get new shoes and backpacks for school and then to the café afterward as a treat."

"Actually…" As the screen door shut behind Bryce's mom, something shut in his heart. His mom wouldn't mind. It would only be for a few days, and she looked after the kids all the time. "Since school starts so soon, my mom can babysit. I'll pay you for this last week, but you'll have more time to get ready for your first competition. Look at any farm and ranch properties too." His heart constricted at the thought of Carrie being so close but also far away. Still, it would be easy to avoid her, and when their paths did cross, he'd be friendly like with any other acquaintance.

"Your mom? But I haven't said goodbye to Paisley and Cam. I can't disappear on them. I also meet my commitments." Carrie's voice was tight, and her eyes shone with unshed tears.

"You can still drop by any day this week. Just let my mom know beforehand." And Bryce would make sure he was in the outlying fields, where there was no cell phone service, so he wouldn't give in to the temptation to call Carrie. "Don't worry about not meeting a commitment. I'm releasing you from it." So why did he feel like a jerk? "You could even take a vacation. Leave Teddy here as long as you need." He wanted to be generous, but even to his own ears, he sounded pompous.

"I'll pick up the things I left at your place when I say goodbye to the kids." Carrie sniffed and smoothed Teddy's mane. "I'll also find somewhere to board Teddy as soon as I can. Maybe at Diana's. She has a few empty stalls in her barn."

"Good." The backs of Bryce's eyes burned. He'd never broken up with a woman before, and it hurt. "Take care."

"You as well." She led Teddy into the barn, and the horse's hooves made a dull clopping sound on the hard-packed dirt.

And as Bryce went to the ranch house, he tried to convince himself he'd done the right thing. He'd miss Carrie for a while. The kids would too. But any relationship, especially a marriage, had to be based on honesty and trust. He couldn't risk his heart, or his family, on any other kind.

CARRIE KEPT HERSELF together while she stabled Teddy and chatted to Heidi as if nothing was wrong. She also kept herself together while she drove back to town. But as soon as she turned into Angela's driveway and parked her pickup in the space beside her aunt's car, the tears came.

She rested her head on the steering wheel and gave in to emotion. Bryce didn't want her. She'd betrayed his trust, and he'd never forgive her. Gulping back sobs, she grabbed a handful of tissues from the box on the console.

She'd never forgive herself either. If only she'd stood up to her parents long ago. If only she'd been honest with Bryce from the start. However, it was pointless to ruminate on what might have been. Somehow, she had to come to terms with what was.

After blowing her nose, she stared out the truck window at Angela's backyard. A vegetable garden occupied one side of the property, while a profusion of flowers and herbs bordered a patio with a lawn swing and glass-topped table surrounded by chairs. Shade trees edged the fence to give the yard privacy, and the two-story, white-painted house with green trim drowsed in the late-afternoon sunshine, blinds closed against the heat. It was peaceful and, in a more rural setting instead of in town, the kind of house Carrie wanted for herself one day.

She unclipped her seat belt, got out of the truck on wobbly legs and aimed for the swing near a patch of purple alpine asters.

"Carrie?" The back door of the house opened, and then Angela was beside her and wrapped Carrie in a hug. "What's wrong? I heard your truck and then when you didn't come inside, I… Oh, honey."

Her aunt's kindness made Carrie dissolve into tears again. "Everything's wrong, and I don't know how to make it better."

Ginger, the small white mixed-breed dog Angela had adopted from the local shelter, hopped onto the swing and nosed Carrie's arm.

"Does this trouble have anything to do with Bryce Carter?" Angela's expression was wry.

"Did my mom—"

"She didn't say a word. I guessed." Angela rubbed Carrie's back in a soothing motion.

"I didn't tell Bryce something I should have, and I said I was sorry, but it's no good. He's paying me for my last week of nannying, but his mom's looking after the kids. If I stay here, I'll see him, and—"

"That's his problem, not yours." With a final pat, Angela released Carrie. "As for Joy looking after Paisley and Cam, I talked to her not more than an hour ago, and she didn't mention anything." Her eyes narrowed. "Don't let Bryce run you out of town. I hope you aren't thinking that way."

Before this summer, that was exactly what Carrie would have thought. She'd have packed her bags and hit the road, leaving her troubles behind as easily as she moved between rodeos on the competition circuit. But she was different now, and despite Bryce, those changes were good.

"It crossed my mind but no. I love High Valley. I have friends here. Family. You." She gave her aunt a tentative smile. "I want to make my home here." In addition, Paisley and Cam had already lost their mom and grandfather, and she didn't want them to lose her too.

"Then let's go."

"Go where?" Carrie raised her tearstained face to stare at her aunt.

"We have some farms to look at."

Angela collected her purse from the patio table and scooped up Ginger. "The old Sutton place is coming back on the market. Something to do with the previous buyer's financing falling through. Billy and Marie Hogue's farm will be up for sale soon as well. For the right buyer, they'd likely take less than the asking price."

Carrie gulped and took more tissues from Angela. She'd heard how fast news traveled in High Valley, but this was the first time she'd experienced the efficiency of the local grapevine herself. "Don't we have to make an appointment with a Realtor and wait until both places are actually *on* the market?"

Angela laughed. "For the Sutton farm, yes, so we'll have to look at it from the road. However, I talked to Marie Hogue after church, and she said we'd be welcome to drop by—informally, of course—any time. My mamma would be so happy the money she left you will go to realize your dream. If you'd told me what you wanted earlier, I could have contributed from the start, but it's not too late."

"That's really nice, but I can't accept your financial help."

"You can, and you will. Come along." Angela gestured to her vehicle, and Carrie followed her. "My husband and I weren't blessed with children, and this summer, well…" She stopped and buckled Ginger into the pet restraint in the rear seat. "You've become like a daughter to me. If you need a bit extra for a down payment, I want to give you money now I'd have left you after I'm gone."

"But…" Carrie settled into the passenger seat as her aunt got behind the wheel.

"No *buts*." Angela gave her an impish grin. "We're family. Although I lost sight of it for a while, family comes first. Understand?"

"Yes, ma'am." Carrie grinned back. Although she could be crusty on the outside, underneath Angela was kind and loving. Carrie would find the means to pay her back, but right now she'd accept her aunt's generosity in the spirit it was given.

"I can see the wheels turning in that smart

and pretty head of yours." Angela accelerated out of the driveway and headed for the highway. "I don't want to hear any talk of repayment. I'm not rich, but your uncle's estate is finally settled, and I have enough. I worried for more than a year about how I'd manage, but now? I have more money than I ever expected, and that's the truth. Having you nearby for keeps will be a blessing, and I'm a fortunate woman."

"I'm fortunate too." More tears threatened, but they were happy ones this time. "Thank you."

"I should be thanking you." Angela tooted the horn at Kristi outside the Bluebunch Café. "After your uncle passed, I was angry. I didn't like myself, and I suspect a lot of folks didn't like me either. Nina stuck with me, though, and made me see I wasn't helping myself or anyone else by being cross, bitter and judgmental. Then Melissa and her sweet Skylar came into my life, along with the Sunflower Sisterhood. Thanks to their friendship and after reconciling with your mother and having you to stay, I'm truly living again."

Guilt slithered through Carrie, and she looked out the passenger window at a garden edged with pink and white hollyhocks. "Apart from when I first came to High Valley, we've hardly spent any time together."

"You're young, and you have your own life.

Knowing you were around made all the difference." She gave Carrie a fond smile. "Bryce Carter will come to his senses, you'll see, but no matter what, you have to go on and live your own life."

Carrie did have to go on, and looking at properties was only the start. "Which place are we seeing first?"

"The Hogue's farm. It's closer to town, and I also hear there's a problem with the septic system at the Sutton place."

"How did you—"

Angela shook her head and slid her thumb and index finger from one side of her mouth to the other.

Yet more information via High Valley's unofficial news source. Carrie focused on the landscape, its vastness healing and filling some of the empty, hurting places in her soul.

Ten minutes later, Angela turned onto a gravel road that dipped into a small valley before coming out again onto flatter land. In the distance, a white mailbox sat at the end of a long tree-shaded lane.

"Did you hear anything about the Hogue place?"

"From all accounts, it's in good order." Angela turned into the lane with the mailbox. "Billy and Marie have done well, and they both come from successful farming and ranching families. Now that I think of it, Marie's related to the Carters on her mother's side."

Carrie hugged herself. She'd have to get used to casual references to Bryce's family. They hurt now, but it would get easier in time. It had to. She looked at the fields on either side of the lane. One was pastureland where two bay quarter horses grazed. The other side lay fallow, and while it looked like an untended pile of dirt, Carrie knew better. There was a lot going on underneath, and this time of rest would lead to higher crop yields in the future.

As they came to the end of the lane and pulled up in front of the farmhouse, she drew in a soft breath. A white frame house, with three upstairs gable windows trimmed in blue, nestled against a low hill sheltered by trees. A wide porch wrapped around the house on three sides, and a white barn, also trimmed in blue, snuggled amidst more trees.

"Pretty, isn't it? A bit like my place in terms of architecture and layout. The house could use a coat of fresh paint, but that's minor. Billy's not as spry as he once was, and he's never been one to hire anyone for jobs he'd rather do himself. They'll miss this place, but Marie wants to move into town to make things easier for Billy." Angela got out of the car and unbuckled Ginger. The dog dashed out to greet a golden retriever, who said hello with several happy barks and a wagging tail.

"It's beautiful." A vegetable patch sat to one side of the house, and in a field beyond, ripe wheat waved against a sailor-blue sky dotted with high white clouds.

"In terms of acres, it's smaller than the Sutton place, but Billy and Marie have made the most of what they have." Angela tucked her car keys into her purse and waved to a couple in their late seventies or early eighties who'd come out of the house and onto the porch.

"It's perfect." And just like that, thoughts of the Sutton farm fled, and Carrie fell in love. She hadn't walked the fields, seen inside the house or checked out the barn, but she felt the rightness of this place down to her bones. Her name wasn't on the title, but the Hogue place was already hers in her heart. She could picture Teddy in that pasture and her own crops growing in this earth. She could also see herself on that porch with friends, family and, one day, when she didn't travel as much, a dog. Maybe she'd raise goats too, along with offering horse boarding.

Unlike men, horses were easy to understand, and a horse had never hurt her like Jimmy and Bryce had. She turned in a slow circle as contentment washed over and through her. She wouldn't run away or give up the life she wanted because Bryce had let her down. And while she'd let Bryce down too, if he were truly the man she wanted to spend her life with, he'd have listened to her, understood her and genuinely forgiven her, instead of pushing her away.

"What do you want to see first? The house or the barn and fields?" A small smile played around Angela's mouth.

"The barn and fields." Although where Carrie would live was important, the barn and surrounding fields would be at the heart of her new life. A life that would be good, rich and full in things that mattered and fulfilled her—even without Bryce.

CHAPTER TWENTY-ONE

"WHEN WERE YOU going to mention you expected me to babysit Paisley and Cam this week?" On Sunday evening, Joy waylaid Bryce as he came out of the barn after late chores. "Who's watching the kids now?"

"Ellie. I hired her to babysit tonight and tomorrow morning until noon. After that, I can watch them while I work from home. I was going to talk to you soon. Like now." He looked everywhere but at Joy. "How did you find out?"

"Angela Moretti called me with a question about the next Sunflower Sisterhood meeting. She mentioned it was good of me to fill in on short notice since Carrie wasn't working for you this week." In the light coming from above the barn door, Joy studied her son. Unshaven, his eyes dark-shadowed, hair unkempt and shirt buttoned the wrong way, he looked almost as bad as he had after Ally passed.

"Did Angela say anything else?" Bryce's voice sounded anguished.

"No, should she have?" Joy resisted the urge to smooth the lock of hair that tumbled across her son's forehead. Even if he was behaving like a child, he was a grown man.

"No, of course not. So, can you look after Paisley and Cam? I let Carrie leave early. She has stuff to do with getting ready for her first official competition."

"You 'let' her leave? I suspect you 'told' her to go because something happened between the two of you."

"It's…over." Bryce shrugged, but the casual gesture didn't mask his hurt.

"I'll look after the children, but I'm doing it for their sake, not yours."

"Thanks, Mom. We can always count on you."

That was one of the problems. "No, you can't. I'm not your on-call free babysitter." Joy had to take a firm stand with her son for his own good and hers. Although Bryce didn't know it, her life was about to change. Once she and Shane were married, Bryce and the rest of the family would have to get used to Joy not always being as available to them as she was now.

"What do you mean?" Bryce finally met Joy's gaze.

"I love Paisley, Cam and you, but one of the reasons I said I couldn't provide full-time childcare this summer was because you were relying on me too much."

"But I—"

"It's the truth, and it's partly my fault. I didn't say no before, but by forcing you to find someone else, I made you take a step forward—a step you needed to start rebuilding your life." She touched Bryce's stiff shoulder. "Carrie made the kids happy, and she seemed to make you happy too. She was a good influence on all three of you, and I was glad."

"I let myself get personally involved with her, and that was wrong." Bryce examined his boots.

"How so? Ally wanted you to find happiness again." And although Ally had also asked Joy to encourage Bryce to be open to a new relationship, until this summer he hadn't been ready.

"She told you too?" Her son's voice cracked.

"Ally and I had lots of talks in the last few weeks of her life. She was taken too soon, but she made the most of the time she had. You could learn from her example." Joy needed to get through to Bryce, but how?

"Carrie's great, but she's not Ally."

"Of course not, and you wouldn't want her to be." Joy exhaled with frustration but also understanding. She'd been where Bryce was, but unlike him, she hadn't stayed stuck there.

"I don't, but it's not the right time. Maybe

when the kids are grown, I'll meet someone. Besides, Carrie's not ready to settle down. She's going back to barrel racing."

"Maybe you're thinking about 'settling' the wrong way. Some barrel racers have husbands and children. If they make it work, there's no reason you and Carrie couldn't do the same." Bryce had always been stubborn, and when he made a decision, he stuck to it. While that was a good quality in many ways and made for a devoted and committed husband, it could also be infuriating. Now, he was making excuses for why he and Carrie weren't right for each other.

"I appreciate you want to help, but it's my business not yours."

"It's partly my business because you're my son, and it concerns your happiness as well as my grandchildren's." Joy glanced at the horse trough filled with cold, fresh water and briefly considered dunking her son's head in it to shock some sense into him. "Breaking off whatever relationship you had with Carrie and not allowing yourself to see where it might go is a big mistake. For you as well as Paisley and Cam."

"Drop it, Mom. I know what I'm doing." Bryce closed and locked the barn door with a clatter.

"I hope so, but if you find you're wrong, it's okay to change your mind." She patted his arm, but he shrugged off her touch. "Remember hockey? You were so determined to play because Zach and Cole did, but it took you most of two seasons, and the coach talking to me and your dad, to get you to admit you really wanted to try curling instead."

"It's not the same. Besides, I was good at hockey. Not like Zach, but at least as good as Cole." Bryce started across the barnyard, and Joy followed him.

"But you excelled at curling, and you loved it. You still do." Joy and Dennis had tried to make sure their kids knew they were valued as individuals and had discouraged them from competing with each other. Even if they'd missed the mark with Bryce, it wasn't too late. "Whether it's in sports or life, as much as you can, you should do what gives *you* joy. There are always chores like shoveling manure." She tried to joke. "But there are wonderful things too, and I thought you'd found something special with Carrie."

"Can I drop the kids off with you at seven thirty on Tuesday morning? I'll make sure they eat beforehand."

"Forget about breakfast. They can eat with your brothers and the ranch hands." Joy bit back everything else she wanted to say. Like that old proverb her nana used to quote, "You can lead a horse to water, but you can't make it drink."

"Thanks, Mom. You're the best." As they

reached the gate in the fence dividing the barnyard from the lane leading to the ranch house,
he gave her a one-armed hug.

"You're the best too." She returned the hug.
"I only hope you realize it."

She'd done what she could to help Bryce, but
now he had to help himself. Changing himself,
and changing his life, had to come from him because *he* wanted it, not because of Joy or anyone else.

BEHIND ONE OF the long tables set up in the ele-
mentary school's playground, Carrie stacked
paper plates and napkins alongside platters of
precut vegetables, bananas, cookies and other
kid-friendly snacks. "I'm glad you asked me to
join you." She smiled at Melissa, who set water
bottles and juice cartons on an adjacent table.
"It's fun to share the back-to-school excitement."
Volunteering at the school's welcome back barbecue, a tradition in High Valley on the Friday
afternoon before school officially started, also
made Carrie feel part of the community.

"Since I'm the newest member of the PTA and
don't know many others yet, I'm glad you're here
to keep me company." Melissa greeted a kindergarten student who clutched her big brother's
hand, a boy Carrie recognized from the field
trip in June. It had only been a few months, but

since then, everything had changed, especially Carrie herself.

Across from the tables, on what was usually the basketball court, Zach, Cole and Bryce manned barbecues along with Ellie and several other teens. "Here you go." Carrie spooned carrot strips and cherry tomatoes onto a paper plate for Skylar. "Have a great year at school." Carrie needed to focus on the kids, not Bryce.

When Skylar grinned and showed Carrie the new sneakers Melissa had taken her to buy, Carrie's heart hurt a bit more. She'd missed back-to-school shoe shopping with Paisley and Cam, and she also missed them almost as much as she missed their dad. Except for a brief goodbye at Bryce's house, when the kids and Joy had been as teary as Carrie, she hadn't seen them in almost a week.

"Carrie." A pair of arms went around her waist as Cam hugged her.

"Where have you been?" She hugged him back and then embraced Paisley. "I looked for both of you as soon as I got here."

"I helped my new teacher put up posters and organize the art cupboard," Cam said with quiet pride.

"I helped too," Paisley chimed in. "Mrs. Benson used to be my teacher." She clung to Carrie's hand. "I miss you. Grandma's fun, but she's not you."

"I miss you." Carrie swallowed a ball of emotion. "But I was only ever going to be your nanny for the summer."

Paisley fiddled with a piece of hair. "Daddy's been really grumpy since you left."

"It's harvest season. He's likely tired from getting the crops in and the cattle moved." Despite that immediate twinge of concern, Bryce's mood wasn't Carrie's business. "Did you hear I bought a farm? I'm staying in High Valley, so that's good news, isn't it?" She made her voice cheerful. It *was* good news. The best. And she was determined to focus on what she had, not what she didn't.

Carrie had made an offer on the Hogue farm as soon as it was officially on the market. Billy and Marie had accepted it, and she'd take possession in mid-October. Between rodeo and everything she needed to get organized before the sale closed, she'd be too busy to think about Bryce.

"Ms. Kristi told us about your farm. It sounds nice." Paisley didn't even smile when Carrie added an extra cookie to her plate.

"If it's okay with your dad, you can both visit me. I bet there are dinosaur fossils there, Cam."

The unhappy expression Cam had had when he was being bullied was back, and he shook his head when Carrie offered him cucumber sticks with his favorite dip.

"How's everything at the ranch?" She missed it too, but to avoid bumping into Bryce, Carrie made her visits to Teddy brief.

"Okay, I guess." Cam shrugged. "I talk to Teddy when I do chores with Uncle Cole."

"Teddy appreciates you checking in on him. I do as well." She'd given notice at the Carters' barn and would move Teddy to Diana's ranch the following weekend. Cam would soon miss Teddy too. "Have a great year at school." She made herself repeat what she'd already said to all the other kids.

"Oh, Carrie." Cam hugged her again and pressed his face into her shirt. "Can't you come back to look after us?"

"Please?" Paisley's voice was pleading. "It's not the same without you. Grandma doesn't play like you, and riding lessons aren't the same with Uncle Cole. He knows about barrel racing, but he doesn't do it himself. And when I asked Daddy if we could go to one of your competitions, he said he'd see. That usually means no."

"Your dad knows what's best for you." Carrie's voice cracked, and she focused on the school's vibrant Welcome Back banner so she wouldn't look at the kids and cry. "You'd better go get a hot dog or hamburger."

"I'm not hungry." Cam still clung to her.

"I'm not either." Paisley set her plate back on the table.

"Come on, kids. Carrie's busy, and you're holding up the line." Bryce joined his children. "I took a break to help you get food."

"Carrie did that already." Paisley made a sulky face.

"Can we go home?" Cam gave Carrie another hug before she gently extricated herself from his grasp.

"We can't go home until my volunteer shift finishes." Above the children's heads, Bryce's gaze met Carrie's. "Congratulations on buying the Hogue farm."

"Thanks. I'm excited about having my own place." And Billy and Marie were thrilled Carrie would take care of the property as they had.

"The soil quality's excellent near that ridge." Bryce took Paisley's and Cam's plates and moved the kids along. "Good luck with whatever you plant. Winter wheat should do well there."

"I'll keep that in mind." Carrie made herself nod and smile as if Bryce were any other parent.

Then he and the kids were gone, and Carrie was once again left with a hole in her heart—and her life—bigger than the big Montana sky.

"Are you okay?" Melissa's face was filled with compassion. "I can look after both tables if you need a break. As long as she sits down, Beth can help too." Melissa indicated Zach's wife, who was unpacking more water bottles from a box the grocery store had donated.

"I'm fine." If Carrie took a break, she'd fall apart, and she didn't want Melissa or anyone else to know how much she was hurting.

"You're not really, but I understand." Melissa's voice was gentle. "If you need to talk, I'm here."

"Me too." Beth joined them. "The Carter guys are great, but..." She hesitated.

"Sometimes they're also maddening and frustrating." Melissa rolled her eyes. "Bryce has to realize how fantastic you are for him and the kids."

"Of course, he will," Beth added. "He's stubborn, but we saw how he acted around you."

Carrie tried to smile. Melissa and Beth meant well, but they didn't know Bryce like Carrie did. They also didn't know how she'd betrayed his trust. While part of her would always love him, she had to move on.

Letting herself hope for a miracle would only lead to more heartache.

CHAPTER TWENTY-TWO

"SORRY WE'RE LATE, MOM." On Saturday afternoon, at the end of the first week of school, Bryce greeted Joy in the ranch house kitchen. "Hey, Molly. Great to see you." He hugged his sister, who'd flown in from Atlanta the night before, and Paisley and Cam welcomed their aunt with excited cries.

Before this week, Bryce had been certain he'd done the right thing by sending Carrie away. However, everything was a mess, himself most of all, and things weren't getting any better. He was lonely, and even when everyone was home, the house still felt empty, as if its heart and soul had been ripped out. And seeing the affection between Carrie, Paisley and Cam at the school barbecue was a poignant reminder of what, and who, they were all missing.

"We've been waiting for you." His mom's face was pink, and her blue eyes sparkled. "Come through to the family room. Everyone's here, as well as Shane and his kids and grandchildren.

The buffet table's ready, but we wanted to tell you something first."

"We?" Bryce glanced at Molly, but she looked puzzled too.

"Shane and I." His mom was almost girlish as she led them to join the others. Bryce's folks had loved hosting informal parties, and after his dad passed, his mom had continued the tradition on her own. This get-together was to celebrate Molly's return home for a short vacation, so why was Shane's extended family here? And why was his usually casually dressed mom wearing a filmy blue-and-gray floral-patterned dress and heels?

"Shane." Bryce shook hands with the older man. Instead of his usual jeans and T-shirt, Shane wore beige dress pants, a white shirt open at the collar and a navy jacket.

"Thanks for joining us." Shane looked around the family room, where everyone talked in small groups. "If I could have your attention for a moment, please?" He took Bryce's mom's hand. "Joy and I want to share some news with you."

Conversation ceased, and expectant faces turned toward them. Bryce joined Zach and Cole by one of the big windows that overlooked the horse pasture.

Standing beside Shane in front of the fireplace, his mom's smile mixed happiness with apprehension.

"Last month, I asked Joy to marry me, and she said yes." Shane beamed. "I'm a lucky man, and I'll be honored to call her my wife."

Muted clapping broke out, but Joy held up a hand to ask for silence.

"Neither of us expected to find love again, but we did, and I'm grateful." Joy looked at each of her children in turn, and her gaze lingered on Bryce. "I'll always love my first husband, Dennis, like Shane will always love and remember your mom, Bonnie." She smiled at Shane's kids. "But there's room in our hearts for each other, and we hope you'll be happy for us."

"Of course, we are." Zach stepped forward to offer congratulations, and then, led by Cole, the room erupted in applause, whistles and cheers.

As everyone surrounded the happy couple and admired Joy's engagement ring, Bryce hung back. He liked Shane, and Shane and his mom were a good match, so why did he feel so empty and miserable? He made himself congratulate his mom and Shane too, join in the toast Zach and Shane's oldest daughter proposed and then, although he wasn't hungry, fill a plate with food from the buffet.

"You're happy for us, truly?" His mom stopped him by the punch bowl.

"Yeah, I am." He made himself smile. "Shane's a good man. Dad would have liked him."

His mom's expression softened. "Me marrying Shane will change things, of course, but I'll still be nearby to help you when I can. As an engagement present, Shane gave me that land your dad and I had to sell to pay some of Paul's medical bills. We want to build a house there."

"That's great." Bryce filled a glass with fruit punch. "It's also fantastic to have the land back in the family. I bet it won't be long before Cole asks to use some of it for his stock contracting venture."

"He already has." His mom laughed. "Your brother never holds back in asking for what he wants."

Bryce laughed too, but it was hollow. His mom and Shane having a new home together made sense, but it also meant his mom was moving on, and their family, the heart of which was this ranch house, wouldn't be the same. "Be happy, Mom. That's all any of us want for you. It's what Dad would have wanted too."

She hugged him before going to talk with Shane's daughters and their husbands.

As Bryce filled glasses with fruit punch for the kids, his thoughts drifted to Ally. Why could he tell his mom to be happy and not put that advice into practice for himself?

He no longer felt guilty or that he was betraying Ally by letting himself care for Carrie. However, Carrie not telling him about her folks expecting her to return to Kalispell and work for the family business stung. It was more than that, though. Faced with her obvious remorse, anyone else would likely have been able to forgive her and go back to the way they'd been with each other, but he hadn't. That was about him, not Carrie.

He set his drink and untouched plate of food aside and returned to the window as the party went on around him. Daisy-May, Maverick and most of the other horses grazed peacefully in the sunlit pasture. Bryce had taught Ally to ride with Daisy-May, and she'd loved the gentle horse. The scene blurred as memories tumbled through Bryce's mind. Ally as a teenager riding alongside him. Their college graduations and then Ally on their wedding day. A few years later, Ally giving birth to their babies. And then Ally getting sick and how Bryce had been so sure the doctors would make her better.

He grabbed the window frame to steady himself as realization shot through him. He'd lost his wife, the person he'd loved most in the world. But until now, he hadn't understood why and how that loss meant he hadn't been able to truly move on.

With Carrie, letting himself love her had gotten mixed up with those awful memories of loving and losing Ally and made him afraid to love and lose again. He'd used Carrie not being fully honest with him as an excuse. Instead, Bryce hadn't been honest with himself—or her.

He finally knew what he wanted and what he had to do to get it, but he had to do something else, something just as important, first.

Whirling away from the window, he asked Melissa and Beth to keep an eye on Paisley and Cam and give his apologies to his mom and Shane. Then Bryce left the ranch house at a run and got into his truck.

Fifteen minutes later, he parked by the fence outside High Valley's cemetery. It occupied several acres of rolling land alongside a small stream tucked behind the town's first church.

He walked past older gravestones to the newer part of the cemetery and found Ally's marker with her name and birth and death dates. *Beloved daughter, sister, wife and mother.* The backs of his eyes smarted as he knelt on the grass by the stone.

"I've been an idiot." He glanced around, but there was nobody nearby except a white-haired man by a grave a few rows over. Now retired, Mr. Kuntz used to manage the feedstore. He'd lost his wife young and had never remarried or, as far as Bryce knew, even dated. Now, with his kids grown and scattered across several states, he was on his own.

In the light breeze that rustled the trees, Bryce could almost hear Ally's laughter. "What have you done this time?" He could almost hear her voice too and picture her teasing expression.

He rubbed a hand across his forehead. How to explain what he'd only just understood himself? "Even though you aren't here, you're still in my heart. You always will be. You're part of Paisley and Cam too. You'd be so proud of them. But now…" He took a deep breath. "I've met a wonderful woman, and there's room in my heart for both of you. I love her. Carrie's good for me and the kids, but I ruined everything."

"You can make it better." Ally's voice was so clear it was like she was beside him. "You make everything better."

She'd always had faith in him, but after she died, Bryce had lost faith in himself and, apart from the kids, everyone else. "The whole time you were sick, and then when you passed, I wanted to be there for you like always…" He gulped. "I did my best but I've been so scared. I was scared of losing you, and since then, I've been scared of losing the kids. I've also been scared of letting myself care for anyone else. I know you wanted me to be happy, but I couldn't. I bet you understood all that, even though I didn't."

More laughter, but this time it was loving, and the wind brushed his face like a tender kiss.

Anyone overhearing him would think he'd lost his mind but instead, Bryce had found it again and found himself too.

"I have to go, but I'll be back soon and with Paisley and Cam. I stayed away because I couldn't face coming here, so I kept the kids away. That was wrong. But now, we'll bring you your favorite flowers, and I bet Cam will want to draw you a picture of Daisy-May. Paisley can tell you about girl stuff she doesn't want to share with me." He looked at Mr. Kuntz, who held a framed photo and, with his head bent, seemed to be talking to it like Bryce was talking to Ally. "I love you, Ally, but I love Carrie too, and I need to go tell her."

If he didn't, and if he let the fear of loving and losing stop him, he'd end up like Mr. Kuntz, alone and talking to someone who could never answer back.

When instead, Bryce could have a life rich in love, family and everything else that, with Carrie by his side, would make the rest of his years better.

While he hoped it wasn't too late for Mr. Kuntz, either, what if, in the end, *he* was too late? *No.* Bryce ran back to the truck and jumped into it to head to Angela's house. He'd fight for Carrie's love as long and as hard as it took. And rather than living his life in fear, from now on he'd live it with hope—in himself, in her and in their family.

CARRIE LED TEDDY out of the barn and into the horse trailer. "I know, buddy. You've been happy at the Tall Grass Ranch, but you'll be happy at Diana's too. Besides, it's only a few days until we're on the road again." She loaded Teddy into the compartment, closed the door and tied him down but left the outside window open so he could look around while she returned to the barn to retrieve a few last things.

From Teddy's peg in the tack room, she picked up his saddle blanket and a set of reins, and then, for the last time, walked along the barn's central aisle.

The horses usually stabled in this part of the barn were out in the pasture, so it was quiet apart from the soft coo of pigeons and the rustle of barn cats playing in the straw.

"Bye, boy." Mr. Wiggins wrapped himself around Carrie's ankles, and she bent to scratch his ears. "Look after Bryce and the kids for me, okay?"

In the barnyard once again, she stopped to silently say a final goodbye.

Cars and trucks were still parked near the ranch house for Molly's welcome home party, and while Carrie had been inside the barn, people had spilled out of the house onto the porch. Although Joy had invited her to the party, Carrie had thanked her but declined. It had been hard enough to be around Bryce and the kids at the school's barbecue. A family gathering would be much harder, and Carrie wasn't ready to face that yet, if ever.

She turned back to the trailer to close Teddy's window, but as she patted him, a pickup truck sped along the gravel driveway and squealed to a stop by the fence.

It was Bryce's truck, but he never drove that fast. Yet, it *was* him. Carrie shaded her eyes against the bright sunlight as his familiar figure, topped by a white cowboy hat, opened the barnyard gate and ran toward her.

"Thank goodness you're here." Bryce skidded to a halt, put a hand to his side and gasped for breath. "I went to Angela's first. She said you'd come out to the ranch to load Teddy an hour or so ago, so you might be at Diana's by now. I'd have gone there next."

Carrie should have been at Diana's, but she'd lingered here because it was hard to say goodbye to a place that meant so much to her. "I'm on my way." She gestured to her truck as Teddy looked at them out of the still open trailer window.

"Please wait. I have to explain. And say I'm sorry. So, so sorry." Bryce's face was red, and his expression was both desperate and despairing. "Please, will you give me a few minutes and listen?"

"Okay." Carrie's heart pounded.

"When your folks were here, and I found out they expected you to go back to Kalispell and take that big, important job, I was hurt and angry you hadn't told me."

"I should have, and I'm sorry too, but—"

"Forget it." Bryce gulped. "Yes, you should have been honest, but what you did or didn't do isn't why I pushed you away. It's because of something else." He came closer, and from the horse trailer, Teddy neighed. "It's about me, not you."

"I don't understand." Carrie stared at his dear, familiar face with the serious, now anguished blue-gray eyes that saw into her soul.

"I only just figured it out myself. As soon as I did, I had to find you." He took off his hat and held it in front of him. "I ended things between us because I was scared. I was so afraid of losing you that I couldn't let myself love you in case I lost you like I lost Ally."

"But I'm not sick, at least, not that I know of."

Carrie's voice shook, and she clutched the saddle blanket and reins.

"No, but I've been letting fear rule my life in all kinds of ways. I don't want to live like that anymore." He took a deep breath and got down on one knee. "I love you, Carrie. Please give me another chance. I'd like us to be a family. You, me and Paisley and Cam. You're going away, and I... I want to fix things between us before it's too late. Will you marry me?"

"Marry you?" Love, happiness and excitement fizzed inside Carrie. When she'd let herself imagine a proposal, it had never been in a barnyard, but this was real, right and perfect. She didn't need flowers, candlelight or a fancy meal. She only needed Bryce.

"Yes, please marry me because I need you by my side and want us to build a life together. I'll support you in rodeo, on your farm and in everything else. I'll be there for you no matter what, to care for you and love you forever. And maybe, if you're willing and the timing's right, we'll have a child or two of our own one day." Bryce's face held all the kindness, loyalty and trust Carrie could ever want.

Teddy neighed again, louder this time, and Carrie glanced back at him. He nodded as if he understood and was giving his approval. Having Teddy nearby made this moment even more perfect.

"Yes, I'll marry you." She dropped the saddle blanket and reins and took Bryce's hands to pull him to his feet. His cowboy hat went flying, but he ignored it, his gaze focused only on her. "I love you, but I need you to promise me something."

"Anything." He moved to draw her into his arms, but Carrie stayed where she was.

"From now on, we have to trust each other with the hard things along with the good and sharing our fears. Can you do that with me?"

"Yes." His voice caught. "It's hard, but I know I'll be able to do it with you by my side."

"Just like I know *I'll* always be able to truly be myself with you by my side. You 'get me.'"

Bryce gave her a teasing grin. "Now can I kiss you?"

"I can't think of anything I'd like more."

As their lips met in a kiss to seal their future, Teddy snorted, and then Daisy-May, Maverick and several other horses joined in from the pasture while a cheer went up over by the house.

"Come here, kids." As Carrie and Bryce drew apart, she gestured to Paisley and Cam, who along with Joy, Molly, Bryce's brothers and their wives now hovered in an excited group by the barnyard fence.

"We've got something important to tell you."

Bryce kept one arm around Carrie and hugged the kids with the other after they ran to join them.

"Are we gonna be a family for real?" Paisley stared wide-eyed between them.

"For absolutely real," Bryce said.

"For always? You promise?" Cam wrapped his arms around Carrie's waist as if he feared she'd disappear, and he was determined to hold her in place."

"I promise. Forever and always." And as Carrie looked at Bryce over the children's heads, her vow was as important as the one she'd make in front of a preacher. "I do."

EPILOGUE

JUST OVER A month later, Bryce rode Maverick across harvested fields and along the lane to what was once the Hogue farm but now belonged to Carrie. On this Saturday afternoon, the October sun lay in mellow ribbons across the fields, and the farmhouse gleamed with fresh white paint with blue trim and a matching blue front door.

As Bryce rounded a curve, Carrie came toward him on Teddy. They met under one of the big trees that lined the lane, its leaves now russet, orange and gold. "I missed you when I was in Texas." she said, leaning across Teddy's saddle to greet him with a kiss.

"I missed you too." He took her left hand, on which she wore the simple solitaire diamond he'd given her to mark their engagement.

"The outside of the house looks great. You and your family did a fantastic job finishing what I started. Thank you. I wish I could have been here for the painting party weekend." Carrie and Teddy rode beside Bryce and Maverick as they made their way along a field where Carrie had seeded winter wheat.

"I wish you could have been here too, but that's rodeo life. It's hard being apart when you're competing, but it also makes our time together even more special." He took her hand again. "It's not official yet, but you're a Carter in all but name."

She smiled and squeezed his hand. "I've been thinking about our wedding. I'm keeping the name Carrie Rizzo for barrel racing, but everywhere else I'll be Carrie Carter." She drew Teddy to a stop under a towering American red maple, the tree now the brilliant autumn red of its moniker.

"And?" Bryce stopped Maverick. He wanted to marry Carrie as soon as possible, but she had a busy competition schedule, and he didn't want to push her. They'd get married when the time was right and they were both ready. They also needed to figure out where they'd live and all the other details that went into making a life together.

"What would you think about having a double wedding with your mom and Shane at Thanksgiving?" She squeezed his hand once more. "Before you say anything, hear me out."

"Okay." Bryce nodded and tried to contain his excitement.

"My mom and dad are finally okay with me not joining Rizzo Construction, and my cousin's doing great at the job that was supposed to be mine. She and Dom have hit it off too, so everybody's happy. But…" She hesitated and gave Bryce a half smile. "Now my folks, my dad especially, want our wedding to be this huge extravaganza with hundreds of guests, a multicourse sit-down dinner and me in an enormous dress and veil flanked by an entourage of bridesmaids, flower girls and all the rest."

"If that's what you want, it's okay. Truly." Although the thought of such an elaborate wedding made Bryce cringe, marriage was about give and take, and compromise started long before they exchanged vows.

"It's not." Carrie gave a mock shudder. "I told my parents that, but they've asked me to take more time to think about it. I don't want a big wedding, and I'm not going to change my mind, but it's still uncomfortable and awkward."

"You're getting good at standing up for yourself." Bryce teased her gently. "You're getting good at winning first-place ribbons too. Between us, the kids, your folks, rodeo, this farm and freelance projects, I'm so proud of how you're handling everything." He was in awe, but together they were learning how to make their careers and family work. He leaned in for another kiss.

Carrie kissed him back and then laughed. "Although my parents will be disappointed that I don't want the wedding they're dreaming of giving me, they'll come around in the end. Look at how my mom and I convinced Dad to semi-retire and spend summers here." She hesitated again. "If we get married at the same time as your mom and Shane, I could have the simple, no-fuss wedding I want. We could also start our married life sooner. And Molly and your other out-of-state family members wouldn't have to make two trips here."

"You'd like that?" Happiness rolled over Bryce, along with love—the kind that would last a lifetime.

"I would." She nodded and patted Teddy. "I'd like to include some of my family's Italian traditions, though."

"I'd like that a lot." Bryce swallowed as emotion threatened to overwhelm him. "As long as my mom's okay with it, that kind of wedding would be perfect."

"Your mom thinks it's a great idea. In fact, she suggested it." Carrie's cheeks went pink. "I talked to her earlier when I was driving home. I called her about that exhibition of Paul's art we're putting together, and then we got talking about the wedding. She asked if I had any ideas about a dress yet, and somehow…she was so kind… I opened up to her."

"My mom has that way about her." Bryce was

glad she did because without his mom's gentle nudging, he might still be mired in grief and loneliness.

"She does." Carrie grinned. "She might have had an ulterior motive, though, because she also asked if I'd be interested in renting my house to her and Shane while their new place is being built. Before the baby comes, Zach, Beth and Ellie are moving into the main ranch house. They'd like more space, and it's closer to town so more convenient for Ellie's school. And Cole, Melissa and Skylar are moving from the house Melissa's been renting in town into what was Zach's house until they build their own place."

"It's like musical houses instead of chairs." Bryce blinked as he tried to follow his family's housing plans. "Does that mean you want to live at my place? I thought… Ally and I lived there, and I don't want you to be uncomfortable."

"I won't. Your house is the only home Paisley and Cam have ever known. I don't want to disrupt the kids' lives, and I'll be happy on the main ranch property with the family nearby. Besides, I'll be working here at this farm most days when I'm in High Valley. If you're open to having another painting party, we could do some redecorating and make your house more ours."

"That sounds good to me." Bryce's voice

cracked. "It was my lucky day when that goat got loose."

"The goat?" Carrie stared at him, puzzled. "Oh, you mean Sammy."

"Without him, I might never have met you." Bryce linked one hand with Carrie's as they walked Teddy and Maverick along a path leading uphill between more maple trees.

"It was my lucky day as well. I love you, Bryce. Now and forever."

"I love you too." And he'd spend the rest of his life showing her how much.

* * * * *

For more great romances in
The Montana Carters miniseries,
visit www.Harlequin.com today!